# conquered

## HONOR BOUND: BOOK NINE

## ANGEL PAYNE

# conquered

## HONOR BOUND: BOOK NINE

## ANGEL PAYNE

WATERHOUSE PRESS

*For Thomas... for being my fantasy fulfilled.*

# CHAPTER ONE

Of all the days to vie for an Olympic medal in tripping over one's own feet, Jen Thorne had to pick this one.

To be fair, however, maybe the circumstances had picked *her*. Most days, the most thrilling thing that happened in and around her little accounting office at Nellis Air Force Base was a freak desert thunderstorm or a UPS delivery. Because the legs on the UPS guy...

She wasn't thinking of the UPS guy right now, though. Or much of anything else except staying upright as she and Lola, her assistant, headed back inside from their lunch break. In the Las Vegas Valley, wind was a fickle bitch. One second, the air could be eerily still, only to switch up and gust so hard, Jen wouldn't have been surprised to see Auntie Em pedaling by with Toto in the basket of her bicycle.

Caught by such a gust, Jen was faced with saving the leftovers of her burrito or the hem of her dress. Normally, the issue would be moot, but the burrito was a Zapatas special, meaning she'd have a decent dinner tonight while working late to close out the pilots' logs for the month. Besides, Lola was too busy trying to see through her own hair, a frizzy mass she'd just had hennaed to a deep purple, to notice Jen was flashing a similar shade in French panty lace—

As the wind rushed in again.

And had her stumbling, one suede-heeled boot over the other, just to maintain *some* semblance of upright balance—

Until a pylon popped up in the middle of the parking lot to help her.

*Shit.*

"Shit!" Only when Lola's echo hit the air did Jen realize she'd blurted it too—for damn good reason. The pylon wasn't a pylon. No pylon on the planet looked like this, with commanding muscles on a six-foot-plus frame that turned even his plaid shirt and jeans into an outfit worthy of Camelot itself. The guy's stance was worthy of nobility too, with posture that bordered on arrogant and booted feet braced to steady both himself and her. None of that was even the most gulp-worthy part of him, as she learned when jolting her sights up to his face.

*Oh, God.*

He was worth way more than another gulp. Full-on gawking was now in order—but could she be blamed? Those thick ginger waves. That deep-dimpled grin. Those eyes, wolf gray and just as keen, seemed to take in every detail about her...

Including her exposed underwear.

*Ohhhhh. Jeez.*

And yeah, *that* had spilled out too—in the highest, most horrifying squeak she could imagine. Not true. Nowhere, in any shoot-me-now nightmare she'd ever had, did she let out a sound as obnoxious as that.

Lola, clearly agreeing, didn't help by barking a giggle and snapping her gum.

Neither did Major Skip Tremaine, a man who'd never matched his call sign better. "Cat Five," with his sharp nose and flawless high-and-tight haircut, rushed forward with the subtlety of an F-18 getting catapulted off a navy carrier. "Thorne! What the hell? You having the vapors or something?"

Lola yipped with another laugh.

Jen groaned beneath her breath. *Kill. Me. Now.*

She meant it, and even considered begging her ginger King Arthur to do it, but the only sound that emerged when she opened her mouth was another ridiculous whine. Why that made the hunk only smile wider and hold her tighter was just as irrational, if not fully dysfunctional—which, of course, only made him more irresistible. Holy hell. *A lot more...*

"*Och*, Tremaine. The *vapors*, man?"

"What?" Cat Five countered. "*You* taking full credit, Braw Boy? What, so the 'lasses' are now falling at your feet before you even meet them? Cocky son of a bitch."

"Lasses." It screaked softly out of Jen, doubling her horror as she also rasped, "Braw Boy." Frantically, she grabbed at the hem of her skirt, newly taunted by a fresh blast of wind. "You're...him. The—the hotshot from Scotland."

"Captain Sam Mackenna." His lips, composed of bold lines that emulated the cliffs of his native land, curled up a little at one end. "Also known as the cocky son of a bitch." He offered his hand for a handshake. "And you are...?"

"Mortified." Jen ducked her head, attempting to yank free from his grip. Though he was in civvies and she was no longer auditioning for the Victoria's Secret Angels, this was still a thousand kinds of inappropriate—an impropriety her whole body begged her to continue. And though Sam allowed her to step free, he remained unusually close while issuing a quiet, easy reply.

"*Bah*. Mortified isn't fun at all. How about...mouse?" Though with his Highland drawl, it came out much closer to *moose*—which pulled a giggle out of Jen before she could help it.

"With the silly squeak to match?"

He didn't return the laugh. Instead, with his hooded gaze dropping to her mouth, he murmured, "Silly wasn't the first word that came to my mind, lass." As the parking lot was hit by another whomp of wind, making it hard to hear anything more than a few inches from one's face, he leaned over and murmured close to her ear, "But adorable, hot, and sexy sure fucking did."

And now, the wind wasn't the only force walloping the crap out of her.

Maybe the gust had simply made her hear him wrong...?

One quick glance over. One stare full of his blatant flirtation.

Nope. Not a thing wrong with her hearing.

Jen concentrated on taking several long, steady breaths. But still, her heartbeat galloped. Her bloodstream ran viciously hot and then ruthlessly freezing. The wind kicked up again, mighty and merciless. *Dear God.* All they had to do was lengthen her skirt a little and then turn his sweater and jeans into a jerkin and kilt, and this would be a reenactment from the Highlander romance she'd finished last night in the tub. Including the part about how connected she already felt to him...

*Fiction, Jen.* Fiction. *Remember? The fun little word bringing the reminder that strapping Scottish hunks* don't *come wrapped in kilts and romance and carnal promises in fluent Gaelic? And technically, this one's not even here for pleasure— though with Sin City right out the front door, he'll likely find his way to it soon enough. Yeah, after talking rockets and guns and blowing enemy jets out of the sky all day, he'll want some recreation—*not *a night pointing at constellations from your* *apartment balcony.*

"All right, all right." She held up both hands, managing to insert a laugh that sounded halfway casual. "Why don't we just try for 'Jen'?"

He tilted his head. The wind whipped hunks of whisky-colored strands across his hewn features. She pretended to clutch her Zapatas bag harder, which helped her resist clearing the brilliant strands away herself.

*You: geek sandwich.*

*Him: alpha male filet.*

*And if the two are offered on the same plate?*

*Grab the stomach pump.*

As if she needed an even bigger reminder of *that* mental sticky note, Tremaine strode up and swept in at once, clapping her on the back as he would one of the mechanics in the hangar. As Jen's teeth found their rightful places again, he declared, "Thorne here is your ace inside the office, Mackenna. She'll keep your ass in line with the administrative song-and-dance, and since this air combat cross-training program with the RAF includes twelve of you Scottish jocks, there's going to be an ass-load of those hoops to hop." He interrupted himself with a hissing grimace. "Annnnd there I go, harshing the girls' Zapatas high. Sorry, Thorne—but once you see what Braw Boy and his crew can do to redefine the High Yo-Yo move alone, you'll be damn glad we invited these boys over for a few weeks of friendly collaboration."

Lola, having locked and come around the car, broke in with a snarky snort. "Oh, I think she already *is*, Major."

Tremaine glanced over as if she were a three-year-old shouting "pwanes!" at the F-35s lined up on the tarmac in the distance. Just as callously, he turned back to Jen and Sam. "So maybe the two of you should get together for a few minutes, after Sam gets to know his way around the hangar and shit?"

Jen clenched her bag of leftovers even tighter while plastering a completely fake smile to her lips. "Sure thing. Whatever will make things easier for Captain Mackenna."

"That's my girl."

She was damn glad she'd kept her teeth clenched. One, it meant the man didn't knock any fillings loose with his shoulder smack of "encouragement." Two, it helped cinch back the rejoinder that never failed to percolate when Tremaine used the diminutive.

*I'm* not *your girl.*

Locked molars or not, she was sorely tempted to fling the words—and didn't even try to disguise why. In the space of three minutes, Captain Sam Mackenna had definitely upended her axis. Flipped the freaking tables of her awareness. Slammed a cosmic can opener on the lid of her composure and made her inhale a scoop of pure, raw, chemical attraction from the inside.

*In three minutes.*

How the hell was she going to see him—talk with him, interact with him, work with him—nearly every day for the next month?

The answer came in a strange, swift, relieving rush.

She simply hadn't seen this coming. Hadn't known the superstar Scottish pilot would look—and talk, and smolder, and flirt—more like a kilt-clad warrior who'd walked out of her favorite novel and right onto her boring old blacktop. And because she was caught with her defenses down and her skirt flying up, she hadn't been prepared for the shock. And *really* hadn't anticipated what Mackenna himself would do with that vulnerability.

Decisiveness was good in a pilot.

So were ruthlessness, boldness, and confidence.

All the reasons why she stuck to fictional hunks instead of real ones.

All the reasons why her wildest dreams involved one of those heroes handling her in the same ways.

Dominating her in the same ways...

But she wasn't a plane. And the man needed to focus on his strategies and his flying.

A realization reached too late—especially when Lola was nearby. Oh yeah, the woman was all over her Sam Mackenna scope-out like white on rice. With a wry chuckle, she twirled a couple of indigo curls around two fingers and nudged Jen in the shoulder. Joined in commiseration, they stood with the wind behind them, watching Mackenna and Tremaine striding off to the hangars.

Lola's humor turned into a wistful sigh. "Ho. Lee. Fuuuuck. That backside belongs in a G-string downtown."

Despite the weird curl of tension still lingering in her belly, Jen laughed. "It's...impressive."

"Ohhhh, girl." Lo patted her forearm. "Something tells me he's going to need the deluxe version of the talk."

"Hm." It was more commiseration than consideration. "Which one? Keep-the-ego-in-the-cockpit, or keep-the-libido-in-the-locker-room?"

"Both."

Jen groaned. "That's what I was afraid you'd say."

★ ★ ★ ★ ★

Jen kept true to her word and gave him the speech. All right, not a *speech* speech, but she managed to drop enough hints about not "flying the flyboys" and "sampling the joysticks in her own hangar" that Captain Mackenna, with his miss-nothing focus and boulder-steady command, clearly didn't miss an iota of her subtext.

And she was secretly, giddily gratified to sense he hadn't.

Not that she would ever change her policy. As policies went, they *needed* to be in place. For circumstances just like this.

For unexpected arrivals like Captain Sam Mackenna.

Because just a week into this "special" assignment of his, she already knew that as pilots went, he was something special—and as men went, she would never meet anyone like him again. And yes, she thoroughly ran both conclusions past her usual internal reality check, because any self-respecting girl with a historical-romance addiction the size of hers was used to situations just like this. The giddy rush from watching him approach, imagining a sword swinging from one of his lean hips and a flintlock from the other. Replacing his olive-green flight suit with buckskins, muddy leather boots, and a broad-brimmed hat molded low over one eye—complete with pheasant feathers angled off the back. Or better yet, pretending the jet mechanics he waved at were actually loyal servants attending his ornate carriages—if billion-dollar planes could be kind of sort of considered "carriages"—along the lane leading to the grand mansion, where she waited for him with a glass of sherry and her pantaloons conveniently "in the wash" for the day...

But then the reality check cranked into gear. Big-time.

Her world was full of straight lines and order, where variations of one-plus-one always added up to the same thing and could never change. Even in her volunteer hours at the library, Dewey and his decimal system put order to the chaos. In every book she borrowed or bought from the used-book sales, there was a happy-ever-after to make the world right.

But Sam Mackenna? Well, if he really *was* the god he looked like, he'd rule over fire or battle or mischief—or a combination of the three. His world consisted of changes that happened by the second and the reaction speed to match: where half the time, the earth was up and the sky was down; where he took risks that meant living very much in the moment...

A philosophy that likely extended to his love life.

Wrong. Not his *love* life.

His sex life.

Because guys like him were always, *always* reminded that the dangers they faced in the cockpit directly corresponded to the action they could get in the sack—and because guys like him usually had the perfect skills to measure up to those demands as well. Because arousing a woman was probably a lot like guiding a fighter jet to Mach Five. And if even half that assertion were true, then Sam Mackenna's prowess between the sheets was probably—

Nothing she should even dare to consider, let alone dwell on.

It was time to move on.

As in, right now.

Despite how the man proved out every single one of her theories, in exquisitely agonizing detail, during his approach across the main hangar. Strolling like the undisputed ruler of everything he surveyed. Then smiling as if his little "inspection of the estate" was a predawn thing and she was the sun who'd just risen on his day.

*Moving. On.*

*Right. Now.*

Only...a funny thing happened on the way to the great land of her noble follow-through. The man got within touching distance again. Not that she was going *there* by any stretch of the imagination—though by now, that distance had been proved in colorful detail—but just one good inhalation of him was making the path a hell of a lot harder to maintain. How could a guy smell *that* good after several hours in a cockpit barely wider than his shoulders? And even right here, where used jet fuel, heated steel, and fried rubber competed for the discretion of her nose? His scent was the stunning opposite, reminding her of a walk through the forest after a storm, with earth and spices mixing in the most evocative, erotic way.

More urgently, why was it easier to think of the mountain of filing waiting on her desk—hell, even the mountain of *laundry* waiting for her at home—than keeping true to her noble policies?

No. Just keeping true to them when it came to *him*.

Magnificent, maddening man.

Magnificent in all the best ways. Maddening in all the most dangerous ways.

Because even as they exited the hangar and started back toward the conference room, the energy radiating off him was palpable...and intentional. She knew it from the curious looks tossed at him by the guys they passed in the hall, as well as what she could see simply observing their hazy reflection in the windows. No doubt about it... Sam Mackenna needed a classification of his own. A category she could never hope to reach—no matter how intensely his wolf grays tempted her otherwise after they rounded the corner into the conference room and sat down.

*After* he shoved a figurative middle finger at protocol and pulled out her chair for her.

*After* he followed that up by striding back and quietly closing the door—doubling the potency of his allure in a single move.

*After* he slid into his chair like that damn viscount beholding a virgin at some carnal castle feast.

And here *she* was, reacting to that scrutiny with everything but the heaving bosom in the corset, attempting to string even two coherent thoughts together. What had they come in here to do again? The symbols on the papers in front of her weren't any help. Ohhhh *shit*, was she in trouble.

"All right, m'lady. Yer the one drivin' the apple cart here. Let's have at it, then."

"Huh?"

No. Not trouble. She was all the way in the damn weeds—and Mackenna looked as if he had all afternoon to watch her struggle out. Did he have to quirk those full, firm lips like that? And brace his elbows on the table like that, emphasizing his shoulders in such muscled glory? And why did her imagination have to pick that second to run away on her, imagining what those shoulders would feel like beneath her spread fingers, bunching and coiling in time to his ruthless thrusts inside her?

And they *would* be ruthless. She had no damn doubt about that. The same way she knew she'd savor every single one of them...

"Yer the one who called the meeting," he clarified as she

tried discreetly rearranging her position. Thank God there was a corner of the conference table between them. Not that her damp panties were even visible to the man—though she wouldn't put it past him to have X-ray vision on top of his other god-level powers. "So I'm here and...at your service."

She wasn't sure whether to deck him or return the smirk he got in with the statement's purposeful pause. Holy shit, the man even smirked with purpose. She just wished that intention didn't feel so aligned with what was happening between her thighs. She also wished he didn't look so much like he thoroughly knew that, even as she reached for the stack of personnel files neatly positioned just a foot to her side, right where she'd left them specifically for reviewing during this meeting.

"Well, I think you have that wrong." She actually *had* to smile then, to dilute the snippy verbiage. Why did it feel like she got the ratio of businesslike and flirtatious all wrong? She smiled at male colleagues all the time and had never second-guessed herself like this—though to be fair, she'd never smiled at any of them while attempting *not* to undress them with her gaze.

*Oh, dear cripes.*

"Yes, errmmm..." She opened the first file with a decisive whoosh. "Wrong. You. I mean, you're not *wrong* wrong; you just—well—this is more about how *I* can be of service to *you*—"

He jogged up a tawny brow, and her guts turned into a nervousness parfait. "Is *that* so?"

"I—" *Oh, gawd.* "I mean—"

"Jen." His soothing tone did nothing for her rampaging senses. Neither did the press of his hand atop hers and how he curled his fingertips around the outside edge of hers. "Take a breath. I don't bite." Then, after he squeezed in a little tighter, "Hard."

Wasn't he the funny one? Like she'd ever be able to "breathe" normally again, after just one tiny contact of her skin with his. And *hell*, his hold was just as warm and firm and confident and masculine as she'd imagined it would be. But his command wasn't restricted there. It permeated his voice. Extended far beyond his not-so-subtle flirtation, becoming a dictate she couldn't—nor wanted to—ignore. So she didn't. She took one deep breath. Another. They were enough to lend her fresh composure, along with the reminder that even their handclasp was violating at least a dozen rules of conduct—not that the insolent Scot seemed to mind or care. Which sure as hell didn't mean *she* couldn't.

"All right, then." Cursing *and* thanking herself for it, she pulled her hand back to rest on top of the first file she'd opened and forced herself to focus on the name at the top. *Rodric Camden.* "This isn't going to take long. Just need to make sure I've got the basics correct for everyone on your squad, along with double-checking that they're getting settled in okay and have everything they need for their stay here."

"Fair enough."

He coiled his tone back to professional coolness, even settling back into his chair and parking an ankle onto the opposite knee. For the next fifteen minutes, she succeeded in cooling her own jets long enough to get through the first third of the files in the pile. Unbelievably, her pulse evened out to a survivable rate again...

Until they landed on the *M* files.

More specifically, halfway through the *M*s.

*Macallister, Macdonnah, MacDougal,* and *Macgregor?*

All completely fine.

But once she got to *Mackenna*...

"Maybe we'd better save this slick skellum for the end of the show."

Yeah, to the point that she even tried joking about it.

"I think the slick skellum has somethin' to say about *that*." And as easily as the man had eased back into his good behavior, he slipped right back out of it—into an even sexier, silkier version of his licentious lord side. Yes, doubling her pulse as soon as he slipped a hand back across hers. Yes, ensuring her throat closed to the diameter of a toothpick as he used the pressure to make her close his file. And yes, drawing her in all over again with the intensity of his gaze, those lupine grays rendering her weak in the knees no matter how solidly her backside was secured in her chair. "And how do you know what a 'slick skellum' is, anyway?"

His perplexity wasn't just endearing; it was adorable. Jen held herself back from a full laugh by twisting her lips into a coquettish smirk. "A girl's got to have her secrets."

Annnnd forget adorable. He turned fully primal, obviously extracting all the naughtiest nuances from her quip—and with the darkness in his eyes and tension in his jaw, Jen wasn't sure she minded. Just for this tiny second, it might be nice to think their worlds *could* collide. That her "secrets" weren't things like reading three books a week, including the colorful slang of lands she longed to visit. Like his. *Especially* his.

"Well then...a boy's got to the right to try unlockin' 'em."

She gave in to a laugh. "Not if he doesn't want the biggest disappointment of his life."

The corners of his eyes tightened, bringing the gold tips of his long lashes into the light. For the love of all that was good, the man turned even fluorescent lighting into a heart-stopping experience. "You know you're just really at it now, aye?"

Jen cocked her head. "I know what *that* means too, Captain. And I'm in full control of my mind, thank you very much—which I'm not sure applies to *everyone* in the room at this mom—"

As she attempted reopening his file, Sam swiped the whole thing from beneath her grip. Like everything else he did, the move was strong but calm, force wielded by a hunk who knew he didn't have to be an asshole about it. He was simply going to get his way, and that was that.

But at this point, what did "his way" entail?

And why was she suddenly a little scared about that?

And why did the possible answers turn her on so damned much?

"You're here to make sure I have everything I need for my stay here, aye?"

She blinked a few times. Where was he going with this? "Affirmative." Humoring him might be the only way to find out. And at least that answer was easy enough.

"Well, I don't."

Several more blinks, along with a frown—until she finally comprehended that *he* wasn't blinking, though he was focusing harder on *her*. "Okay, Braw Boy," she huffed. "Now that's just enough."

"Oh, I haven't had nearly enough, Miss Thorne."

"*I* am not a vital need for you, Captain Mackenna." And before he could expand *that* into about a hundred different innuendos, she borrowed from some of her growing aggravation to snap, "And if that *is* a vital need for you, then ask some of the guys from our squad to show you some local places where the jet jockey fans hang out." There was more colorful vernacular for the girls who liked regularly wrapping themselves around the pilots' "cockpits," but she refused to use the crass terms. Long story short, she'd never be one of them, even if she wanted to be. Genetics hadn't given her lush mermaid locks, generous curves, or the balance necessary for five-inch designer heels. "I guarantee you, there are curvier, prettier, and *way* more graceful choices in Vegas."

For a long beat, the man didn't falter. Through the moment that followed, in which the air got thicker and his jaw clenched tighter, Jen interpreted his tension as her victory—of sorts. Clearly, he was weighing the avenues toward a graceful concession, which should've brought a wave of relief, right? But in the ocean of her mind, there wasn't a ripple. Just many gallons of salty disappointment and contemplating how she was going to deal with life for the next month, working side-by-side with this Scottish god of a man while knowing he was out taking his pick of the stiletto starlets across the city.

And remembering the way he held her hand like this. Then slid his grip up to encircle her wrist instead. Then matched the grip with his other hand around her other wrist. And officially awakened so many latent needs in her body. In her psyche. In her sex...

In all the parts of herself so carefully hidden through the years...because surely no normal or decent man would want a woman who begged him to restrain her...and then take her as hard as he could...

No normal man.

But she jerked her sights up and confronted the stunning features of the man who'd tethered her body—and robbed her breath—all too easily. And clearly didn't intend to release her anytime soon.

And clearly liking it very much.

And clearly daring *her* to say she didn't like it.

But God help her, she did.

So very, very much...

"Jen?"

"Y-Yeah?"

"When are you going to stop fighting this?"

She gulped. It hurt a little. Her throat was parched, and her lips were dry. But holy shit, she even welcomed that pain too. "This...what?"

Sam stood. With noiseless steps, he moved around the portion of the table between them and then filled the space directly in front of her. But he didn't stop there. Bracketing her legs with both of his, he only halted once his knees abutted the front of her chair, and she had nearly a straight-on view of his crotch. And the way it punched forward when she *did* savor that sight. And how she felt her eyes widen, knowing how flight suits were meant to be roomy down there but how the man's shaft made use of damn near every inch of it...

*Ohhhh, holy shit.*

"Look at me."

His voice only added to the spell begun by his erection. Gone was his vocal swath of velvet confidence, burned away by the peaty husk of his grate. The second she tilted her head back, she saw a matching mien across his face, his high cheekbones jutting into torrid angles that pointed the way to the noticeable parting of his lips and the pronounced flare of his nostrils. It was a look she'd not seen from him before, but right away she knew why.

He was as consumed by lust as she was.

And confirmed it—as if she really needed the affirmation—by looming an inch deeper over her. Increasing the torque of his grip by half as much. Just enough so she knew he wasn't going to relent. Not anytime soon. Though right now, she prayed it wouldn't be *ever*...

"You are just not gettin' this, are you?" he rasped.

For a couple of seconds, Jen worked her lips up and down. *Words*. She knew a few of those, didn't she? "I—I don't... Not getting what?"

He dipped in by another inch. A treacherous one this time, since the man's fluorescent light voodoo conspired against her, exposing new depths of his eyes to her. They weren't just gray. Dashed into his irises, there were also shards of cobalt as rich and breathtaking as a Sicilian lagoon. "That I don't want the girls in the bars across town. That ever since I got here, I've only wanted the chance to know *one* sweet lass a little better. And that if I'm not mistaken, that lass feels exactly the same way."

Jen rolled her eyes, despite how the move narrowed his. "Is this the part where you hit me with the line that *fate* made me trip in front of you last week?"

He didn't surrender an iota of his laser focus. "Would it be so wrong if I did?"

Jen forced herself to look away from him. But not even the coffee spatters on the floor, likely left over from the tactical training they'd had before the hops this morning, could dim the magic of his words in her system. It was true, then. The man affected her far beyond his physical glory. He was a force in her senses...

But a destiny in her life?

"There's a huge gap between attraction and fate, okay?"

She let her shoulders sag to emphasize the point, since fighting the man's hold wasn't something she wanted to consider. But her surprise about that was eclipsed by his quick response.

"Fair point," he conceded, going again for his silken baritone. "I'll rephrase. Would it be so wrong to deny our *attraction* from last week?" He readjusted his hold, working the rough pads of his thumbs across the pulse points in her wrists. "Christ. Our attraction from right fucking now."

As he punched out those last three words, Jen sucked in an equally tormented breath. They were doing it again. Syncing even the cadences of their lungs to each other without trying. Because they didn't have to. Because they just *were*...

"Tell me you don't feel any of this, Jenny." His demand, even without the heart-halting enhancement of her name, was like vocalized magma. "I dare you, woman. Look straight at me and tell me that when we so much as lay eyes on each other, your blood doesn't turn to fire, your chest isn't a poundin' chaos, and your skin doesn't feel three sizes too tight." He enforced his hold, scraping his thumbs up to the middle of her palms. "And tell me that every inch of your senses doesn't scream at you to come to me. To be held by me...exactly like this. To be connected to me, even tighter than this. Just tell me, damn it. Tell me just once, and I'll be gone and leave you be for the next four weeks."

She dragged in a shaking breath. Another. But what did she expect to happen? That the billion knots in her senses would suddenly unravel? That her brain would cease to be a soup of arousal and denial and confusion?

She couldn't need this.

She couldn't want him.

"Damn it. We've...been through this already, Sam."

"Right," he spit back. "Your personal 'policy' and all."

"Even if we chucked that out the window, this—us—just isn't a great idea."

He gritted out a tight growl. "Aye, well neither is flyin' a fighter jet into a Pugachev Cobra, but it sure as fuck feels good."

As he finished the last of that, he bent even closer over her. Still, Jen managed to get in a thorough huff as the man lowered her arms along the chair's rests while maintaining his grip on top of her wrists. "And if you crash that jet?"

At once, he pursed and twisted his lips at once, quelching her ability to take that huff into a full grumble. To her horror, a sound *did* spill from her, though it was more a mouse's squeak than a lioness's growl. But when the man smirked like that, she couldn't be held responsible for any wayward sounds— especially when he followed it up with a line that was a little cocky-ass pilot and *a lot* bold, brash Scotsman.

"Oh, my little mouse. I don't *ever* crash."

# CHAPTER TWO

Sam finally—though reluctantly—let up on his hold. While Jen's unthinkin' little squeak had been the most adorable thing *he'd* ever heard, her furious blush told him she couldn't be further from agreeing with his assessment. Still, before he pulled away, he allowed his fingertips to feather along the backs of her hands—and his spirit to rejoice in the visible shiver with which she reacted.

Which meant he longed to do it again. Right this fuckin' second.

Though next time, he might not stop just there.

He'd use his lips along with his fingers. Take hers beneath them, using gentle brushstrokes at first, until he couldn't resist sweeping his tongue to taste hers—though he already knew what she'd taste like. She'd be warm as whisky but sweet as wine and have him as plastered as if he'd downed a gallon of each. And he wouldn't regret one damned second of it. Not with her. Not with this woman who did so many *things* to him. Heady, giddy things.

Things he never imagined he'd feel again...

Because despite bein' an arrogant bastard, he was also a deeply damaged one. The huddy who didn't believe it when everyone told him this break in the States would be "good" for him, perhaps even help with his emotional healing. In truth, he'd agreed to come and do the cross-training just to shut everyone up. He'd *never* expected to admit they were all right. And certainly not within the first hour of his arrival in the middle of this land so foreign, it was like another planet...

Giving him the nectar that had never felt more like home. The elixir of this woman's gaze.

The startled light in them, torn away from him too fast that first day...not even cognizant of half the magic they held.

Not even aware of her true submissiveness.

His sweet mouse...awakening every leonine instinct inside *him*...

Especially in moments like this, in which he was entranced by her smile but wholly unsure what it meant. Forced to delve deeper into the nuances of her quirking lips and twinkling eyes, attempting to determine exactly how her reaction to his comeback was comin' along. Because she *did* have one—of *that*, he was as certain as a g-force *whomp* at takeoff. He just wasn't sure if he were about to be throttled or kissed.

"*Never* crashed, Captain? Well, there's a first time for everything, you know."

And then there was the concept of both.

And no, that technically didn't qualify as a kiss—though it wasn't a direct beating, either. In a word, it was...

Oh, fuck the words.

Fuck anything that would cage this incredible, unpredictable little mouse to something as ridiculous as words. She was far more than that. *They* were already far more than that. This morning, he'd flown a jet to the edge of heaven but not known half of *this* adrenaline, pulsing and pounding through him, calling like freedom and feeling like fire—all from just being this close to her. And damn it, she had to feel the attraction too. Hell, the journey between the hangar and here had shown him how semi-strangers could see and feel it.

She had slammed on a hell of a pair of mental blinders about it. But he was prepared to yank 'em off. To fight for the right to, if that was what it took. He'd already laid down his life for much less, on too many occasions than he wanted to remember.

Jen saved him from the ugly track of *that* thought by suddenly rising from her chair, bringing the entire length of her body just an inch away from his.

And already, he began the battle to get to her blinders.

One simple tug and he obliterated the inch between them, fitting all of her softness against him and keeping her locked there. And by every saint he could remember, she felt good. At once, his cock swelled even more. His blood roared even louder. His arms ached to wrap all the way around her, until they were filled with what they wanted. With his fingers aligned along her spine and his face dipped to meet the upturned expectancy stamped on hers, he gave in to a new desire: his slow, cocky smile couldn't be controlled any more than the seas her eyes evoked and the wind her hair smelled like.

"Hmmm," he rumbled, pausing just long enough to enjoy the cute little hitch of her breath. "A first time for *everything*, you say?" Then jutted his chin, just far enough for stressing his point. "Like...reconsidering certain 'personal protocols' when a lonely pilot from across the pond simply wants the chance to know you better?"

Truthfully, he was as perplexed as Jenny looked. He'd met her lacy bits before even shakin' her hand, and their raw sexual pull had been turning the air into a fireworks show for seven days straight. So why his sudden game with the Victorian-style wooing? *A lonely pilot from across the pond? The chance to know her better?* He wanted her. She wanted him. It should be that simple. It *had* to be that simple. He couldn't do complicated or courtly. Before this week, he didn't know he even had the capacity for sheer lust anymore. While this was familiar territory, it was still terrifyingly new. A stretch of life he never thought he'd have to deal with again.

Clearly, his cock had other plans.

And every drop of his bloodstream. And every neuron in his mind. And every speck of fascination in his imagination.

"You mean like...becoming friends?"

"Well...sure." And what the fuck was *that* all about? *No,* not like "friends." Not unless the Yanks had redefined that as two people getting naked, sweaty, and screaming together. If so, then aye, he was pure dead brilliant for the proposition. But one lengthy look at her, with such fresh hope across her face and keen interest in her eyes, and he beheld the truth of it. *Her* truth. This idea was the loophole around her "protocol." A way to spend time with him but not give in to what she really wanted to do with him.

What she was just as terrified of too.

And just like that, he could've swan-dived off the cliffs at St. Kilda and been less stunned by the impact.

This really wasn't just protocol for her.

This attraction had her just as malkied as him. But why? She wasn't afraid of *him,* per se; that much was clear in how easily she enjoyed their banter and even counterin' his arrogance with her adorable sass. But this, right now? The way he held her perfect little form flush to his body? It had nothing to do with the possibility of being discovered and everything to do with the intimacy itself.

Which was why he reluctantly released her. Why he followed that up with a move as awkward as it felt, halfway between a nod and a bow. Why he added an equally ridiculous smile, though he completely forgot his embarrassment as soon as she grinned in return, the edges of her lips kicked up into the blush returning to her high cheeks.

By God, she was gorgeous.

And so different from any other woman he'd ever met.

Which was why he kept up the stupid smile, even after all the huddy bowin'. Why he approached her again, scoopin' up only her hand this time and liftin' her soft, small fingers into the press of his lips—his soul rejoicin' like church bells on Easter from the second she spurted out her answerin' laughter. Which sounded even better than those damn bells...

Aye. So different.

So sweet.

So worth having to do things in different ways for her. To *win* her.

"If 'friends' is what you're easy with, lass, then 'friends' it is."

She released a long breath, though it carried the hints of a sigh—and just those traces, which he easily imagined leading to her cries of arousal, had bells pealin' through his system all over again. This time, they as hell weren't *church* bells. "Yeah. I *am* easy with that," she murmured. "Thank you, Captain." She punctuated that with a crunched forehead, instantly respondin' to the similar look from him. "What?"

"Friends don't call each other 'Captain.'"

Her furrows deepened as she drew up with a look remindin' him of fussy Mrs. Stewart from the Aldeburgh fish counter. "Well, at work on a US air base they do."

"Then maybe we should skedaddle this show to somewhere more tidy."

"Huh?"

He chuckled. At least her confusion turned her scowl into history—and it came with the accessory of a half smile, indicating his Scottish-isms actually fascinated her. Which of course opened his mind to all the *other* slang he could teach her. The secret, nasty, only-for-whispering things...

"Friends do things like have lunch together, aye?" he explained by way of furthering his quest. "So what're you going to do about that wee beastie in your stomach, woman?"

Silently, he thanked the growl in her belly for complying with its second loud snarl within the last couple of minutes. It was goin' on well after one o'clock, and there was no way she could deny her belly's very vocal reminder of the fact.

After her cheeks turned a darker shade of pink, she recovered enough to jerk a distinct brow at him. Fuck him, even those auburn arches had personality all their own. Would there be an end to the nuances he discovered about her with every passing moment? He suspected the answer was no—a possibility that hardened him for her all over again.

"What the hell, Mackenna?" She added a saucy toss of her short but thick auburn waves. "You angling for 'friends with benefits' already?"

He closed the space between them again. How could he resist, with her lookin' so bonnie and beguiling and confident and resplendent? "Hmmm." With a dip of his head, he honed every speck of his attention on her. "That depends."

"On what?"

"Is it workin'?" He hoped to fuck she said yes. If so, even if half the base intruded on them right now, he wouldn't be able to resist conquering her mouth with his. Boldly. Brutally.

"Well." Perhaps more than brutally—if she kept up with threading her responses with that arousing spritz of a sigh.

"You're certainly making sure I keep paying attention."

"I'm not one for favorin' the trite, my friend."

"Clearly," she laughed out. "My *friend.*"

He dared to slip out one hand, forming it to the side of her waist. She wasn't a skinny thing, but nor was she filled with a thousand curves to negotiate. In short, she was the perfect medium, filled with planes and lines he couldn't wait to explore better. Borrowing from that theme, he stated, "So why don't we meet in the middle on this?"

"The middle?" Her laugh faded, but her smile didn't. "Dare I even ask what that is?"

Sam glided his hold around to her back. "Why don't we just call this...*friends with possibilities?*" As her mouth popped open, all but broadcastin' her perplexity about how to answer that, he went for it and plunged on. "Possibilities we can explore over lunch."

She slammed her mouth shut, which only seemed to serve as the cue for her stomach again. Still, even as the growl sent tangible vibrations into the air between them, she settled into a resigned stance. "That sounds like...a super intriguing proposition, Captain..."

"But?" Sam went ahead and filled in the obvious.

"But I already have a lunch date today."

Only after she gave him the declaration, addin' one of the most delectable bottom lip bites he'd ever witnessed, did he realize just how much of his *other* secret sides she'd made it okay for him to let out. Not all the way, of course, but enough that he now recognized 'em for what they were—as well as how long he'd missed having 'em out for a nice stretch. How much he now wished it wasn't just a "stretch." How he wished it were going to be a full, fun play date, filled with plenty of this woman's moans and screams and acquiescences—because of what he did to her with his hands and fingers...and then his crop and flogger...maybe even his ropes and cuffs...

"A lunch date with *whom*?"

But first things first. Lettin' her have the brunt of his possessive snarl, along with the glower he wasn't about to apologize for. Whatever pissant wanker she had plans with, it was clear the "friend" wasn't meetin' a skoosh of her most important needs—not just the ones between her thighs, either. She was hungry for fulfillment between her *ears* too. Her fantasies weren't gettin' heeded. Her desires weren't gettin' sated. If they were, her gaze wouldn't still be lookin' like a pair of fairy bathin' pools right now. All those eager sparkles had never come from any well-satisfied woman *he* knew.

"It's...complicated."

Strangely, her mincing answer made it easier for him to push back by a step. To lock his purpose on her with a posture consisting of his spread stance, folded arms, and narrowed stare. "I'm a big boy, mouse. I can handle complicated." Armed with the information he was already damned certain of— that "Complicated," whoever the fuck he was, wasn't close to meetin' her needs as a lover—he was as certain of those words as his own dick. Aye, the one that throbbed yet now, needing the feel of her. The one that would likely be lurchin' like a stud stallion all day long because of her—and now, because of "Complicated."

"You really think so?"

He tightened his glare as *her* features grew more animated. She was enjoyin' the hell out of this, wasn't she? Watchin' him squirm just from her playful dance around the subject of "Complicated"? What the hell was she about, anyway? And just how gleeful would she be if he went ahead and trumped her fun game with his own? Wasn't the keenest of moves, since he figured "Complicated" had been in her life a lot longer than a week, but if the guy was set on nobody trompin' all over their lunch dates, he should've been meetin' the woman's needs a hell of a lot better than this.

Leading to the exact reason why Sam rocked back on a heel, assessin' the woman with a hooded gaze before leveling, "If you don't believe me, invite me along."

He prepped his victorious smirk for the moment her jaw dropped to the floor.

And never got the chance to use it.

The only thing the woman dropped was an invisible mic, returning his lording arrogance with a stunning dose of brazen glory, imitating his pose while spreading a bigger grin across her lush lips. "I'd really love it if you came along. I think they will too."

*They?*

So the victorious smirk got dingied as well.

Unless one counted the look on *her* face, eruptin' into a bright and brilliant laugh, as he stood there like she'd just told him to drop trou and go full bangers on her. So the thought did have its merits, though right now only served to remind him that he still stood here in the clothes he'd been in since dawn today. "Well, all right, cannie pants," he quipped. "Just give me ten to change, then, and—"

"Negative."

He stopped halfway to the door. "Excuse me?"

"I said negative." She glanced at the clock. "We're already almost late, thanks to your own case of—how was that?—bein' a cannie pants?" As he bore a glower-grin at her, she finished gathering up the personnel files from the table. "So I can give you five while I lock these away. Give yourself some slides of the stink-good stick and meet me out in the parking lot."

"Hmmm." He waggled his brows. "The parking lot."

That earned him a giggle, along with a motion down at her tailored navy slacks and crisp cream blouse, complete with a silky bow at the apex of the V-neck that lent her a secretary-ready-to-be-unraveled vibe. "Sorry, buddy. Don't think I can make your day in this."

He was ready with a brazen grin. And, from the looks of the sensual smoke that appeared in her gaze, had outdone himself with the glance before even letting his cocky comeback fly.

"I wouldn't be so sure about that at all, little mouse."

# CHAPTER THREE

She'd teased him about not making his day—but the truth was, he'd just made the hell out of hers.

Times twenty-four.

The two dozen faces in front of her now, ranging in age from seven to nine and encompassing every color from Anna's pale freckles to Paki's rich mahogany, were still locked on Sam in wide-eyed wonder. Their faces hadn't been that way when she'd first entered with Sam, about twenty minutes ago. Plenty of the guys from the base had already come with her to Vegas Valley Elementary's afternoon story hour, where she volunteered once a week—and sometimes more than that, if the teachers and staff were having a not-enough-hours-in-the-day thing going on. Which meant she was usually here more than once a week and that the kids had definitely gotten their fill of details about the intricacies of a fighter pilot's life.

So the fact that Sam made his living at Mach speed was as worthy as last year's memes to these kids.

The fact that he usually did it in the skies over Scotland, however?

*Now* they were speeding with some new gas.

And by this point were giving Sam a thorough bath of the stuff. Then tossing matches at him too.

So far, the man was handling the blaze like an epic pro. And maybe, crazily, seemed to be *enjoying* the whole thing. Jen knew she was smiling in wonderment and didn't bother hiding an inch of the expression as she looked to where the man now sat—sort of—in a yellow plastic chair, his long legs hitched so high, he looked sort of like a praying mantis perched on a small rock. But his grin was still all lion, and thoroughly entrancing, as he pointed to Lindy and the arm she patiently pointed in the air.

"If you're really from Scotland, why aren't you wearing a dress?" she blurted.

At once, Oliver spun toward her with rolling eyes. "Duh. It's not a dress. It's called a kilt, and boys in Scotland only wear them on special days now."

Martha, practically seated in Lindy's lap because best friends *had* to be that close, bared her teeth at the sneering boy. "How do *you* know, Ollie? You're French and Spanish, *not* Scottish."

Oliver was already prepped, narrowing his gaze and jutting his chin. The boy was strikingly handsome and already knew how to use those looks well. "My mom told me. She likes reading those same books as Miss Jen. My dad says it's because there's lots of kissing in 'em, and plus, the boys don't put on underwear under their kilts."

Lindy and Martha shrieked. "Ewwww!"

At the back of the big carpet mat, Shawn popped to his feet, rascal's smirk already in place. "Do *you* put on underwear with *your* kilt, Captain Mackenna?"

"All right, all right." While Jen's shout was underlined by a new outburst from Lindy and Martha, she secretly thanked them for the extra pause to suppress her laugh. Sam was no help, openly giving in to his. "That's enough of *that* subject. Shawn, have a seat, please. If nobody else has any questions for Captain Mackenna, perhaps he can continue reading for you..."

But as she spoke, at least six hands popped up across the room. Jen sighed in frustration, looking to Sam for some support of her initiative, but he was prepared with a devastating—and smoldering—glance of his own, assuring her he really was having the time of his life.

He kept things diplomatic, calling on a boy for the next official question. Taio was already a little bruiser and had a fondness for the Green Bay Packers as well as any animal bigger than a breadbox. His question came as no surprise and even earned him a bigger smile from Sam.

"Can you throw a tree?" the boy asked. "One day, when there was no football on TV, my dad was watching a show where guys in kilts were throwing trees."

"Well, we call 'em cabers," Sam explained. "And they are indeed made out of trees, with all the green stuff cut off. Each caber weighs close to eighty kilograms. That's nearly two hundred pounds."

Well, *that* had every head in the room snapping back around.

"Holy guacamole," Martha finally blurted, her big brown eyes wide. "That's heavy!"

"So are you any good?" Taio raised his chin, clearly enjoying the grown-up bro vibe he could get in. Jen's chest swelled with emotion when Sam honored the boy by emulating the motion. Taio was being raised by a single mother, and camaraderie with a role model like Sam had probably made the boy's week.

"I have no clue," Sam admitted after that, spreading his hands. "Takes a mate with special talent and years of trainin' to toss a caber with true aim. I've been flyin' jets steadily for nearly ten years now, meanin' there hasn't been a lot of spare time for heftin' cabers."

The next one to be called on was Xylie, who contradicted her exotic name simply with her long blond ringlets and large green eyes. "What's the name of the castle you live in?"

Jen bit back a chuckle—and noticed Sam having to rein back the intensity of his. "Unbelievably, lass, not everyone in my land lives in castles."

"Well, of course not *everyone*," Xylie returned. "But *you* do, right?"

"*Pssshhh*." Martha waved a dismissive hand toward her princess-perfect classmate. "'Course he does. You ever seen Miss Jen look like that *unless* she's swooning over some guy from a castle?"

Jen had made the mistake of turning to open the snack-sized bags of chocolate-chip cookies for snack time. Thanks to Martha, the bag upon which she was tugging got a Herculean effort, and the cookies turned into exploding meteors, flying out to all corners of VVE's little library. At once, the kids burst up as well. Two dozen cries of "I'll get them!" collided atop each other, overridden only when Jen threw some lung power into her corresponding bellow.

"If I see *anyone* sneaking one of those cookies down their maw, your entire snack is forfeit for today and the rest of the week!"

Thank God it was only Tuesday. Thank God, as well, for Sam, who actually caught one of the flying cookies barehanded and then scrambled another up from the floor near his foot. After the four remaining cookies were returned whole, barely fifteen minutes remained of what was supposed to be story *hour*.

"All right, you little goofballs." She put her hands on her hips, resigned to chalking today up as a kitten herding day. "Why don't you all enjoy some extra time looking for books to check out while Captain Mackenna helps me open the rest of the snack bags?"

Shawn was among the first to pop back up, his silly grin breaching even more of his face. "More explosions! More explosions!"

"Annnnd there's a future IED man for you," Sam muttered while she shooed the throng toward the stacks.

"Come back in fifteen minutes with books, you heathens," Jen teased them. "And remember: your pile should have at least two from your grade's required reading list. No loading up on manga and nature picture books. I'll be looking for those gold 'approved reading' stickers, ladies and gentlemen."

She turned back to help Sam with the rest of the cookie bags, but he'd already finished—with no more explosions—and was on to pouring cups of fruit juice and milk. "*Och*," he murmured as she leaned in, transferring the cups to the end of the table where the kids would be eating. "Miss Jen, you're pure skyrocket on the ball bustin'."

A chuff escaped her. "Captain Mackenna, I thoroughly represent that remark." Even though the last couple of words were the only part that made real sense. She could infer the rest, which might be a good idea at this point—because reaching in and getting that close to him again was definitely *not* her most fabulous move. Not already knowing what the man's nearness did to her whole nervous system. Not after how the kids had just frayed it even more, outing her as "swoony" like that. Not with how the man cocked a sideways stare at her, obviously not about to give up on the memory so easily himself.

"Glad we've got that out of the way," he stated, reprising the voice so silken, it belonged in a pinned cravat around his neck and topped with a velvet doublet—all but guaranteeing she'd tilt up a responding stare. Which at once crunched into a curious scowl.

"Which means what?" she demanded quietly, though interrupted herself the next second, calling at the two kids in her periphery, "Sheila, stop trying to kiss Anthony. And Anthony, stop trying to let her." Without veering the angle of her stare, she cut the volume to demand from Sam again, "Which. Means. What?"

This time, he was the one to extend his arms to either side of her, two juice cups in each hand, and place them on the table behind her. The push made her scoot back a little, sandwiched between the table's edge and all of his...*edges*. Which had been molded against a lot of *her* just an hour and a half ago, so why the hell was her body being such a rebel and forgetting all of that now? Why was she even more on fire, more out of breath, and more out-of-bounds on rational thought than she'd been when he was this close back at the base? And during a few key moments had been even closer? The only thing that had really changed was the setting—and the fact that they were now surrounded a bunch of squirrelly second, third, and fourth graders. So officially, he couldn't really touch her. But more exigently, *she* couldn't touch *him* in return.

She was tied back...

Held down...

And undeniably, uncontrollably wet from the mere thought of it.

And suddenly, restlessly, licking her lips because of *that* simple thought.

And perfectly, maddeningly, aware of how she riveted the man in front of her as well. No. Not just in front of her. Still around her, his arms bracketing her, his impossibly long fingers stroking the tabletop next to where her ass cheeks were braced. Still not touching her...but close enough that she could feel every steady, slow stroke along the fake wood surface... every caress he was thinking about delivering to her skin. And yes, she knew that too. After one glance up, letting her stare drown in the dark soot depths of his, she *knew*. She *felt*. So many perfect, bold vibrations, carrying all the way into her skin through that cheap laminate...

Until she recognized exactly why she was so sensitive to all those sensations.

The room had become so quiet, she could hear *herself* breathing. And her heart thudding. And perhaps even her blood rushing, having been turned into the Colorado River after the spring snowpack melt, by one dazzling male clad in a dashing flight suit and an I-rule-everything-including-you stare.

But it was never a good thing when *this* crowd went silent.

As she and Sam learned while turning their heads together, pushing the edge of their foreheads and then slowly rolling to the side...

Twenty-four sets of eyes. More eager than ever.

Twenty-four matching grins. Wider than ever.

And now, twenty-four raucous laughs, which got halted only because a few of the kids began a chant, which caught on through the crowd like wildfire.

"Kiss. Her! Kiss. Her! Kiss. Her!"

Oh, dear *hell*.

Out loud, Jen opted for the more acceptable choice—a

mortified groan—just before Sam broke out in a laugh that shook his shoulders and ignited silvery glints in his eyes. His mirth was contagious, at least to the point that she didn't argue as he scooped a hand behind her head and tucked her face close to his shoulder. Though he was far from an asshole about it, his firm grip nonetheless spoke to her with one forceful message.

*Stay. Put.*

And remarkably, she did. Even more amazingly, knowing that she *could*. That she had complete trust in Sam's ability to handle this mini mob, even if they all decided to become *real* squirrels, chitter their way up his tree trunk legs, and run around both their heads in the chanting demand for their kiss.

But thank God, this was Sam Mackenna: the pilot who made her think jets were his personal livery and hardened military mechanics were his loyal horsemen. The man who could, with one swoop of his free hand, silence every one of these squirrels like a thunderstorm in their forest.

And did.

"Awright now, you wee beasties. You want to stand here and clamor about somethin' that is not—I repeat, *not*—going to happen—"

"Ever?" Martha looked like the squirrel who'd just dropped all her nuts.

"—or would you like to think about gnoshin' on some yummy snacks real quick so we have time for a quick Scottish ghost tale?"

A collective squeal pushed at the confines of the library before the kiss chant was quickly replaced by a new war cry.

"Snacks, snacks, snacks, snacks!"

It was just as good a time as any for Jen to release a relieved sigh. And to follow it with a soft laugh, mixing hers to the sound of Sam's rich chuckle as he followed her into the stacks to help re-file books from the returns cart. It was easier to relax with him now, after an hour of seeing him acclimate on her "stomping grounds" instead of his, especially in the wake of his patience and charm with the kids she'd come to love so much. And with the cart between them, it was easier to resist the hot, heady temptation of the man's pull on every shred of her self-composure. Not that she wasn't still aware of it or wouldn't be even after he flew all the way back to Scotland. How far *could* a giant magnet pull on helpless particles doomed to be drawn to it? Or had he bypassed the magnet and gone straight for some Gaelic gypsy spell, entrancing her forever even if oceans separated them instead of a four-foot book cart?

At this moment, she was inclined to believe the latter. The heady force of his presence had only strengthened over the last week, which had brought her to more than a few full stops of astonishment. Until now, she'd written off this kind of allure as something that only happened in fiction, but here he was between *Little House Biddle Mouse* and *Little House in the Woods*, though standing like he was about to transform those tomes into Chaucer and Shakespeare, his long legs and proud shoulders making even his puke-green flight suit look like a nobleman's vestments. And here *she* was, trying not to look like she wanted to be wearing a corset and five layers of crinolines instead of slacks and heels, just so he'd shove the cart aside, pin her against the Warrior Cats shelf, and claim her mouth with a conquering lord's groan. Then he'd slide one of his large, powerful hands up under her skirts...and he'd use the other arm to capture her sighing swoon as she turned the texture of moors mist in his arms...

"Miss Jennnnn!"

When Sam started as violently as she did from Lindy's shriek, she bit back an instant giggle. His quirking lips warmed her heart even more—while dampening everything between her thighs. Clearly she hadn't been the only one to fall prey to their pull. And while the anomaly couldn't last forever, she took a second—just one—to enjoy it while it lasted.

"Lindy." She issued the calm reprimand while rounding the corner back toward the snack table. "Unless you see fire or blood, you stick to your inside voice, please. And sit down correctly. All four legs of the chair on the floor."

Lindy pouted. "But—"

"On. The. Floor, missy."

"But Anthony's about to upchuck!"

"Oh, dear freaking..." But by the time she got that far, Sam already braced his huge hands around the boy's ribcage, hoisted him out of his chair, and got him into the bathroom. Two seconds later, the poor kid's retching noises were overridden by a fresh wave of horrified *ewwww*s, as well as the boys' celebratory shouts. "All right!" she broke into the din. "Showtime's over, gang. Change of plans. You all now have some bonus playground time. Clean up *all* your trash before you leave. Remember, your cups go into the green recycle bin."

The group wasn't exactly ready with the gleeful cheers she expected. A sulking Martha supplied the reason why. "But Captain Mackenna promised us a ghost story."

More warm feels across her chest. She barely knew Sam but instantly interpreted the heartfelt nod he dipped from the open doorway of the bathroom. "I think Captain Mackenna would be happy to come back again soon in order to get that ghost story in."

"Yaaaaay!"

Just five minutes later, Anthony himself was piercing the air with the same word, having convinced Jen he only ate something weird and was feeling fine enough to go enjoy the bonus playtime. Imagine *that*.

Jen had just wrapped up the call she'd placed to the boy's teacher, warning the woman that a trip to the medical office might be happening before Anthony agreed to go to after-school homework club, when Sam sidled up to her side with a paper towel still in hand. *Incredible.* The man had just played nurse to a vomiting kid but still smelled like a mixture of balmy sun and spicy rain. More unbelievably, he was still grinning like a laird who'd merely been out romping with his wolfhounds in the heather fields.

As Jen stared at him in unguarded amazement, he murmured, "This was a much better afternoon than I ever thought it would be."

She couldn't help spurting a laugh. "Remind me to send *you* to the medical bay when we get back to Nellis."

He pivoted a little, regarding her with a thickening gaze and a smoldering mien. "But my aches can't be helped by doctors, lass."

So screw the damp panties. As Jen acknowledged the hot lump in her throat, she also accepted that the man had made her completely wet. Yes, right here in the afternoon sun. Yes, between the tetherball courts and the swing set. But the man and his inference, in that lush Highland growl and with that anticipating wolf's intent, swept her to the middle of a sexual forest, where anything could happen in the shadows...and she prayed that it would.

Only through sheer force of will, along with the nails she jabbed into her palms and the air she ordered into her lungs, was she able to avoid looking back at him and exposing all of those illicit fantasies to him at once. Somehow, she feigned her way through a light laugh instead. Then a flippant toss of her head, freeing her hair from where sweat made her shoulder-length waves cling to the back of her neck. "Don't be so sure of yourself, Captain. You haven't seen how cute they grow the nurses here in the great Mojave Des—"

She was cut short, in the most breath-halting way, by the invasion of a warrior-sized pilot into her personal space. Sam pushed nearly as close as he'd gotten in the conference room back on base, making damn sure she was very aware of every huge, taut muscle in his tall, tense form—and how they all seemed ready to obey the vexation in his eyes at his slightest command.

His command.

And his vexation.

What *would* the two be like when meted out, especially combined with the third factor about his new vibe?

*His desire.*

So apparent, she couldn't even write it off as chance.

So potent, she didn't want to.

"Jenny."

"H-Huh?" she managed to blurt.

"Why the fuck do you keep doin' that?"

"Keep...doing what?"

He leaned in even closer. Again, not as close as he'd compelled her before, but near enough that the sunlight sparked into his mesmerizing eyes, flaring the lightning-bright specks of silver in them. Over and over and over, he streaked that electric heat across her face until dropping right onto her lips as he drew in deep air through his flared nostrils.

"Maybe I'll have to take *you* back to school, Miss Thorne."
The gruff edges of his voice spoke the truth of the words—as
much an invitation to pleasure as pain. "You seem to have
forgotten a few...key lessons."

*Dear God.* As the outcry echoed through her senses, Jen
sneaked the tip of her tongue through the seam in her lips.
Sam's fascination with *that* turned into a flash of boldness
she'd never possessed before. "Lessons...have to come with a
plan of enforcement. You do know that, don't you, Captain?"

He gritted something in Gaelic beneath his breath. She
had no idea what it was, but the emphasis alone sent a new
gush of arousal through her entire core. Yep, she'd definitely be
driving the man back to base with soaked panties...

A theory proved to its fullest when they left VVE in the
rearview and headed back up I-15 toward the base. At once,
Jen hoped to resettle her nerves by cranking on the radio
and silently thanked the alt-rock gods for a well-timed block
of broody tunes designed to promo the "Emo Halloween-o
Weekend" that was coming up—but not even a string of AFI,
The Cure, and My Chemical Romance was daunting Sam
from twisting in the passenger's seat to fully face her and then
even reaching a hand over to the exquisitely sensitive spot on
the back of her neck.

"S-Sam..." She fought to get it out as a request instead of
a groan. His touch was pure heaven, making her want to melt
and quiver instead of navigating the mix of impatient locals
and lookie-loo tourists on the highway.

"Hmmm?" His voice offered an even more decadent
escape, lousy with a mix of seduction and command...the
perfect mix required for a Highland laird. Only this wasn't
medieval Scotland, and clan lairds were only something

traipsed out at costume fairs these days. In short, no matter how heady the fantasy he offered, she *had* to keep one foot grounded in reality. And hopefully take all her intimate bits along with it.

"You...that...feels wonderful, but..."

"But what, little mouse?"

One foot. Reality. Intimate bits too.

Even if he had gone ahead and turned "mouse" into an entrancing version of "moose" and had found the tightest wad of tension in her entire body to start kneading on...

With gritted teeth, she pulled herself away from him by leaning toward the steering wheel. Though she now looked like a blue-hair on her way to Bingo Night, the distance served her well with delivering fortitude—at least enough to state, "You don't have to. I'm all sweaty back there."

But damn it, the man simply slid his wickedly long fingers up and over her headrest, as if waiting for her to resettle before continuing to have his way with her nape. "Who says I don't *want* you sweaty, *a leanbh*?"

The man was *not* making this easy.

Not by one damn particle.

He did, however, provide her with a diversion—maybe something they both needed by this point. "So, what does that mean?" she queried, swiping her mind free of every torrid innuendo he'd just evoked. "*Lan-uhv?*"

Sam echoed her pronunciation, only finessing it with a lot more sex. At least that was what it sounded like to her, especially when he began his incredible rubbing as soon as she focused more on his voice than her Granny Thorne posture and resettled into the seat. "It's similar to how you'd say 'little one' or 'baby' here."

She side-eyed him with considerable snark. "Not 'OMG, this is the sweatiest neck I've ever massaged in my life'?"

He stopped his hand—but only long enough to snarl, "I thought I'd made my views clear about that."

She cleared her throat. "Yes, sir. You did."

His grip got tighter. A gruff grunt escaped him. "Say it again."

"You did." Jen issued it without thinking. But the man's beautiful brogue, layered over that leonine growl, would've had her agreeing to drive the car all the way to the edge of the Grand Canyon at this point. Probably right over the lip as well. "Made your views clear, I mean. I—I got it. You're fine with sweat. We're—We're clear." Only *were* they? Through her babbling, the man just kept clenching his grip tighter and harder.

"No," he finally uttered. His growl was gone. In its place was a tone more dangerous, like his throat had become a cold steel pipe—matched by a cuff he locked around *her* throat. And her mind, because she instantly knew the words he wanted.

The words she craved to give him.

"Yes, sir."

At once, he eased up on his hold to her nape. Dragged it up into her hair until his long, forceful fingers dug in against her scalp, kneading the back of her head. "*A leanbh*," he husked. "Good girl."

★ ★ ★ ★ ★

Before they got back to the base on the day they spent at school with the kids, he used the word at least six or seven more times with her—each time, seeming to reach inside her brain and discern exactly what they did to her. What *he* did to her with them, coupling every occasion to a touch or a smile or a look that served as a wordless, flawless reminder of a new connection they shared with each other. A connection leading them to a bridge...a bridge that would be burned once they crossed it. At least for her.

But then Jen remembered the foot she'd anchored in reality.

The reality that told her a masterful god like Sam Mackenna had probably crossed the Dominant/submissive bridge a long damn time ago. And that since then, he'd probably taken a spin around the dungeon with a lot of gorgeous, willing submissives. And that in a city like Vegas, she'd just be the first of many he'd meet and fuck, even in just four weeks here.

But for her, it'd be different.

He'd be her first.

And he'd be good.

Yes, she knew that—*knew* that—after just one perfect neck massage in the car.

He'd be that damn good—and she'd be that damn ruined.

But after her first taste of the sexual dynamic she'd craved ever since recognizing that it had its own name and rules and practitioners, would she be able to settle for anything else again? Was she doomed to be in some BDSM book nerds' purgatory forever, having found the only man who seemed to have brought all her fictional fantasies to life? And if so, wasn't she doomed to be there—if that was the standard she was holding living, breathing men up to?

It was all messed up.

Which meant she likely was as well.

And ever since Sam had walked her back to the office that

day, seeming to have figured that out for himself, she'd gotten in some long damn days to really hammer herself with the point. As in, a trio of twenty-four stretches in which the man didn't insert himself into her world at all. No hunk appearing filling her doorway every morning, interrupting her routine with his insolent smirk and a dumb joke. No dust-covered pilot reappearing in the afternoon with a cute pout of befuddlement, begging her to help him enter the flight logs correctly. And damn it, no striding stud in the hallways or across the tarmac outside her window, always accompanied by the slight jog back of his head, as he knew he'd just made her stop whatever the hell she was doing just to ogle his backside in that flight gear...

It had all just come to a screeching stop.

Yeah, even the damn tarmac strut.

Which, to be fair, she had no right to play pity party about, since the two flight squads had gone up on night hops for the last two nights. But where there was a will there was a way, and Jen would've bet solid money on the cast-iron texture of Sam Mackenna's will. No word from him in three days. The ghosts in the Mob Museum were seeming more real than him by the day.

Which shouldn't have stung so damn much.

But did.

Okay, so she hadn't expected him to drag her off to the nearest kink club, even after their potent exchange in the car. But the couple of hours *before* that moment—the afternoon in which she'd opened up a special part of her life to him—had earned her a kiss-off better than—well, a *kiss-off*. Not *this* kiss-off, that was for damn certain. But she wasn't going to give the issue the benefit of her stress. In the end, she had to realize that no matter how thoroughly Sam Mackenna had already rocked her world and awakened her libido, she'd be just a blip in the narrative of *his* life. It was the way of things, no matter how "incensed" the whole matter seemed to make him whenever she'd touched on it. Maybe he'd just finally seen the light. Or maybe the guys had really convinced him to go have some drinks and he *had* gotten a chance to see what the "local selection" was like for a guy like him. Or maybe he'd thought about the long game on all this, as she already had, and confronted the realities of being with a girl at least five notches down from him on the social totem pole.

All valid recognitions.

All doing absolutely nothing to ease the sting.

She had to approach this with her big-girl panties on. Like the week after she'd gone cold turkey on peanut butter pretzels, Jen knew she just needed time to feel like herself again. She'd get there...eventually. She'd be able to look at her mortal normality and realize it wasn't a half-bad place. She'd know again, very soon, that a girl *could* be happy, even if Mount Olympus and her own private god weren't going to be waiting over the horizon. Vanilla could still be a super decent flavor...

She just had to keep reminding herself of that.

Especially tonight.

Especially during this long minute of an elevator ride up to the Nyte Hotel's wedding level.

Okay, granted, showing up for an engagement party and "advanced wedding rehearsal" in one night, especially at the newest and hottest hotel in the city, wasn't exactly her idea of pressure-free fun at this point—but her best friend was worth it. It seemed only yesterday that Jen was joining Tess Lesange in the play-food kitchen in preschool; now they both had real-life kitchens of their own—though she wondered how much time Tess really had for whipping up things from scratch these days. The woman was a little over a week away from marrying one of the world's rising billionaires. Life at the side of Dan Colton, the golden-haired hunk who helmed Colton Steel and its gazillion subsidiaries, had been a whirlwind for Tess so far. Though Tess had moved to Dan's mansion in Atlanta, where the Colton Steel headquarters were located, Vegas had won out as an easier destination to access for most of the wedding guests, including Dan's Tacoma-based Army buddies and all of Tess's family, who still lived here.

Which was why Jen breathed a sigh of relief with the knowledge there was a different set of elevator banks in this place. No way could she imagine some of Dan's business associates, let alone Tess's oddball parents, using *this* lift car—though no way in the world did she refuse the chance to take what the cute girl at the concierge desk called the "Anything for Love Express." The alternate lift, the "Crystal Car," bore a much more mother-friendly title—and decorative theme.

"Vanilla is fine. Vanilla is fine. Vanilla is *great*, actually," Jen muttered as the lift doors closed, sealing her into a space that was covered in mirrors on the two longer walls, with padded leather surfaces consuming the others. She kept up the mantra while examining the rest of the car, blatantly recognizing why the Nyte was *the* Resort everyone talked about lately, in a city where "pushing the envelope" was what the competition was doing *last* year.

"Holy shit." *Not* the mantra but more than fitting, now that she spotted at least six different leather cuffs attached to strategically-mounted chains in the leather wall to her left. The control panel next to the door didn't just have options for floor numbers. There were illuminated buttons underneath the standard ones that gave options for activities like "Dim Lights," "Fun Swing," and "Scream Stop."

"Scream Stop?" she rasped to herself. "The hell? How could anyone get *that* far during an elevator—" Good thing she finally snapped more than two brain cells together, though when she continued, it was in a nearly breathless mutter. Blushes that felt more like hot flashes could definitely do that to a girl. "And thus, the Scream Stop. Nice work, Thorny-boo."

She saved the awful nickname only when feeling like a true doof, like all the falls she'd taken to earn the damn thing in the first place—and of course, right now. But she was still upright, which was a plus, and she was *alone*, another plus. If Mattie and Viv caught her gawking at the Scream Stop button, they undoubtedly would've found a way to turn her into "Thorny-boo" from their derision alone. Tess's sisters took special glee in the slick torment they'd dished out over the years, capitalizing on the fact that Tess had been the "circle the one who doesn't belong" part of the Lesange family portrait. It was why Tess and Jen had bonded into pseudo-sisters in their own right—and why, when Tess had first fallen for Dan, Jen had become her main sounding board for the years-long tale of unrequited love, insane spy adventures, and finally, the shocking news that *Dan* was secretly the Dom who'd been making all of Tess's D/s dreams come true.

And now, she was going to become the man's wife as well as his submissive.

The fantasy come true.

So yes, the kinky fairy tale really *did* happen for some. Just not all.

Right now, while exiting the lift, Jen ordered herself to thrust back her pity party because of the latter and focus on her heartfelt joy because of the former. It was past time to become a team player for her very best friend in the world. To turn her frown upside down. Get on board the happy-la-la wedding train. And, if she wanted to get historical book nerdy about it, to saddle up and stop burning bloody daylight.

Except there was one not-so-teeny hitch in that whole plan.

Saddling up a horse and swinging into the saddle probably would've been a simpler task than what she tried pulling off at that moment.

Marching into the wedding salon in four-and-a-half-inch-high Louboutins.

While attempting to take in the grandeur of a room that rivaled European cathedrals for gilt and fairy tale glens for beauty.

While trying to smile at the small throng gathered near the altar, including a glowing Tess and a beaming Dan, as if she saw places like this every day. Yep, even with fiber-optic lights that were suspended to look like stars and flying buttresses that were surely a scaled-down copy of Notre Dame's iconic architecture.

But forgetting every damn detail she'd just catalogued as soon as her gaze veered a little to the right...

And beheld the last person she expected to see here.

All six-foot-plus, gray-wolf-eyed, gloriously ginger-maned inch of him.

"Holy. Shit."

The doors of her consciousness blew back better than a Michael Bay movie clip—taking her precarious balance right along with them.

She went down, ass over elbows, sprawling face first

across the Italian marble floor. In two-point-five seconds, she found herself wondering why the hotel had ponied up for ornate carved cherubs at the *base* of each pew in the salon.

Before realizing she had about another two-point-five seconds to come up with the cleverest one-liner a woman could conceive after announcing her own entrance at an occasion like this.

That was how it was supposed to happen, right? Out would pop her inner Sofía Vergara, giving up the va-va-voom to make everyone dissolve into relieved laughter—especially the man who'd taken over all of her erotic fantasies within the last ten days? Yeah, the same chiseled Scot who led the pack to rush over to her...

"Holy. Shit."

The whisper deserved repeating as she dared a fast glance up, confirming her perceptions hadn't played tricks on her—that she hadn't been thinking about him so much, her imagination hadn't conveniently manifested him from thin air.

He was here. Really here.

And Sofía wasn't coming to her rescue—though somebody sure laughed *somewhere*. The giggles weren't in her head. They were as horridly real—and easy to recognize—as her fogged breath on the expensive floor.

Mattie and Viv Lesange were definitely in the house.

And ready to exploit her fall of infamy to their full advantage. And any *other* tangible weakness they could expose while they were at it. Which wasn't going to be too hard, since she was certain she already wore that truth across every inch of her face.

Right now, her only real weakness was Captain Sam Mackenna.

"Mouse?"

Especially when he leaned that close over her, engulfing her in his forest and ocean scent, turning *his* special name for her into a velvet caress on the air. And looking that damn good in the process. She'd seen him in civvies before, but his normal jeans and T-shirt combo hadn't prepared her for the deliciousness of what his long, lean muscles could do for a gray sport coat, white dress shirt, and black dress slacks. Business casual had met its poetic perfection.

Just like her embarrassment had met its sickening ceiling. "Sam," she squeaked, ordering her stomach not to join her heart in doing handsprings against her ribs. "Please—"

*Please, seriously, just go away. Let me deal with this like every clumsy girl attempting to acclimate to a pair of custom wedding Louboutins. Alone.*

"You need a hand?"

"No." *Especially not when you look good enough to make my damn toe hairs tremble.* "And don't call me that."

"Why the hell not?" He sounded confused, even a little hurt. Right. Like a demigod needed the validation of a paper pusher.

"You know why."

"Because I get beautiful 'yes, sirs' in return when I do?" So much for his puzzlement. He was back to insolent laird mode, rededicating himself with an intensity that had her breathless—and even a little scared. "Because I've been dreamin' nonstop of the next moment I'll get one?"

"Yeah?" She pushed to a sitting position, shoving dark strings of hair from her face. She'd actually thought the sleek, sophisticated look would be cool for the party, a combination engagement party and wedding rehearsal due to it being the one night *everyone* was available prior to the actual wedding date, but Audrey Hepburn she'd never be. "You have a funny way of communicating that to a girl, Mackenna."

He had the decency to purse his lips. "I know." And to drench that in enough remorse that she believed him. "And patchin' you was my last intention, I promise."

"All right, all right. I...believe you."

"Thank fuck."

She didn't expect the huge whoosh he used as punctuation, bringing on her rushed disclaimer. "Mind you, I don't *want* to, but..." Suddenly conscious of the sea of humanity approaching them, she gritted, "How are you here? *Why* are you here?"

When he kicked up the corner of his mouth, she wasn't sure whether to be reassured or unnerved. "I'm a plus-one."

And unnerved it was. "For who?" Though the amused glints in his gaze had her tacking on a good case of incensed as well. Which was irrational, she knew—unless fate was feeling really frisky this week and had managed to introduce him to Viv or Mattie within the last three days. Both of those wenches had been known to dip their well-pedicured toes into the Nellis flyboy pond from time to time, especially if a pilot as devastating as Sam showed up at one of the regular bars.

"The best man." Sam celebrated her confused scowl by nodding toward the half-Samoan giant standing at the altar, chatting with Dan. "John Franzen is a good mate. I think he took pity on me after calling to check in and seein' I was mopin' about over a certain emerald-eyed local lass." He paused to let that sink into her, his dimples deepening with knowing meaning. "Once I started bletherin' on about her, he told me I'd be wise to accept his invitation for this pure barry revelry."

She blinked for two seconds before deciding to focus on

what she *did* understand there. "You two...served together?" But really, no other explanation made sense. Franzen was a career army man and had been raised on Kaua'i. According to Sam's file, he came from a town just outside Edinburgh.

Sam grunted and then nodded. "Camp Bastion. Never underestimate its magical brotherly bonding powers."

The man's sarcasm was grim on purpose. Jen knew way better than to laugh. People rarely did when Bastion was invoked. The Brits' operating base in Afghanistan was no humorous matter. Located in the lethal Helmand Province, it was a dirty, dangerous compound sitting in the middle of nowhere, making it ideal as an airstrip and very little else. When the Americans joined the party too, the base became an even bigger play toy for the enemy—often with lethal results.

Suddenly, she found herself battling a violent urge to yank him close and not let go. Yes, right here and now. Yes, after just a glimpse at the demons he'd just exposed for her—though even that flash was likely too long a look for him. She was doing the overall math about Sam Mackenna now. The hundreds of tactical flights on his service record, spread over four deployments that had taken him to the shittiest parts of the globe. Then the sudden, seemingly inexplicable stop to it all...

That suddenly made a whole lot more sense...

But at the same time enforced why *she* wasn't the woman in the room he should keep devouring with his stare like that. The man didn't need a damn Catherine for his Heathcliff. He needed a Scarlett for his Rhett: a woman who'd force him to dance and laugh and drink sherry with her before letting him kiss her senseless while she sighed and swooned in submissive bliss.

A woman exactly like the one approaching them now.

Since hitting puberty, Mattie Lesange had elevated "blonde bombshell" into an art form. Jen should know because she had been there to witness every stage of the transformation, finely finessed from the second Mat learned she had curves and could use them to her maximum benefit. The woman was as well-schooled as a reality TV star about skating to the edge of slutty but never over it. In short, she was a perfect stateside diversion for Sam and would help him take the edge off his Dominant side with perfect, pouting skill. As she strutted closer, Jen saw the gears in the woman's head spinning no doubt about hooking up with Sam tonight. Probably dreaming up appropriate nicknames for herself, like *kitten* or *princess* or *sugar sweetness*.

Not *mouse*.

"Well," Sam went on then. "Looks like I'll be owin' Franzen a few pints for his pure magic suggestion." Though his expression instantly grew another few shadows of sardonicism. "Though the alternative activity of choice was a guys' trip to Disneyland tomorrow." He chuffed and shook his head. "Fuckin' Franz can be a glaikit bawbag when he wants to be."

Jen's return smile came all too easily—not great for maintaining her Catherine Earnshaw side but pretty fun for coaxing out more of his entrancing new dimple. "What? You really don't want to get a pair of plastic mouse ears to take home and show off? They have all kinds to pick from now, you know. I think pink fuzzies with your call sign in purple bling would be perfect."

Sam mock-glowered—for all of a second. As soon as the look moved into real seriousness, his eyes gained a new gleam.

Jen swallowed past a sudden cotton mouth. Fought against getting sucked into that stare of his, so sizzling and brilliant...

Hopeless cause.

Especially as he leaned over, both hands raised, knuckles brushing her cheeks...

Before yanking on her earlobes and cracking a broad smirk. "Don't think the plastic ones will compete with these beauties."

She spurted a laugh. Good thing. It disguised the quiver conquering the rest of her body...and then the heat in the tender tissues between her thighs. Even after he lifted up, her pussy thrummed and pulsed in accentuated awareness...

*Hell.* He'd only indulged some playful tugs on her *ears.* What the hell was wrong with her? She surely wasn't any Mattie, but she wasn't a shivering virgin anymore either. Men had touched her before. In *lots* of places.

But none of them had been Sam Mackenna.

*Danger zone, girl. You are way behind the boundaries of what's good for you here. Get out now, while you can still sprint back to the border. Get out while your important parts are still safe. Parts like your heart....*

"Captain Mackenna?" she finally murmured.

He gave in to a new smile. "Yes, Miss Thorne?"

"You're so full of shit."

He dropped his hands. Chortled harder. Making him laugh shouldn't have felt so damn good...

"Well played, *a leanbh.* Well fuckin' played."

But it did—in the exact same way his comeback made her belly tingle, her heart race, and her libido gallop.

*A leanbh.*

It didn't mean a thing. Or so she kept ordering at herself.

Sam was still an outsider in this country and simply felt comfortable enough with her to sling the casual flattery. And Jen was just an outsider, period. He'd get that point soon enough—especially as Mattie sauntered near enough to wrap a hand to Sam's shoulder.

Her nails, painted in a trendy reverse French, tightened on his broad muscle with their shiny ebony tips. In a voice as smooth and glossy, she crooned, "Everything all right here, Thorny-boo?"

"Sure." *Except for the ride back to the worst parts of adolescence. Thanks so much, Mat.*

Mattie's laugh was as perfect—and fake—as Marilyn Monroe's on a press junket. "Sweetie, don't pout. It brings out yucky lines in your face. Besides, I kind of like all those cute memories."

Jen wasn't sure whether to drive Mat insane by pouting harder or confuse the hell out of her by giggling as Sam purposely slid away from her grip. Fortunately, the man made it possible to stay in a neutral zone between the two by rendering his own reaction, tagged with an openly curious stare. "Memories?"

And God, was she glad for that neutral zone. Poor Sam had no way of knowing that his politeness had just sent a deeper dredge into her humiliating past, but she wasn't about to give Mattie any more fuel for her gluttonous gloat.

"We all grew up together," the woman explained, damn near pulling off the act of an affectionate school chum recalling "the good ol' days." "Jen was always the most adorable thing with her pratfalls. Then when her auntie came to pick her up from school, the woman would kiss all over her 'boos.' After a while..."

*You and Viv turned it into the nickname I hated more than any other.*

"I think he probably gets the idea," Jen blurted instead. This evening was Tess's special time, and she wasn't about to taint any of it by dragging either of her sisters through the mud they enjoyed slinging. Besides, it was clear Sam *did* get the idea, evidenced by his tightening brows and hardening jawline. At once, Jen hated his new expression. She knew the beginning of pity when she saw it, and it was awful even on his beautiful features.

And no, it wasn't any better when he growled, sounding wrathful and protective, before uttering, "Mattie."

"Hmmm?" The woman didn't flinch at a note of his warning tone. She was either really clueless or had the biggest pair of girl balls Jen had ever encountered.

"Cool it."

"*Please.* Jen doesn't mind. If anything, her little stumbles made us all adore her more. She used to send us all into fits, always walking around with her nose in some book. We often joked that the aliens could fly right over from Area 51, land in the school's quad, and Thorny-boo would barely notice—until she took a header into the bushes. Or the wall. Or down the stairs. Even the teachers excused her from being tardy all the time, because—"

"*Mattie.*" A heftier dose of Sam's tone finally silenced her. Still, Jen couldn't pick stupidity or girl balls when the woman returned Sam's glower with a blithe little grin. With those deep furrows in his forehead and heavy breaths flaring his nostrils, the man was even a little...scary.

In all the right ways.

All the most arousing ways...

She couldn't go there. She *wouldn't*. Her racing pulse and electrified nerve endings had *much* different ideas.

This was insane. This was incredible.

"Honey! Is everything okay?"

Tess to the rescue. *Thank God.* Her friend grabbed her by both hands, a huge grin on her face as she helped Jen gain her feet once more. That was also a damn good thing, since she now had the treat of viewing Tess from head to toe.

Her friend was nothing less than stunning in a red sleeveless sheath that hugged her cute figure, as well as showing off her shoulder-to-elbow tattoos. Tess's latest ink, a heart emblazoned on the middle of her chest with Dan's initials in the middle, peeked from the dress's sweetheart neckline. Everyone would be able to see the full tattoo in a couple of weeks, thanks to the breathtaking cut of the cream-colored gown Tess had selected in which to become Mrs. Daniel Colton.

*Mrs. Daniel Colton.*

Holy...cow.

A smile split across Jen's face now as she reassured her friend, "I'm fine, girlie. And *you* are gorgeous." An understatement. Her friend's beauty, so similar to Mattie's on the surface, with a button nose and heart-shaped chin, went so much deeper than the surface. Tess had a soul as vivid as the color wash that turned her hair a blazing red and a generous heart that burst through in every sparkle of her brilliant green eyes.

And oh yeah: a bullshit meter that was wickedly accurate, even *before* her stint with the FBI. "Why do I not believe you?" the woman accused, clearly putting the meter to good use with the force of her conviction.

"Because you're a dork," Jen teased. "Come on, Tess. Chill. I just need a little more practice in these heels, which was exactly why I wore them tonight."

"Well." Mattie's matter-of-fact tone was likely the closest she'd come to comfort. "At least nothing valuable seems broken."

"Of course not." The rejoinder came from Viv Lesange, who'd slipped in next to her sister. She clearly didn't have the same designs on Sam as Mattie, being the girl who gravitated toward pretty boys who had twelve opinions on every trending Twitter tag—with a matching number of piercings. "Our Thorny-boo is made of Teflon."

Jen didn't bother with a glare. Tess flung a strong glare for them both. Mattie and Viv blinked back, as clueless as sticks of chalk, before Mattie offered, "Maybe it's best that she rests. I'm more than happy to walk the aisle again so she can get how the heels are handled."

"No." Jen borrowed more of Sam's growl. Owing a "favor" to Mattie Lesange, however small, would've been equal to jabbing a spike into her brain. "I'll get it right," she insisted, pushing off the pew she'd been using for some extra support. "I just need to—"

And right on schedule, her balance protested the Louboutins again. Just two seconds, and she teetered precariously...

Directly into Sam.

# CHAPTER FOUR

"Oh, God!"

Jen's outcry sent a fan of heat across Sam's chest as she grabbed him tight, digging her pretty fingers into his biceps and awakening even more primal urges through his entire system. Especially as her thighs slammed hard against his. And her luscious breasts mashed into the wall of his chest. And her heartbeat pounded relentlessly next to his, practically in unison to the wild, lusting gallop of his...

But he didn't let her go. He gripped her even harder than she grabbed him, knowing she didn't want to fall again—

But unable to think of lettin' her do anythin' else.

And how she'd look if she took him down with her...

Until they were prone on the floor together and she was beneath him in all her sighing, sweet, passionate resplendence...

Makin' him wonder what she'd say if he ordered everyone—politely, of course—to adjourn themselves for dinner already. Everyone but her. She would stay right here. Gaspin' and writhin' as he hiked her filmy skirt to her waist. Sighin' and keenin' as he ripped her panties away and took her here and now like the cretin she'd undeniably turned him back into.

Holy fuck, he was so hard.

And so ready.

Like he had been for three goddamned days now...

"Shit, Sam. I'm so sorry."

"I'm not." It spilled from him as breath more than volume, zapped that way by the energy arcing between their bodies. The hot, torturous force sizzled through his nerves and bubbled in his blood before shooting down to invade the length of his cock, causing it to punch the front of his pants even harder.

He wanted her.

Despite knowing she still didn't believe that.

He needed her.

Even more so as she jerked her head up and locked her gaze with his.

Her gaze.

Ah dear God, her eyes.

The dark, endless seas of them were a force on his senses, makin' him pull her even closer, until the cadence of her heartbeat pulled on his like an ancient siren's song, awakenin' more primeval instincts inside him. Oh aye. He was a painted Pict, huntin' a graceful she-stag across the moors. He was a medieval archer, trackin' a wild hawk across the crags of Skye. He was raw lightning, chasin' her rain across a gray and violet horizon...

"Why?"

He started from her sudden blurt, though it barely dented the primordial images dominating his imagination. "Why... what?"

"Why are you not sorry?" She crunched an urgent frown. It had to be one of the bonniest sights he'd ever seen.

Sam swallowed hard. It was no proper answer but with any luck might lead to one. She had, after all, asked the perfect question for it. *I'm not sorry because I came here on this exchange thinkin' I would be. Thinkin' I had nothin' left to offer my country but a man carved hollow by too much blood on his hands and too many hours in the cockpit. Thinkin' I had nothin' left to give the world but a soul full of disillusionment, and a heart full of loneliness. A Heathcliff who'd never really find his Catherine...*

*Until you, Jenny.*

*Until you.*

But while he had the answer, he still didn't have the right opportunity. Her furtive glance around brought him back to that recognition. Clearly she was already a ball of anxiety about becomin' the main attraction, instead of the friend for whom she'd showed up for, even in heels that had damn near been her ruin. He was glad to see that no one seemed more aware of that fact than Tess Lesange herself, who was still eyein' Jenny for damage from top to bottom.

"Hmmm..." Though suddenly she was including him along with her assessment. And throwin' in that weird little commentary on top of her perusal too—which in turn didn't escape Jen's attention.

"Hmmm...what?" she challenged to Tess, twisting enough in Sam's hold to prop a hand against her waist.

"Yeah." Dan moved in behind his fiancée. "Hmmm what, my little ruby?" The man took Jen's threads of suspicion and wove them into a full vocal tapestry, framing the whole thing inside a watchful scrutiny. Sam, continuing to secure Jenny at his side, looked on with a nod of appraisal—and approval. Franzen had supplied enough hints about Dan's darker Dominant tendencies that Sam already had a good idea about the fuller aspects of the couple's relationship, but watchin' Dan finesse his Dominance over Tess with more subtle techniques was like observin' a master martial artist at work. It only looked easy.

"I was just thinking"—Tess tapped a finger to the side of her chin—"about how nice Jen and Sam look together."

"Well, thank ye." Sam laid on the charm enough for Tess to clap in delight, giving him time to dip a deferential nod at Dan. The way Dan held Tess with protectiveness but not possessiveness, along with his subtle squeezes to her nape and wrists, were all just subtle affections to the majority of the room—but likely carried a huge world of meanin' between the Dominant and his pretty subbie. *Well done, mate*, he conveyed silently to Colton. Out loud, he continued to Tess, "I couldn't agree more."

"Right?" Tess's face lit up as she swiveled to face her fiancé. "He couldn't agree more. That definitely means I should go to talk to the banquet captain about scooting around the place settings for dinner, and—"

"No."

"No?" Tess spat it from compressed lips but backed off on her rebellious salt the second Dan swung around to fully face her, arching his left brow so sharply, it pulled on the swath of burn tissue along that side of his face. During the drive here, Franzen had given Sam the tweet-length explanation about Dan's scars, because both of them had lived with stories like it for a long damn time. A mission, an explosion, a fire, and some trapped nurses. Dan had gotten the job done. Enough said.

"I said no, my little rose." A new tug at the back of her neck was as gentle as his murmur above her forehead. He officially turned the woman to mush by bussing her hairline with the same firm forbearance. "You've been working yourself ragged on all of this for weeks, and tonight, I am instructing you to do nothing but be in this moment, with me, and enjoy the beauty of what you've created." He slid a thumb beneath Tess's chin, coaxin' her face up, and Sam swore his breath snagged right along with the woman's pleasure-filled little gasp. The look Tess blessed her Dom with...soaked with her trust and adoration and love... He'd not ever had the joy of such a moment with a submissive yet, but getting to witness such a connection was a gift as sacred and perfect as a sunrise over the Trossachs. The magic was really possible. If fate had brought him to the States just for this message, then the trip would've been worth it. But by God, he hoped he'd been brought here for more—and that the bonus included creating some special times with the gorgeous brunette in his arms.

"Yes, Sir."

He'd been so lost in spinning up some new fantasies about Jen, it took a second to identify the breathy little sigh had emanated from Tess instead. Dan rewarded her with a low, satisfied growl before shifting his tender kisses to the bridge and tip of her nose. "I mean it, sweet one. From this moment on, you're to relax and enjoy the hell out of all this. If Jen and Sam want to sit together, I'm sure they'll find a way to sit together." He emphasized that by tossing a look to Sam as clear as it was quick. *Just fucking do it, man.* "My little ruby is going to simply revel in this special night...and all of its fun surprises."

"Yes, S—" Tess stopped short, her face swapping out languid and submissive for stunned and alert. "Wait. What? Surprises?"

As she spurted the last of that, a handful of hotel staffers pulled open a pair of double French doors on the far side of the salon—to reveal a spacious terrace awash in the dark amber rays of early twilight. In the center of the space was an elegantly set dining table. It was surrounded by towering palms, their graceful trunks wrapped in white twinkle lights.

The table glowed as well, since LED lights were embedded beneath its surface. Red- and gold-colored roses floated on a miniature reflecting pool that extended the length of the table. Nearby, waiters in tuxedoes stood at the ready with trays of champagne and chilled flutes. Sixty stories below, the city's iconic Strip blazed to life, lights flickering and traffic bustling, as the night approached.

"Oh...my." Tess's exclamation matched the awe across her face, meanin' her man was equally lousy with emotion. In the space of a snap, Dan had abandoned his growlin' hound of command to simply simper like a lad who'd given his special lass a fine gift from the depths of his heart—and probably had. That explained why Dan hadn't wanted her footerin' about and chasin' down the banquet staff too. He'd wanted this moment all to himself.

"Do you like it?"

At first, Tess didn't utter a word of reply. But her teary gaze spoke a thousand to everyone in the salon, making it inconsequential when she rasped her answer right into Dan's ear. Everyone broke into applause when she sealed the perfection of the moment by popping up on tiptoes and dragging the man down for a ravaging, rolling kiss that left very little of her intent to the imagination.

Aye. Perfection.

"Ohhhh, you crazy kids." Franzen, obligin' a pointed look from Tess's mother, moved in to disengage the lovers from their public gobble under the guise of movin' the party along. "Let's save some of the fun for the wedding night, yeah?" Spreadin' out his massive arms—over here, they called them "guns," but when it came to Franzen, the moniker fit—he clapped one huge hand to Dan's back and then the other over to Tess. "We know eight days sounds like forever, but—"

"That might be how long you'll need to get out of traction, Pineapple Smoothie," Dan cut in. "Unless you choose to get your charming paws off my subm—my fiancée."

Franzen chortled, along with most of the gents in the room, at Dan's little slip. "As you wish, Dungeon Fun Ken."

Another round of laughter, for which Sam was instantly grateful. The moment presented a prime opportunity to gauge Jen's comfort level with talk like this: thinly-veiled references to the BDSM dynamic that her best friend clearly indulged in with Dan. He set his expectations for everything from matching laughter to a discomfited squirm...

Everything other than what he did observe.

The two women were actually eye rolling at each other. As if the "boys" were preoccupied with their innuendos, and they were sneakin' in the chance for a shared titter before the Doms got serious again...

Sam almost nudged Dan so the mate could catch his subbie red-handed—red eye-rolled?—but he let the girls have their fun, even enjoyin' what he witnessed. In many ways, he was reassured. Clearly Jen came from a crowd in which Dominance and submission were approached with respect but not held up as religion. That was good. Really bloody good. But at the same time, kind of bloody bad. Now more than ever, it was so easy for him to envision sweet Jenny surrenderin' to him. Tied down by him. Cuffed for him. Naked and spread and ready for him. Utterly vulnerable to his every desire and pleasure but knowin' the power she gave up was his to borrow, not to keep.

And damn, did he have some brilliant ideas about how to return some incredible dividends to her with that loan.

Naughty, nasty, filthy things. Decadent, flagrant, wild things that would leave some sweet, sexy marks on her for a few days, remindin' her of exactly who had conquered her body and then looked into her very soul.

Shit. Shit.

He forced down a deep breath. Directed his imagination to hit the fuckin' showers—and to crank the knob all the way over to C.

He'd only been in the same room with her again for fifteen minutes, and he was already doin' it again. Dreamin' up scenes that weren't what "friends" did with each other, in any fuckin' culture across the globe. Worse, he was glommin' extra details that were five steps past the edge of dangerous. Looked into her soul? What kind of mince was that, and who the hell did he think he could fool with it?

Fuckin' hard to see into a person's soul, when a man wasn't sure if any of his was still left.

Not after what he'd seen.

Not after what he'd done.

*So maybe you should stop moonin' over the woman like you're on a desert island and she's the only biscuit left on the beach.*

But he looked anyway.

To find her peerin' back at him. Just as intensely.

Fuck.

But now that they'd started this, no way could he even think of endin' it.

No. He'd already started it—from the second she'd blurted her first "Yes, sir," to him, three days ago when they were on the motorway back to the base.

Two small words...but he savored what they did to him.

Throughout his body...and yes, deep in his soul.

No. He hadn't savored them.

He'd treasured them.

And he did again now, in every relevant way, while watching Jen twist a delicate fist against the middle of her stomach. While observing her heartbeat thud at the base of her throat, savoring the telling dilation of her pupils as he kept gazing at her, and securing her a little tighter to his side. While she answered that subtle move with the tiniest jerk of her hips, coupled with the tiniest clench of her jaw...betraying exactly what he'd done to the hottest, tightest grottoes of her body...

"Oh," she whispered.

"Christ," he gritted back.

Just before more servers entered, bearing trays of hors d'oeuvres that layered the balmy air with savory, delicious aromas. But as everyone hummed in delight and started moving toward the terrace, Sam let them pass his unmoving form—as Jen took advantage of the moment to extricate herself from him, murmuring about a need to use the ladies' room.

A need he should let her attend.

A break they both needed.

A space he should recognize, giving them room for rational regard, sober perception, sensible breaths.

But that was what he'd told himself for three damn days. Had assured himself would be a positive for them, lending the distance and clarity they needed about this—whatever the hell this was. Yet with every sway of her escaping backside, those glorious ass cheeks moving so perfectly against her silky dress, the only label he could assign to the last three days was a matching number of words.

Fucking wasted time.

And one of the few important truths he'd learned from years in the world's finest hellholes? Time liked being wasted the way death liked being disrespected. Both ended up with a guy's balls strung up in a sling, watching his own hand twisting the counterweight.

He was done with the sling. Same way he was done with figuring out "friendship" with this woman. Same way he was damn sure Jen was done with it too.

He just wished he could still be sure about that once he rounded the corner of the terrace, onto a smaller side patio consumed mostly by a comfortable seating area around a modern fountain. Box hedges framed three sides of the setting, with the fourth bein' a sheer glass wall overlooking the Vegas Valley all the way out to Red Rock Canyon. In the last glow of the day, the canyon's edges were majestic silhouettes against a sky as glorious as any back home, autumn colors setting the firmament afire in shades of orange, amber, purple, and red.

The splendor was perfect for Sam's intentions. He sprinted toward Jen, calculating how many steps it would take to rope an arm around her again and then how many more to carry her to one of the couches and finally kiss every damn thought out of her mind and protest out of her senses, until all she felt was all of his passion and all of her need for it...

Except that Jen wasn't making a beeline for the bathroom anymore.

Jen wasn't going anywhere anymore.

She'd stopped so suddenly next to one of the hedges, Sam almost wondered if she'd gotten snagged by the bush, except that the silent panic on her face didn't match that motivation. Unless there was a serial killer clown or soul-sucking wraith hidden in the bush, he didn't know what had her looking ready to throw herself off the tower rather than move another muscle...

Until laughter gashed the air.

It was more like caustic giggles, but semantics weren't his primary concern at this moment—in which the whole, sudden mess of a situation became clear in one blast of a look.

There was Jenny, caught behind the closest hedge. There was the entrance to the privies, located at the other side of the patio.

And there were Mattie and Viv Lesange, lounging on a couple of couches in that patio as if they were going to be there all night...prattlin' in gossip about Jenny herself.

"Ohhhh, whatever are we going to do with our darling Thorny-boo?" Mattie crooned, suckin' long on a fag and then blowin' out the smoke with her head tilted back.

"You're asking me?" Viv drawled. "Bitch, please."

"Honestly, if you aren't laughing at her, you're crying for her." Mattie Lesange lived up to her sister's label by deep-frying her words in a vat of snide.

"Speak for yourself on that one." Viv rose and turned, but the sole glass of whisky in Sam's system had barely dulled his reflexes, and he ducked behind a planter of palm trees before she saw him. Not that the woman seemed to care about the world beyond impressin' her older sister, no matter who she had to throw under the bus to do it. "I'm not going to waste the tears. I mean, that 'look, I'm so clumsy I'm adorable' shit was semi-excusable when we were kids. Who does she think she's fooling anymore?"

"Right?" Mattie took a long swig on her wine before reaching into her bag and popping open a makeup compact. While foofin' her hair and checking her lipstick, she muttered,

"She has to know how to walk a straight line in heels by this point. Isn't that just a basic thing, like learning to shave your legs or brush your teeth?"

"Well, she does work at the base." Viv might as well have been disclosing Jen was walkin' the streets for a living. "She's in HR, or whatever they call that in the military. Maybe the work keeps her on her feet a lot, and—"

"Heels aren't outlawed on military bases, V." A feline sniff from the woman still primpin' in the compact mirror. "I have seen *Top Gun*. Whose side are you on?"

"Are you even asking me that right now?"

Mattie lifted a gentler stare. Pursed her lips as if an actual apology was about to emerge. Instead, she justified, "I'm just tense. You know that. A little off my game."

"I know. It's all right." Viv's heels clacked on the tile as she grabbed up her own wine and paced in front of the windows. Sam was about to give the girl credit for at least stopping to admire that eye-poppin' sunset, until he realized she was using the glass to assess her own reflection. Not that there was much to check out, since it seemed the girl had bought a roll of tinfoil and chosen to call it a dress.

"I just...didn't expect someone like Sam Mackenna on the guest list. I mean, Dan knows some fine, fine men, but that Scot is in a class all by himself..."

"No shit. And you were definitely letting him know that!"

Sam grimaced into the palms. Was that what Mattie's glaikit glances were all about? He thought she was just suppressin' gas or battlin' female cramps.

"Right?" Mattie returned. "But then Thorny had to pull her little face-plant and get him all worked up over her precious, petite little ankles. And then whisper and giggle at him like some tourist flirt in the Encore pool."

Sam was damn glad the palms were well planted. Though if much more trash came out of either of those witches, he'd go ahead and uproot a couple anyway—and then replant each of them in the women's laps. For now, he restrained his rage. The trees provided an equal shield from Jen's view, and he already knew that she'd be horrified about him witnessing her reactions to the sisters' exchange. The tears shimmering on her lashes. The stubborn quavering of her chin. Firsthand, he'd seen what the wars of men did to entire countries—but witnessing what women could do to each other was nearly just as harrowing.

"Wait." Viv spun around so fast, her wine sloshed. "Do you really think she's making a play for Sam?"

"No. I don't think it." Mattie clamped her compact closed and hurled it back into her bag. "I know it."

Fortunately, Jen gasped at the same time as Viv. Sam clenched his fists, fighting not to rush to her, as she clamped a hand over her mouth. Her eyes, still visible to him, shimmered brighter with moisture. She looked hurt—but something more.

She looked...convicted.

"Oh, come on." Mattie huffed at her sister. "Nobody's that much of a train wreck just because."

"Good point." Viv hummed. "But you're not actually worried about this, are you?"

"Bitch, please." Mattie waved her nearly drained glass in an adamant sweep. "The day I sweat a drop about little Jennifer Thorne is the day I buy a cat and look for assisted living." She drained the last puddle of wine and then set the glass down with an angry clang. "Let's get real. Even if I wasn't in the picture, Captain Mackenna wouldn't be tapping on that girl's front door—or anything else of hers. He's out of her league."

"True..."

But the catch in Viv's voice was blatant.

"What?" Mattie charged.

"It's just..."

"Just what?"

"We said the same thing about Tess and Dan."

"Which supports my theory further."

"Oh?"

"Nature's not going to allow another lightning strike under their geeky little rock so soon."

Viv's laughter was so pronounced, the water in the fountain jerked from the vibration on the air. It matched the visible shiver that coursed through Jen as well. She held on to the tension from top to bottom as the girl queried her sister, "So what's your plan of attack now?" but Mattie took her time about contemplatin' that answer as she re-shouldered her handbag and started leading the way back to the party.

Because in truth, she didn't have an answer.

Because deep down, that bitch knew there would be no fucking plan of "attacking" him. An attack implied a territory or victory to be gained—and Mattie Lesange, while cunning and seductive, was nobody's warmer; she knew damn well there'd be no territory to "win" with him beyond social niceties.

But he wasn't leaving a shred of that surety to chance.

Or a syllable of his message to nuance.

Or a single more minute to the time he and Jen had already wasted in their senseless dance around the bush with each other.

And fate, finally giving him a break, happened to present the perfect opportunity to accomplish all three.

Despite how much he hated the circumstances in which it was startin'. With Jen's heartache, evident on every inch of her lovely face as she emerged from behind the hedge, stumblin' onto the patio and fallin' into one of the chairs across from where Viv and Mattie had held their court of ruthless judgment. With the blatant shakes of her shoulders once she dropped her face into her hands, unloadin' a long, hurting groan against her palms. With the transformation of that pain into angry tears, as plain as her sadness had been, as soon as she reared her head back up again.

With her furious surge back to her feet and then her stormin' retreat from the patio.

But not his direction. Not toward the privies either.

She shoved through another glass door, which Sam hadn't seen from the alcove of his position. And though he was able to swiftly tail her, his chest fisted when seein' where she'd ended up.

At the elevator bank.

Callin' one of the lifts that were rigged like shoebox dungeons.

Which might have been a damn fine thing, if not for how the woman pounded on the call button like Trinity from *The Matrix*, standing in the phone booth and waiting for Morpheus to pick up.

Goddamnit, how he yearned to be her Morpheus. And her Neo. Her hero but also her ruin. Her pleasure and her pain. Her bad idea but the best brainstorm she'd ever had. The one she'd break the rules for—only to realize that the greatest risks brought the sweetest rewards.

Maybe that was going to be the prize she got out of all this—but again, fate's higher purpose wasn't his picture to see here. Not yet, at least. That was the thing about big lessons. They were usually mosaics, not watercolors. And they usually only came one tile at a time.

And right here and now, he could only control how this tile got painted.

And knew it sure as hell wasn't meant to have her tear-streaked face all over it.

"Jen."

Which was why he sprinted faster as she started jabbing the button harder.

"Jen!"

Then even faster as the lift on the left slid open.

"Jen!"

And he went completely Neo on her, diving into the lift head first, split seconds before the doors whumped shut.

# CHAPTER FIVE

"*Shit.*"

Jen choked it out as soon as the elevator doors opened and she processed enough of Sam's behavior to arrive at one indelible conclusion.

He'd been spying on the exchange between Mat and Viv too.

*Damn it.*

All right, hopefully not the entire conversation—though he'd seen enough of things to know she'd opted to come this way instead of the restrooms, which probably meant he'd heard the words that had turned her belly into a swamp of disgust and her heart into a forest of anger.

It hadn't just been the petty shit they'd accused *her* of. The way they'd dehumanized Sam, like he was a slab of prize game they could stalk and bag, had had her debating whether to break out of her hiding place and "bumble" her way into tossing their drinks back into their faces. She'd held back out of respect and love for Tess. The woman, who did so much for so many, deserved a night of celebration with her family and friends, not hours of stress filled with her piece-of-work sisters going off about her dorky best friend.

And ergo, her sprint for the elevators instead of the ladies' room. Along the way, she'd tapped out a fast text to Tess, explaining she was going to her car to change into more reasonable shoes—not a lie, but she also needed the self-imposed time-out simply to get herself under control again. Not just because of the rage ball from Viv and Mat. She'd already been a massive tangle of nerves and emotion, thanks to John Franzen's "surprise" plus-one to this thing—and oh yeah, the "fun" elevator ride she'd been on right before *that*...

And now here she was, back at square one for all that.

No. Was there such a thing as negative square one? Whatever the hell *that* was called.

Worse, because she now realized she'd punched the wrong damn floor number too. And there was no way she could reach around to correct her blunder. Sam made *that* part clear as soon as the doors closed all the way and crowded in on her, consuming her immediate sights with the raw wolf hunger of his unblinking stare. Then blocking out all her light with the looming cliffs of his shoulders. Then filling up her senses with his intoxicating smell, all forest and cedar and leather. Then paralyzing her with the wavelengths of his energy, volatile and virile and focused. Completely on her.

"S-Sam." And her inner Sofía was still on an extended break, leaving her to scrape together a coherent voice from the awkward, exposed tatters of her self-composure. Five minutes ago, she'd been shaking in protective rage for him. Now, she was trembling in giddy, smitten awareness *because* of him. And it felt completely ridiculous. And utterly miraculous. This was the part where her corset was supposed to feel too tight, only in no world was a silk wrap dress from the last Nordstrom Rack sale even close to a corset. This was also the part where he was supposed to lean in tighter, letting his hooded stare drop to her gasping lips, but then pull back, bussing her knuckles instead before softly growling if he was intruding in on her tender sensibilities...

Sam definitely had the lean-in nailed.

And the smoldering viscount fixation on her mouth, from which she was frantically inhaling and exhaling as he got closer. Then closer...

But no way was there going to be a dignified retreat. Not by an inch. Not by a breath. As her breaths came with more merciless force, the huge Scot scooped up her wrists beneath his hands, pinned them against the leather wall, and then used his thigh to secure her from the waist down—by pushing it directly between her own.

"S-Sam!" She wasn't sure if she wanted to yelp it from sheer shock or cry it from sheer joy. As a result, the sound was a weird combination of the two. He seemed to get the gist, since he went right on rocking his boulder-hard quadricep directly against the part of her legs. Her whole body trembled in support of what her pussy had already begun. "S-S-Sam..."

"Hmmm. My sweet Jennifer."

For a second, her glare eclipsed every shred of her nerves. "*Jennifer?*"

"Would you prefer Jennifer Josephine Thorne?"

"Would you prefer to keep your teeth?"

The elevator started to ascend. He tilted his head, letting his eyes dip over her face and then back up again. Though they glittered brighter than ever, his mouth stuck to a no-nonsense line—as he started working her crotch with the flat of his beautiful thigh again.

"I'd *prefer* that we finally cut the bullshit." He barely lifted it past a murmur. He didn't have to. Oh damn, he was so close. So big and hard and—

"A-About wh-what?"

He pulled in such a deep breath, she felt the point that it

shook his whole chest. "For starters, all the utter keech from those two shrews that nearly turned you into a gingin' mess."

"Huh?"

His lips thinned. His gaze sharpened. The expression might've been only nominally daunting if he didn't reinforce it by working his fingers over her inner wrists and palms of her hands. Holy *shit*. How did the man *know* all the nerves there seemed to be wired right into her arousal centers? *All* of them...

"Mattie and Viv were spewin' raw shit, *a leanbh*. And if tonight wasn't so important for your friend, I would've made certain I melted all the makeup off their faces while informin' them of that. 'Course"—he narrowed his eyes and seesawed his head—"that might've taken a spell to accomplish, seein' as they piled themselves like six-layer trifle..."

Jen spurted a laugh. He didn't. As best as she could tell, he was still brutally serious. She watched his pulse throb at the base of his throat. Let her gaze descend to where his taut, golden skin disappeared into the V of his shirt. "So...what else are we cutting the bullshit about?"

He was silent. For way too long. Which only curled his heavy, dark growl deep into her blood.

"Jen."

She gulped again.

"Jenny."

*God.* When was the last time she'd been called that? Never. And had it ordered at her in that deep purr... Her senses felt punched through the elevator's roof, up the shaft, and into the endless stars outside.

"Wh-What?"

"Look at me."

She had no choice. He controlled her then, his voice like

velvet strings, tugging her sights up. Over his taut jaw. Across the defined curves of his lips. Into his quicksilver eyes, fixed on her.

"This is going to happen."

*Shit.*

She gulped. Really hard.

"You know it, Jenny...and *I* know it. We're not in control here anymore. This is..." He grunted, shaking his head before lowering his forehead atop hers. "I'm not fuckin' sure what this is. Nature? Fate? Destiny? Chemistry?" Then another grunt, darker and grittier. "Torture? Tragedy?"

She laughed again, though softer this time, because it couldn't be helped. Because *he* couldn't be resisted. The man was beyond beautiful, especially in the throes of his desperate confusion. His vulnerability called to her, and his dichotomy entranced her. His angel's flawless face atop his demon's perfect body. His molded mounds of muscle, outlined by the same shirt that stretched across his intense, passionate heart...

"Well," she murmured to him. "Torture *may* still apply, now that you're on Mattie Lesange's radar."

A vicious sound vibrated in his throat. "She's a pure, petty minger."

"But she's also smart as hell, Sam—and that can be a crazy combination. We can't ignore the writing on the wall."

He growled again and moved against her with a motion that combined a hip roll and a groin thrust in ways she'd only dreamed of before now. "Writing on the wall isn't as fun as a sweet mouse up on the wall."

Though with those words, along with his delectable undulations, she might soon be nothing but *mush* on the wall. Still, she compelled enough mental neurons to pierce her mental mush to say, "You...you have to listen to me, mister. That woman wants you bad."

"Well, she can't have me."

"Thank God. Holy *shit*." The last half escaped as soon as she realized the first had been spilled. "Okay, so I'm just saying—" She wetted her lips. Instantly regretted it, as soon as Sam's gaze flared like a wolf scenting fresh prey. "I only mean that—"

"I know what you meant, Jenny."

Damn. *Damn*. She'd aroused a new beast in him all right—and the result enflamed her blood, thrilled her pulse, cartwheeled her entire belly. She'd read somewhere that life became its most vivid right before death. While the man wasn't about to literally rip her throat out, it constricted around her air nonetheless, confirming she was about to surrender something just as significant. Part of her was about to vanish...

So a new part could be awakened. Enlightened. Molded anew, beneath his masterful hands. His lover's touch.

His perfect dominance...

"I know what you meant." He repeated it while trailing his mouth down the side of her face and then into the indent between her jaw and neck. "Just as you understand everything *I've* meant, aye?" The question came with the emphasis of his bared teeth, which he dug gently into the space in front of her ear. "And everything I want. And crave. And *need*."

He bit her again, a little harder, tumbling the words through her like gravel in an hourglass. Every inch of her body was freshly scratched and compromised, in danger of being the breach that would completely shatter her. Slaughter her. Then open her back up, into something brand new...

She'd never been more terrified in her life.

She'd never craved anything more.

And tried to show him so, arching her chest up to his while letting her head drop against the leather wall. Closing her eyes. Feeling for his breath on the air. Matching hers to it...

"Yes."

And reaching for that word in her soul.

"Yes, Sir."

And adding that extra, special syllable to it.

"Yes...I understand."

Sam's soft, approving snarl turned into a thousand fingers of electricity down her neck. They fanned into the fullness of her breasts until pinching perfect heat into her nipples, and she was conscious of the stone-hard nubs fighting the confines of her bra. She answered him with a sharp gasp—

That became a protesting cry as soon as the lift doors whooshed back open.

"Shit," she muttered, though was actually grateful to see an empty guest room floor instead of the lobby. Despite the blatant kink-vitation these "special" elevators offered, she wasn't used to dealing with an audience when she was this high on arousal. She could only imagine what she looked like right now, caught beneath Sam with her legs splayed, her arms pinned, her lips swollen, her eyes misty. To her understanding, this was the kind of thing that only happened to *other* people. *Fictional* people.

Finally, she succeeded in blurting, "S-Sorry. I—I punched in for the wrong floor..."

"*I* didn't."

She swung her head around, impaling him with a gape. "Huh?"

Sam stepped back, preventing her mushy knees from

giving way by wrapping one hand possessively around her elbow. He plunged his other hand into his front slacks pocket, his pose as slick as James Bond, with a steely gaze to match. "Fail to plan; plan to fail."

"*Huh?*"

With a smooth swoop, he held up a room key between two fingers. "When Franzen filled me in on how I might know Tess's cute maid of honor from the base, a certain lass with bright green eyes and a wicked sense of humor, I dared destiny to let me down again."

As he pulled her out of the lift, she hit him with her perplexed scowl. "Again?"

Without stopping his march down the hall, he murmured, "Dropping you back at your office after we returned from the school"—his jaw turned the texture of the diamond-inspired wall sconces they passed—"after you whispered those words to me in the car...was the metaphysical version of bein' kicked in my fuckin' baws." He stopped in front of a door near the end of the hall. Secured her tighter in his hold as he whipped around to face her with an expression defined by stark lines and unfaltering purpose. "But I could see that you were spooked by it all," he grated. "That maybe you needed some time to figure it out. We don't live in a world that makes it easy for a lass to admit she likes submissiveness, even if it can be the greatest gift she gives to her man and herself."

Jen blinked. Then again. Despite every rugged detail of his face being perfectly clear and brilliant, it was as if the man had blinded her.

With his undeniable truth.

"The...gift?" Despite her questioning lilt, she recognized it too. Yeah. *Truth.*

"Jenny." He wound his hand up and around the back of her neck. His gaze was more sure than ever, beyond even a wolf's stare. His grays were intense and focused, filled with need and lust and adoration...all man. "I've confronted enemies of freedom at speeds that would turn your stomach and spin your mind. I've had to make life-and-death decisions while starin' at the earth through my canopy, and usually in split seconds. I'm a creature trained and wired to follow my instincts—and since the moment I met you, every instinct in my body has told me to conquer *you*." With breaths audibly rushing in and out of him, he raked his grip up to her shoulder. "But only if you're sure, *a leanbh*. Only if *you* want this too."

Somehow, in some way, Jen managed a hard gulp. But while it gave her mind a second to form coherent words at her lips, it didn't ease the burn of the truth now raging through *her* instinct...and blazing through her soul.

"I...yeah," she finally rasped out. "I want this, Sam." She moved all the way against him...unable to ignore the shaft of heat pressing at her from the center of him. It only made her more sure as she reiterated, "I want *you*. I...I need you."

Sam wasted no time in turning and waving the key at the pad on the door. He swung the portal open by bracing it with his weight. With an equally swift tick of his head, he commanded her forward.

"Get inside."

With her nerves racing, her heart exploding, and her brain screaming, Jen immediately, silently complied.

The suite was dark except for the dancing colors across the walls, thanks to the digital billboards along the Strip, forty floors below. Jen reached and turned on the lights.

Sam turned them back off.

In the same sweep of motion, he backed her against the wall. Kept her locked there with the press of his huge body, the force of his steeled glare...

And the crush of his dominant kiss.

A stunned mewl quivered up her throat. He snuffed it before it reached her lips. Consumed her with the sweep of his tongue, not stopping for innuendo or permission. He took over every corner of her mouth, licking into every crevice, leaving no confusion about his passionate purpose.

*Holy shit.*

Was this really happening?

She'd dreamed about it so many times for ten days straight. Tried to imagine how he'd feel, smell, taste, and look. But all of this was so much better. So much more. His muscles, big and dense, molded against hers. His fingers, long and forceful, twined into hers. His kiss, deep and consuming, took over her. He definitely wasn't her charming "friend" anymore. Gone, as well, was the suave rogue he showed to everyone at the base, as well as the funny entertainer for the kids at reading hour. In his place was a lover, bathed in golden light but defined by dark intent, pinning her wrists to the wall over her head...leaving her only one option with which to answer his passion.

Complete surrender.

With a groan, she softened, melted...gave in.

With an answering growl, Sam plunged deeper, harder, hotter.

Minutes—hours, perhaps, as if she cared—later, he dragged away far enough to bolt his gaze into her. A slow smile spread over his generous lips. "I've been dreamin' of doin' that for far too fuckin' long."

"That makes two of us." She punctuated with a soft laugh.

"Though I think Eveready really likes me now. What I've spent on vibrator batteries over the last week probably rivals the state's budget for the year."

His lips parted. His gaze glittered. He lunged into her again, kissing her as if she'd turned into his life support. "Mention vibrators like that again, Jenny, and I'll forget the private promise I made when bringin' you in here."

"What promise was that?"

"The one about makin' love to you like a gentleman."

She rolled her wrists against his hold. "*This* is being a gentleman?"

"Compared to what I really want to do with you right now?" As he nodded, his forehead fell against hers. "Yes. This is bein' a gentleman."

He finished it by bending in, once more fitting their lips together. This time, the contact was a gentle brush. Jen didn't hold back on the effect of it: a tremor that rifted the fault lines of her control. Her knees weakened. Her clenching cleft rubbed against her soaked panties.

"Sam?"

"Yes?"

"Don't be a gentleman."

A snarl ripped from deep inside him. As his mouth tore into hers all over again.

They groaned. Thrusted. Shifted. Needed. Jen hitched one leg around his waist and then the other. Sam adjusted his weight, securing her hips to the wall by sliding his crotch against hers. *Dear...God.* The man's erection, even shielded by his clothes, matched the rest of him. The bulge between her thighs was big, broad, throbbing...irresistible.

Which made the next moment a little unnerving.

All right...*a lot* unnerving.

Deep furrows of conflict creased his brow. He slowly shook his head. "Bold, bonnie girl," he finally rasped. "You still don't understand."

"Then make me," she countered. "Please, Sam. Make me understand."

He slid one hand to the side of her face. Angled his thumb beneath her chin, bracing her to continue gazing at him. Like that was a huge problem. "You can already feel how badly I want you."

She couldn't help giggling. "Sam, they can probably feel it two rooms over."

He didn't return her humor. "But things aren't just that easy."

She pushed her lips up at him. When he deliberately pulled back, she pleaded, "Why?"

"Because...I want you completely, Jen. All of you... surrenderin' to me." The skirmish across his face continued until he seemed to reach some bold inner decision. Jaw newly firmed, he went on, "It means I want to put you on that bed, strip every thread of clothing from you, and then bind you down"—he pushed harder on the wrists he still held—"a great deal like this."

Jen fastened her stare deeper into his. "Only the bonds won't be your hands."

New light flared against the smoke of his eyes. New blood surged into the girth of his cock. "My hands would prefer to be busy with other things."

As her own blood rushed south, Jen sucked in a long breath. "But is all that even...possible? I mean, here? This is a hotel, not a kink club."

"This is the Nyte Resort." He stepped back a little, only to slide open the door to the entry hall closet. Inside of that, there was another cabinet, containing a backlit display, much like a custom liquor array. But in place of Belvedere, Bacardi, and Patrón, there were items like wrist cuffs, blindfolds, and riding crops. "An honor bar for every thirst."

"No shit."

Her face heated all over again. It had nothing to do with the toys and everything to do with the new intensity of Sam's stare. She couldn't bear to return the scrutiny, for fear of what it would do to her bloodstream...and the little lake pooling between her legs.

"Is that a good 'no shit' or a bad 'no shit'?"

Time to look up. Even if she spontaneously combusted from it, she had to let him see how much she meant her response. "Could anything be bad with you, Sam Mackenna?"

An expression suffused his face, something between humility and pleasure. It warmed her so deeply, she wished she could tell him to do it again so she could fetch her phone and make a GIF of it. But even a digital reproduction wouldn't compare to the energy he gave off, a heat that made her wonder if her extremities would turn into fireworks. It made her response to his next words an absolute no-brainer.

"Very well, then. Get on that bed and let me watch you take off every stitch of your clothes."

# CHAPTER SIX

*Holy God.*

By the time she'd stripped to nothing but her panties, Sam didn't know if he'd last much longer. The last ten days—hell, the last *three* days—had been eternities. At first, simply wantin' her—but with every passing minute in her presence, startin' to need her. To crave her. To feel the utter rightness of her laughter and light in a world that had, for him, grown so hopeless and grim.

She was his way back to the light.

Back to feelin' in control of *something* again, for once.

And perhaps, after that, takin' control of the rest of his life too.

As she tugged at the edges of the buff-colored lace at her hips, he tore at the fastening of his pants. He'd already shucked his jacket and shirt; they were tangled with her dress on the love seat next to the bed. Still, he held back on freein' his cock all the way. Damn thing was already a rod of ragin' heat, fed by the blood that pounded his veins like a firestorm of lust. And the mirror along the wall already showed him what he knew: he was an equally daunting sight, with veins standing out against his biceps and urgent air puffing up his tense chest.

"Oh my God." Her breathy burst spiked his concern, despite how delectable she looked while complying with his exact instructions, positioning herself in the exact center of the bed.

"What is it, mouse?"

He stepped over, seeing nothing but her now. Forgettin' even the throb in his tadger because the exquisite dawn of her arousal was too fuckin' good to miss. He raked his stare across the gorgeous dew across her skin, shimmering even brighter between her slightly parted thighs...and then up to the sweet concave from her ribcage, especially because she was breathin' like she'd just climbed Ben Nevis itself...and then admiring the pert peaks of her erect nipples and the dazzling gems of her eyes. Damnation, her *eyes*. They shined like peridots had collided with emeralds beneath the brilliance of a thousand candles.

"What is it?" He spoke it as a command this time. "If this is really goin' to work for us, *leannan,* then you must answer a question when I issue it—especially if it's about your health or well-bein'."

"Of course. I mean, yes, Sir." She nodded so fervently, it instantly pulled at his chest. And a lot of other parts that fed his Dominant's desire. "I just..." She stopped to lick her lips but ended the move with a saucy smile, easing his worry by surprising degrees. Mostly because he had no idea he *was* that worried... "It's just that...*holy shit*..."

"It's all right, Jenny." He leaned over, brushing a thick strand of her auburn waves off her face. No way in fuck was he goin' to miss a moment of how this experience affected her... of how his authority took her mind and body to its greatest, grandest heights. "Take your time. Tell me what you're feelin'."

"My heartbeat's turning my chest into a rave party."

He lifted his brows and quirked half a smirk. "Sounds like fun."

"Speak for yourself."

"Oh, I thoroughly intend to." He said it while returning to a full stand, confirming she watched him through every inch of the movement—including the tiny tug he gave his pants zipper. "I'll show you mine if you show me yours."

Her moan was guttural and delectable. "Oh, yes please."

"You first." He jabbed his chin her way. "Take 'em off, sweet Jenny. Bare your juicy beauty to me."

More of that aroused moan, making the column of her neck all taut and gleaming, as she hooked her thumbs around the lace covering her core. With a slide of motion that maddened him—*faster; fuck, faster!*—but delighted him—*that's it, my sweet mouse; just like that*—she got the garment down to her knees before Sam declared his composure a total loss, and he sank a knee to the bed, taking over for her.

As soon as he freed her of the lace, he wadded the panties up and lifted them to his nostrils. The nectar of her, tangy honey and delicious musk, took over his senses. He sucked in two more lungsful of her sweet scent before growling, "Oh, my gorgeous girl. You're wet. *Very* wet."

Jen's pulse still visibly thudded at the base of her throat. "Is...is that good?"

"That's very, *very* good."

She attempted a smile, but besides bein' soaked for him, she was also still nervous as a kitten in a rocker factory. And completely clueless about how stunning she was, propped against the mound of pillows, every lush line of her flawless nudity on display for him. Offering herself to him like one of those thousand-dollar fruits they sold over in Asia. Only difference was, she was a million times more beautiful than a bunch of golf ball-sized grapes or a rare apple embedded with diamonds. And he already knew—*knew*—she'd be a million times more succulent.

"Holy fuck."

But clearly, his snarl did nothing to assuage her jumpy nerves. While it *did* have a gorgeous effect on her puckered nipples, she still started turnin' her bottom lip into hamburger while twistin' wrinkles into the pristine white coverlet. But that was just the beginnin' of her beauty. With a short tilt of his head, Sam gave himself a perfect peek at what her trepidation did for other parts of her exposed body. Her pussy...*fuck*. Just this glimpse of those dark-pink lips, drenched in her shimmering, thick arousal, and he had to twist his balls through his pants, terrified he'd blow in them like a goddamned teenager.

"I—I know I'm not exactly the definition of 'stacked and sleek,' but—"

"Jenny."

"I try to take care of myself, at least, and—"

"*Jenny.*"

"What?"

"You're perfect, *a leanbh.*"

She answered his rough confession with an elegant blush that suffused her from head to toe. With equal charm, she murmured, "Thank you, Sir."

"Now lie back," he told her then. "All the way, with your legs open and your arms up over your head. I need to see you. All of you."

His emphasis on the final three words brought on another gorgeous flush—though remarkably, her agitation mellowed a little as Sam leaned over and secured her wrists into the leather cuffs that were revealed in a sliding compartment built into the headboard.

"Well." She smiled as he slid a finger between her right

wrist and its cuff, double-checking he'd left enough room for her proper circulation. "Isn't that convenient?"

He dipped a soft kiss onto her lips, using the excuse to admire her beneath him already. With her arms stretched, her breasts were high and taut and exposed, the bold red tips jutting from perfectly round areolas. "The whole place is booby-trapped," he teased, waggling his brows. "Won't it be a bit of fun to take a roam about?"

He expected her to pull a case of sassy mouse and glare at him. Instead, her face lit up and her eyes gleamed like a pair of jaunty high-step dancers. "Booby-trapped? You mean better than in the elevators?"

Sam almost laughed—and likely would have, if a resounding realization didn't hit him so hard that very moment. And expose his every nerve. And make him giddily aware of every fuckin' breath he took...and sensation he felt... and tremor he endured...

"Jennifer Josephine Thorne," he murmured, dragging a knuckle down her sternum and savoring the soft keen she let out as he trailed lower and lower and lower.

"Yes, Captain Samuel Mackenna?"

"Where the fuck have you been my entire life?"

She curled an impish grin. "Is this a multiple choice or fill-in-the-blank answer?"

"Why do I think you'd prefer the fillin'-in kind better, *mo luaidh*?"

She answered with nothin' but a louder purr as he descended his hand, turning it over to hold her abdomen down with the flat of his palm. "Oh," she finally blurted. "Ohhhh, my goodness..."

"Easy, lass," he directed. "Easy, now. I need you to stay

right here for me, aye? I want to explore this sweet cunt before I *fill* every inch of it."

His tease had her shudderin' beneath him and then around him as he dipped his other hand between her thighs, breachin' her swollen folds with a questing finger. Jesus *God*, she was so slick and soaked and ready—and from the second he slid inside, he was a hundred times harder and hotter.

At once, he added a second finger. The second her clenching channel welcomed him, he gritted and slurred the filthiest Gaelic oaths he could remember. Didn't do the trick. He switched to English. "Fucking *hell*, you gorgeous woman. I'm lettin' out precome like a geyser. What you do to me, sweet Jenny. What your beautiful, tight gash does to me..."

"*Oh!*" Her outcry was a damn aphrodisiac, as she flushed and flailed and began bucking her hips, all but begging him to plunge his digits deeper and faster. "Oh, shit! So good, Sam!"

He shifted his free hand down. Used those fingers to rub her labia, working those inflamed lips so they indirectly stimulated her clit.

"Want more, little mouse?"

"Y-Yes, please..."

"Another finger inside you?"

"God, *yes!*"

"Then ask for it nicely." Though in truth, he was ready to bury his whole fuckin' fist inside her if that's what she needed.

"Please. Oh, p-p-please, give me another finger...Sir."

As soon as he did, the extra pressure in her tunnel broke her clit free from its hood, and Sam watched the erotic nub get bigger with every invasion of his fingers. Jen groaned and gasped in time to his lunges, filling the air with a sharp but slippery rhythm, her voice pitching higher as her clit turned redder and he pumped away with more ruthless abandon.

Stretching her.

Testing her.

Celebrating her.

Spreading her.

Still, Sam dictated, "Farther. Open wider, sweet Jenny. Show me exactly what my cock is goin' to conquer."

"L-Like this?"

He lifted his stare. Captured her gaze with the undaunted intent of his. "Do you *really* think you're getting a grade here, little *leannan*?" He extended his strokes, turning them into more contemplative caresses. "Listen to me. You don't worry about *any* of that, Jenny. Not here. *Never* with me. There's no right or wrong, or good or bad, or black and white when you're with me." When she suddenly looked like an inquisitive kitten, baffled but curious, some dark barrier inside him melted—perhaps forever. Not *all* the barriers, but it was a damn fine start. Oh aye, a very good one.

He leaned forward, taking her perfectly parted lips beneath his. "You are perfection, sweet beauty—so all *you* worry about is rejoicin' in every sparklin' drop of that." He captured the gasp she gave as response with adorin' brushes of his lips—while commencin' the deep drive of his fingers inside her body once more. "*Christ*, my little one. Look at how you glisten for me. And feel how you tremble for me. Now I can smell how hot you are for me too. So soft and luscious..."

She looked up at him through her dark sable lashes. There was nothing coy about it. Desire was already a thick, potent force in her lush green eyes. "All of it's for you. All of *me* is for you."

The words spilled from her without hesitation, workin'

heady magic inside him in return. She gave every damn syllable to him without reserve, without hesitation, without expectation—and, most importantly, as her complete truth in the reality they forged with each other right now. A door they'd chosen to walk through together, without cares or concerns about the next portal to come—or even *if* there'd be another door. The next door didn't matter. Tomorrow didn't matter. The explosion of this and *only* this was the key to her freedom—and now, the heights to which he looked for his own desire.

"Those are wonderful words to hear, lass." He tilted his head, fixated with the sight of his fingers driving into her... absorbed and consumed by her soft, glistening sex. "Since that's exactly what I plan on taking."

Jen bit her bottom lip as she bore down on him. Sam cocked a wicked grin, savoring the feel of her tangy juices gushing all over his fingers. So naturally, he plunged in harder. She jerked and trembled, releasing another long, worshipful moan—and spearing him with a bright, pleading stare.

"Then do it." She squirmed and writhed and dug her heels into the bed, seeking traction to arch her core up at him. "Take it." A new roll of her hips, a fresh gush of arousal from the center of her desire. "Take it *now*, Sam. I—I can't hold on for much—ahhhh!"

The scream escaped her as he withdrew his fingers, though the erotic sluice on the air was hacked short by a sharp smack and her startled yelp—as he used his soaked fingers to land a couple of expert spanks across the top of her mound. Though Jen's gaze burst into a stunned glare, Sam purposely ignored her look. He knew where he'd aimed his fingers and had purposely spared the slit where her sensitive nub still thrummed in swollen desperation.

"You'll be holdin' on as long as I tell you to." As he anticipated, the undaunted order made her jaw drop—and her nipples as hard as arrowheads. "Is that clear?"

"Are you freaking kidding—" She yelped as he spanked her once more. Then quivered harder than before. "Okay, okay. We're clear!"

He sent her a choir-boy smile. She shot him an angel's avenging stare. And damn if that wasn't the best comparison of this whole week, with the last of the day's light spilling in across her perfect seraph's body, makin' her look just like one of heaven's own creations, dropped here just to show him a new definition of paradise...

Especially as he rose up, unzipped his slacks, and freed his aching erection.

And her sigh washed over him like the most quality choir of angels in the most quality firmament in the universe.

"*Sam.*"

"Aye, darlin' Jenny?"

"You're...magnificent."

He let a slow smile spread across his lips in correlation to how his shaft grew against his palm as he stroked the hardness to greater life. "Not half as magnificent as you, my bonnie mouse."

No words were truer. He had to fight not to sink himself into her right away, with how she looked like an angel, whispered like an enchantress, and mesmerized him like a goddamned goddess. But after the speech he got from the check-in manager to the enforcements on the key packet and bed stand note, the Nyte was all about people doin' lots of *safe* sinkin'—so he opened the nightstand drawer, found a packet emblazoned with the telltale Trojan's head along with the

Nyte's starry logo, and efficiently tore it open with his teeth.

After he slid the latex from inside it, he quickly gloved up the shaft that had become practically a flagpole between their bodies. A groan took over as he got the condom to the end and had to squeeze his balls again. Another moan swept in as he pushed her knees out with his own, fitting his body into the apex of hers. But even as he nudged her entrance with the hard purple bulb of his sex, he paused for one more moment. Probably the most important one.

"S-Sam?"

Her query was guttural and rough. So was the long breath he pulled in.

"If we're going to stop, you must tell me now." He inhaled again, raking a hand up until his fingers bracketed the chain connecting her cuffs. "The torture's been cruel enough, stayin' away from you for ten damn days."

He watched a maelstrom of emotions flow across her face, through her eyes. Deep furrows across her forehead gave way to a half smile of wonderment. Then a more sober look again before she lifted her face up toward him with conviction that came from clear, determined desire.

"I don't want to stop, Sam."

His answering growl was long and fierce. "Thank God."

Without saying anything else, he entered her.

And reveled in her sharp, shivering outcry. "Hell! Ohhh, *hell*!"

"Fuck," Sam grunted, lost to an instant dilemma. He was stretching her, probably more than she ever had been before, but the reason he knew it so clearly was because she squeezed him so tightly. Her pussy was unlike any heaven he'd known. Unlike any sheath he'd ever filled. Beyond any warmth that had ever welcomed his cock. But he wasn't even all the way inside her yet. Would that even be possible?

It had to be.

It *would* be.

"Fuck," he repeated, withdrawing far enough to give him some leverage for the next thrust. As he clenched his buttocks and rolled his hips forward, Jen shuddered and mewled beneath him. "Easy, little mouse," he urged. "Easy. We'll get there. You're just so perfect. So fuckin' tight... *Easy*..."

So much simpler said than done.

But she guided him there. Inch by fierce, blissful inch. He watched her every second, taking cues on how to move from the slightest twist of her lips, glints in her eyes, tension in her body. Her breaths were his brightest guides. In their squeaking sighs, he knew her arousal. In their sudden hitches, he felt her pain. Slowly, she got used to him. At last, she harbored all of him. By the time his balls knocked against her skin, he was panting in a combination of triumph and torment. Never had he had to be more attuned to a lover like this. But never had one made him feel more alive in the process.

"Fuck!" It wasn't his most original word by this point—but God's bloody tits, did it handle the job well—until he lost the ability to speak, only capable of a primal yell that blended flawlessly with Jen's lusty scream. He reared up high enough to watch her for a moment, rejoicin' in the gorgeous lights of her eyes and the hungry part of her lips, silently beggin' him to copy the fusion of their bodies by fuckin' her mouth with his tongue.

He was all too happy to oblige.

Fully. Ferociously. Damn near fanatically. Jenny returned all his passion ten, twenty, a hundredfold, blowing apart his senses with her open, unbridled heat. There was a not-so-latent beast inside him—he'd known that for too damn long now—but he'd never anticipated that his demure bookworm of a mouse was the disguise for an equally wild creature inside *her*. His gentle angel Jenny was actually a hot, heathen fire fairy...

His mouse was really a she-beast.

They sucked at each other's mouths the same way they fucked each other. With hungry abandon, starving satiation, unhindered desire. But there was more to this than a physical coupling. Sam knew it in the depths of his spirit and the fiber of his being, while he saw its plain proof in the symbolism of the cuffs he'd placed on her. His she-beast wanted to be caught. Needed to be conquered. Craved to be opened for his evisceration and splayed for his desecration...

And he adored her for it.

Yearned to worship her all night because of it.

And fucked her harder in thanks for it.

As he kept pumpin' in and out, he laved her breasts and nipples with new licks and bites. Explored her flesh with eager hands, strokin' every perfect curve and crevice of her. And finally, oh God *finally*, he inserted a hand between her legs, seeking the bundle of nerves that pulsed strongest for him. Needing her to follow him. Coaxing her right over the precipice with him, into the blinding void they both stretched and gasped and yearned for...

"Sam!" She shuddered as he flicked her flesh, over and over and over.

"Yes, *mo luaidh*?"

"Oh...*shit*...that's—that's—"

"Just the kind of commentary I like." He smiled against

her lips and then her neck, his blood rocketin' with arousal as she dropped her head back, her eyes closin' and her breasts thrust up toward him.

"It's—oh *God*." She gasped. "It's...oh, I can't..."

"Of course you can." He dug his teeth into the succulent dip at the base of her neck, continuin' the path of his lips into the creamy valley between her sweet breasts. "Tell me, *a leanbh*. Tell me. *All of it*, sweet Jenny."

"I just—oh my God, I'm seeing stars."

The words alone had him lunging deeper and harder. "And that's a *bad* thing?"

"Yes! I mean no. I—I just—" Her thighs trembled against his. Her gorgeous chebs now had nipples erect as red candies. "It's...so much. It's too much. I don't know if I can—"

"Of course you can. And you will." He doubled the tempo of his thrusts. Her sex shivered around him. God *damn*, she felt so fine. So tight. So wet. Engulfin' every hot, demanding inch of him—and beyond. She didn't just surround his cock anymore. She swallowed his senses. Transformed his reality. Engulfed him in a special kind of reality...

Called her submission.

And in doing so had given him a gift beyond what he dreamed.

A power he'd never thought to know in full again.

A part of himself he'd mourned a long time ago...

But it wasn't dead. It had only been sleeping. And it was reawakened now. Holy Christ, was it *awake*.

"God, *yes*. Take it, sweet Jenny. Take all of me...and all of you too. Let it all in, darlin'. Let it take over."

Through a fog of feeling he heard his voice, sounding like he'd swallowed a crate of glass. He was beyond caring. His resistance was fraying. Pressure pulled and growled at him, prowling the base of his spine until descending through his ass cheeks. He fought to give the beast room, but there was very little lead rope left for it. Once it ran the rein taut, he'd break.

Jen's scream grabbed at the final inches of that tether.

A bellow, hoarse and harsh, exploded from his lips. Heat, wild and wonderful, pumped the length of his cock. He could think of nothing but the orgasm that tore him apart and the incredible, beautiful woman who'd given it to him. The sweet creature who'd stumbled into his path ten days ago but who'd been part of his imagination for so much longer than that.

Because he'd been asking fate for her.

No. Not asking. Taunting. Daring the universe to prove that someone like her could still exist. A woman—hell, a *person*—who could connect to him on every level there was. Even the dark ones.

*Especially* the dark ones.

The levels he showed her now, even as she locked her legs against his back, urging him to take her even harder, fixing him with a stare as clear and adoring as it was unaltered and unafraid.

Making him think...

Or possibly even hope...

She really was strong enough for the darkness.

*All* of it.

As if the bloody enchantress had read his mind, her eyes narrowed a little. Not a lot—certainly not enough that he held back on his lust—but enough to tell him that she *saw*. And she *knew*. Just enough to know that she *didn't* know. That she didn't have *all* of him. Not yet.

"Sam." And though she panted it out, the dictum in her

voice was also there. Just enough of a husk beneath her breath that *he* now knew...

She wasn't going to relent until she saw it all.

"*Sam*. Damn it!"

"Ssshhh. I know, sweet one. I know."

"I will not 'ssshhh.' And you *don't* know, because if you did, then—*oh!*"

She finished that with a strangled choke.

He reared back, until his shaft was simply kissing her outer lips again—

And then fucked into her with everything he had.

Everything he was.

Every inch. Every force. All the brutality. All the darkness.

"Oh. My. *Ahhhh!*"

Her sex convulsed around him. Then again. And again.

And all over again, as soon as he reached beneath her and then searched deeper, finding the forbidden pucker with its ring of sensitive nerves...

"Sam! Oh, God!"

He breathed hard and heavily into her ear while working his two forefingers at her most illicit entrance. "Good girl," he grated. "Naughty girl. You'll let me in here too, won't you? You'll take it because I want you to. Because this is what you want from me."

Her hips bucked. Her lungs pumped. A menagerie of sounds vibrated in her throat, whines and growls and mewls and hisses conveyin' her new arousal so much better than words could. That was just dandy by him. If she needed words, he could supply them. If she needed *anything*, he would give it. The woman was all his now. Spread wide, soaking wet, and panting hard. His perfect little mouse. His darling little treasure.

"That's my girl. *Yes*, sweet Jenny. That's right. Let it happen."

"D-Do I h-have a choice?"

He considered the question for all of two seconds—while pressing his fingers a little farther inside her perfect rectum.

"Not especially."

Her response came just as fast.

In the form of a shocking, dazzling smile, stretching nearly from one of her gorgeous ears to the next. "Good."

As soon as she blurted it, her orgasm hit.

And was easily one of the most dazzlin' sights of his existence.

It moved through her like a tsunami, quiet but devastating, until she was well rocketed to a stratosphere of screams from it. Her composure was ripped away from what little moorings it had left, making her babble with more animalistic noises, along with I-don't-give-a-damn-who-hears lust. Her fervor washed over him too, spurrin' him to a pace that could barely be described as "fuckin'" anymore. This was definitely no longer a fuck. This was a pound. A blast. A cataclysm. A conquest.

Only who was conquerin' whom?

And did the answer even matter?

The slaps of their bodies were like erotic gunshots on the walls, dueling with passion and power, straining through every muscle in his body...through every inch of his cock.

"Jenny. Fuck. *Fuck*."

As the fire grew in his balls, he punched deeper into her. And as the blaze took over his cock, he gave in to it. Surrendered to the cosmic force that took hold from the inside out, turnin' him into a star gone supernova, consumed by silver-white light as he stiffened and pulsed...

And then exploded.

*Deep*. So damn deep inside her.

And as he did, recognizin' the strange part of himself that burst along with it. A wall, tumblin' in...

A cavern, newly exposed...

Fuckin' hell.

What had she done to him?

And did he even have the fortitude to sift through the rubble right now and figure it out? If he did, would it matter? Jenny lay beneath him, still limp and languid and possibly in just as many mental pieces as he was. A smile worthy of a spring meadow adorned her lips, leading him to think she was even baskin' in those fiery fragments. At once, he recognized his own mind turnin' the facts into somethin' new too. Maybe that catastrophic explosion actually *had* been epic fireworks. Or maybe it had been both. Could there really be beauty in destruction sometimes? Was it possible to raze something to the ground—like a man's damn soul—but have something left afterward to build on? To make better?

"Hey."

Thank fuck for the return of his soft mouse and the single word strong enough to haul him out of his metaphysical brood.

"Hey." He gave his head a solid but swift shake, getting his shit together before focusing fully on her again. "You awrite?" With a couple of deft twists, he freed her from the cuffs— though the longing look she flicked up at them was enough to melt away a few more fences inside him. Still he charged her, "Did I hurt you?" When she didn't reply after an obligatory two seconds, he rolled to her side and took her head in his hands. "Shit. I *did* hurt you. Where? How? Why didn't you say—"

He stopped as soon as she reached up too, yanking hard enough on his hair to bring his mouth slamming down on hers. "I *would* have said something, had there been anything to say." Though she gentled her hold, she repeated the kiss with twice as much passion, working her tongue along the seam of his lips until he opened for her, letting her roll her tongue along his with devouring devotion. At last, while letting him go with a long and reluctant drag, she whispered, "I'm not hurt, Captain Mackenna."

"So what is it?" Because it *was* something. He just couldn't get a proper bead on exactly what. Even threading his voice with a deeper growl and jerking a commanding finger beneath her chin didn't impel her to give up any feedback beyond her self-deprecating smile.

"Honestly, Sam...it's nothing. I'm just being stupid. Indulging in too much Jane Austen lately." She shrugged. "And Emily Brontë. And Diana Gabaldon..."

"I like Jane Austen."

"Because you had to get more perfect than you already were?"

He speared her with a tighter gaze. No way was he buyin' the sweet talk she was peddlin', even with the sarcastic tone— but that decision meant he had to shuffle through at least a little of his mental rubble to reply. "I'm far from perfect, Jenny." And then the disconcerting conclusion that brought him to. "You've seen enough of my file to know that." Fuck, even the declassified parts of the thing were harrowing to read through. If she knew everything she wasn't *supposed* to know... about the missions that officially never occurred, in places they weren't supposed occur in, on targets that were never supposed to be authorized...well, she'd have probably thought differently about even mentionin' the word "friends" to him, much less lettin' him lock her down and have his kinky, filthy way with her...

Which said *what* about him now?

He couldn't fuckin' go there.

Because if he did, he already knew the conclusion he'd reach. The explosion he'd see, instead of the fireworks. The resolve he'd make to roll out of this bed this very second and get himself—and his secrets and his darkness and his violence—as far away from Jenny Thorne as he possibly could.

But he didn't move a fuckin' muscle.

Because he was a selfish wanker, and he was brilliant at math.

Three: the number of years the woman had been employed at Nellis Air Force Base.

Nineteen: The number of days left in his assignment here.

Which added up to the number of chances they had of workin' this insane chemistry into any entity more than a solid case of animal attraction.

*Zero.*

So the selfish wanker was stayin' right where he was. And did so with a clear-as-hell conscious and steady-as-fuck nerves.

With those odds, he was more than happy to be her fireworks and meadows for a little while longer. No. He *needed* to be.

That was why he had no trouble about dustin' off his finest, cockiest smirk and wielding it along with his comeback to her. "So what do I get if I admit to reading *Wuthering Heights* and *Outlander* too?"

She narrowed her gaze. "All *nine* parts of *Outlander*?"

"There's more than one part?"

She chuckled. "Doesn't matter. Your guy card is already seriously in danger."

"Which is why I may need to fuck a vow of silence into you."

Her laughter quickly dissolved into a sigh. And then an appreciative moan as she slid a hand down to the center of his chest. "Why the hell did I fight this so hard?" she whispered. "Why did I fight *you*?"

He abandoned the smirk. He needed her to see and feel the sincerity behind his next words. "Because your principles don't get just your lip service, Jenny." He curled a hand atop hers, locking her fingers over his heart. "Which has been, and continues to be, one of the reasons you fascinate the hell out of me." He dipped his head as he raised their joined hands, brushing an adoring kiss atop her middle knuckle. "I know it was no trivial choice for you to break your code for this, no matter how magnificent this sorcery seems." He moved his mouth along her hand, purposely scraping the curves of her fingers with his stubble. *Balls*. He'd slipped out of her no more than fifteen minutes past, and his psyche already clamored at him to mark her in a new way. In *any* way. The stubble burn would have to do for now. "No," he muttered after a long, silent pause. "Not sorcery." Then delved his gaze back at her, selfishly drinking from the depths of her jade lagoon eyes, before committing to declaring, "This is a miracle. *You*, Jenny Thorne, are my pure, bright, bonnie miracle."

Her breathing noticeably snagged. Her features widened as if the word he'd spoken had levitated them off the bed. "Miracle? *Me?*" But she interrupted herself with a sharp chuckle. "Riiight. And all the other girls on your base stops across the world, right? Do I get some kind of an engraved edition number and a certificate of authenticity?" But when he gave her the only response that would truly set in, a longer-than-comfortable silence and a colder-than-steel stare, she traded the saucy giggle for a hard gulp. Then another. "*Sam*. All right, come *on*. I've been pretty damn forthcoming with you. Don't you think it's time to return the favor? No bullshitting, buddy. What *is* my number in the lineup? You know it won't piss me off. You trying to pull off coy and cagey, on the other hand? *Now* I'm getting pissed off."

For another long moment, he didn't say anything. Simply turned his head, released her hand, and then stretched out her fingers so he could fit his cheek against her palm. At last, he murmured, "You're on the magic money, mouse."

Her lips twisted. "Excuse me?"

"It's time for me to return the favor," he stated. "Which starts with askin' you this, then." But the words were harder to get out than he expected, even after forcing air down into every available crevice of both his lungs. "You do know...there was a specific reason why they sent me over for the cross-training here."

"Besides the fact that you can turn a fighter jet into poetry?"

Her compliment could've been in Swahili for all its effect on him. "I wasn't in a good place, Jenny," he confessed. "I... haven't been in a good place for a while now. The deployments have finally started taking their toll—or so everyone keeps telling me. Iraq, Afghanistan, Syria, Afghanistan *again*..."

"I know," she rasped. "And nearly all of them on top of each other." And then screwed her lips together until the elegant ribbons were more like mashed-up twine. "Why the *hell* did they—"

"*Stop.*" Another intention gone awry, as the bite emerged more violently than he intended. But enduring her pity was like forcing him to swallow rat poison. "You also need to know...I wanted them, Jen. Every single one of those assignments"— *along with the ones I signed agreements to never talk about—* "was an honor. A statement of my country's ultimate trust and belief in me. I would've gone again had they called. I *wanted* to go again."

"Why?" She didn't hide her confused scowl. "You've carried your fair share of torches for the cause. You know that, yeah?"

Sam rolled back against the pillows. Though he looped an arm around her shoulders to keep her close, he stabbed his scowl toward the ceiling. There was a seam up there he hadn't noticed before—wasn't as if he wanted the grand tour of the room when they first got here—which, he imagined, operated at the command of the zillion buttons in the headboard. He imagined the panels slid back to reveal a massive mirror, but then he imagined it no more. Forced it from his mind in order to do the hard shit here. Jen had trusted him with her very control. It was time to trust her with his truth.

"It was easier." And that *was* a truth, though he didn't like it. "The missions, the pace, the noise, the violence. When your world is consumed by all of that, it's effortless to block out the rest. The rest of life just...freezes, I suppose. At least in your mind, yeah? You just think of it all like leaves caught in ice."

"Until they're thawed out."

"Until they're thawed out."

"And you hope they're still there."

"And you hope they're still there."

"But they're not." She trailed the center of his sternum with her fingertips again. Though he stiffened beneath her touch this time, she didn't relent with her gentle comfort—nor her quiet words of wisdom. "You find out that the ice turned into a river and carried them away."

It was his turn for the harsh gulps. And then to grunt hard, throwing a hand across the backs of his eyes. "And you don't even recognize the river anymore."

"Sam..."

"Even the bridges over the fuckin' thing are gone. And everyone who meant anything to you before...is standing on the other shore."

Jen pushed up until her face hovered over his. "But I'm right here. On *this* shore."

She shook a little as she proclaimed it. He dropped his hand in time to see that the words were huge for her. A gargantuan risk. But again, she'd never been so right. "I know," he rasped, tucking her head down against his chest. "I know— which is why I'll never stop thankin' them for sendin' me here." His whole body rose and fell with his deep breath. "For sending me to you, Jenny Thorne."

He said no more than that but knew the husk in his tone already gave away his thick emotion beneath the innocuous words. Even before tonight—but especially *after* tonight—he was convinced more than ever in some higher cosmic hand at work here, guidin' the hundreds of operational gears that had to click to land him at Nellis for this program. And that was fine and dandy, but why did he have to go and confess as much to her right now? They really were working toward a solid base of friendship—and the Almighty already knew how much he probably needed a friend more than a lover right now. An arrangement much more than wall-rattlin' sex.

But there was where his mind sixed-and-sevened with his soul once again.

She hadn't just rattled the walls.

She'd spun his axis.

But that didn't mean *he'd* just spun *hers*. That she didn't want something now more than a little pillow chatter. That she wanted—or needed—him to go spillin' about how deep he'd been flyin' in the darkness before she fell down in front of him last week and drenched his world in light. About how bein' inside her tonight had been like takin' a long, incredible bath in that light. About how he just wanted to pin her down to this mattress, possibly even lock up her legs as well as her arms this time, and drench himself inside her all over again. And flood her with his essence, over and over and over again...

Wasn't going to happen.

*Couldn't* happen.

Not right now, when they both laughed from a telltale ding inside her purse. Trouble was, he had to feign his mirth. This whole pulling-away-with-fake-regret thing...he'd done it so many times, except right now, it felt as comfortable as getting a prostate exam. Fortunately, as she scooted away and padded over to where she'd dropped the little bag near the door, she gave him a great excuse to cut loose a groan that sounded just as tormented.

"Sorry, gorgeous," she teased, adding a giggle as delectable as her backside. "But I think I'm needed in good little bridesmaid mode again."

"But you're so much more fascinatin' in good little subbie mode."

"And if I'm a *bad* little subbie?"

He narrowed his eyes. Not that she was noticin', with a hip cocked and her attention riveted on her phone for a second. He didn't care. Even with her gloriously in the raw, he could envision her in naughty schoolgirl knickers, a plaid miniskirt, and a wee bra just coverin' her assets upstairs, ready to play naughty student for him.

"Bad subbie is even better."

"Why did I know you were going to say that?"

"Why do you ken anythin' about me already, Jenny?" And again, it was more than he should have revealed—but since he was already committed, he rolled up and then over until he was perched up on his knees, whippin' off the condom with one hand and reachin' for her with the other. When she placed hers back against it, his chest swelled with warmth. When she blushed and averted her eyes, he leaned over and claimed her lips in a solid, searing kiss.

And when he flipped her over, keepin' their lips just a breath apart and their bodies together like bangers and mash, he curled a broad, knowing grin, sure that *he* now knew somethin' certain about *her*, as well.

"Guess I can start by being a bad bridesmaid, hmmmm?"

Sam started his answer out by sliding his lips over hers again. Then stabbing his tongue between them, giving her own no mercy with his long, merciless swoops and rolls, making sure she knew exactly what her wicked words did to him. The hunch that she likely hadn't uttered them to any other lover before was a headier turn-on too. He knew he wasn't her first in the most obvious of ways, but bein' the first to take her into new realms of sensuality made it much easier to accept that she was *his* first in some ways too. She was bringin' him back to some old parts of himself...parts he'd written off as incinerated in the violence-filled skies over the Middle East. Because of that, the parts he *had* taken home were somehow easier to face...

To accept.

Maybe, one day, to appreciate.

For that, he had no words with which to thank this woman. Yes, this miracle.

No words. So thank fuck, at least for now, he could use actions.

And set about doing exactly that.

# CHAPTER SEVEN

"Wait a second," Jen blurted. "John Franzen learned *what*?"

She was distracted from her bewilderment by the adorable twitch that took over Sam's lips as he placed her newly poured glass of Cabernet in front of her, atop the counter separating the living room from the kitchen of the rustic two-bedroom house Nellis had set him up in for the duration of training. Outside, just beyond base perimeter, the last rays of the setting sun kissed the top of Sunrise Mountain, and a blessedly cool breeze ruffled the palm trees in the backyard. But the scenery was the best in here, where that arrogant smirk threatened to turn the triple flip in her stomach into a quadruple special. The man himself was rumpled and gorgeous in a plain white T-shirt and jeans, having finished several early morning hops, six grueling hours of debriefing, and then the mountain of personnel paperwork *she'd* thrown at him—which had been, as every other interaction they'd had in the last three days, a tantalizing mixture of function and flirtation. Every signature he'd given up had come with a price: a subtle reminder that while he was happy to do her bidding in the confines of her little office, he was damned and determined to repeat a night—or more—of *her* doing *his* bidding elsewhere.

And so, as the saying went, one thing led to another.

Especially as the man had scribbled his final signature right as the clock officially ticked over into quitting time.

And he'd looked up at her, face a mass of smoldering intention, saying he had a lonely bottle of Cab back at his place, all but screaming that it wanted to meet her.

And now he regarded her, his gaze about as Thor-meets-Loki as she'd ever seen it. Drenched with his hammer-god intensity but sparkling with his mischief-god flippancy.

Which turned her answering gape a hell of a lot more interesting. "Okay, now I just don't know whether you're messing with me or not."

"Now, mouse, I mess with you about a lot of things—"

"You don't say." While they'd dropped a lot of innuendo on each other over the last three days, their dynamic had eased into casual ribbing that indeed included the man messing with her threshold of disbelief.

"But this is a bit different than makin' you believe my tale about the Demon's Penis."

"Well, if you'd stopped after proving that the mountain exists, rather than telling me you climbed it in nothing but your kilt and a beanie, in the February..."

"We're digressin' from the point."

"You mean the one where you make me believe stories that aren't true until I hunt up real facts and discredit your ass?"

He scowled over the rim of his own wine. "You *like* my ass."

"Your ass is mighty fine, Captain." She arched a brow while taking a sip as well. He *had* been right about the Cab. The wine was a perfect blend of berries and spice, making it a great choice for an autumn happy hour. "But not when it's helping your *mouth* as you stand there trying to tell me that Franzen found out there's a secret kink dungeon hidden in the

Scene Lounge at the Nyte Hotel and offered a hundred bucks to the first guy who goes and finds out."

He trailed a finger along the bowl, and then the stem, of his glass. Though his expression barely changed, Jen could feel his watchful wolf prowling past Thor and Loki to lurk closer to the surface of his urbane demeanor. *Holy shit.* The man did attentive wolf better than anyone she knew.

Perhaps because she knew he meant it.

"Might be a pure rocket way to make a hundred spondoolies."

She was damn glad she decided not to get in another sip of wine. "Spondoolies? Hold on. Let me get you some free shevacadoo to go with those."

"Huh?"

She gloated without remorse. It was a rare but fun moment when she knew a meme and he didn't. "My point exactly."

"Which is what?

"Hmmm." She canted her head and grinned, unable to ignore the pull of the new grin he attached to that. Regrettably, it did nothing for the Sam-the-Wolf Fan Club's dance party in her belly—taking inspiration from the larger dance *she* was doing with him. "What *am* I saying?"

He tilted his head the same direction she had, hiking the opposite eyebrow. On any other guy, it'd be weird. On him, it was more fodder for the fan club factor. "That you're up for the challenge of checking out Scene with me?"

And there it was, all but written in black and white—making her feel like she'd had a lot more to drink than two sips of really good Cabernet. *So what now?* Sam wasn't going to kick her out if she backed up the truck and just said she was comfortable with dinner, Netflix and chilling—which was still a win-win for him, considering he'd been clear about his intent in telling her the Cabernet was "really ready to be devoured" and had "a stiff opening of berries" that promised a "robust, rousing finish." But was comfortable what she wanted from this...from him? Nothing about Sam Mackenna, even just being in the same room as him, had ever been comfortable. He'd given her every speck of uncomfortable she'd ever craved—and because of that, she'd never felt more alive. The last two weeks had been a couple of the happiest in her life.

Who the hell was she kidding?

They'd been the *best* of her life.

Especially those two hours he'd given her, on the night of Tess and Dan's party.

Would returning to the scene of the sizzle add an even better chapter to their story or just hasten the "awkward goodbye" ending that would be coming in a couple of weeks anyway? And why was she even brooding about that and not trusting that any time she spent with Sam was going to be incredible? Wouldn't she rise to his challenge if he said he was searching for the tackiest tourist shop in Vegas? Arguably, that would take hours longer than *this* mission...

"Oh, mousie..."

His singsong prodding had her thoughts circling back to the moment and her backside scooting off the barstool.

"I...I..."

And her mind utterly unable to make a damn decision about this.

"I...have to pee."

Which wasn't a lie. And bought her the space she needed to get her damn head screwed on straight—or to twist it the way it needed to go, if that was the case. Just to get to a decision not based on how breathtaking he was, so muscled and messy-haired and stubbled, bearing wine and a smirk and a double-dog dare that terrified but thrilled her...

Okay, so not anywhere in there had the man mentioned "dares." Not verbally, at least. If she counted the Loki-lupine tease in his eyes, however...

It was a *damn* good thing she'd had to pee.

Before she even shut the door, she started to make columns and comparisons in her head.

He was halfway through his time here. So if tonight went awesome? Major win. They'd have two more weeks to float through heaven. Maybe even some damn fine social time to really get to know each other. He owed the kids at VVE another visit, after all.

But if not?

How was she going to keep her disappointment and despondency off the public shelves? How would she pretend all was—how did he like saying it?—*pure dead brilliant*, when it really wasn't? Worse, how would she be able to stay civil in five days, knowing Tess had openly invited Sam to join in their wedding celebration but having to watch Mattie and Viv move in all over him with their classic man-eater tricks?

Did she draw the line, or didn't she?

Did she run with his double-dog dare or protect what was still left of her heart?

What did she continue to keep locked up in her emotional cabinets?

But the ambient lights in his bathroom, flickering to life as she entered, already shattered those cabinets to pieces.

No. Not the lights.

What they illuminated.

A set of clothes, hanging perfectly from the hook on the back of the door.

A dress blazer in dark gray. A white silk shirt to go beneath it, along with a brocade vest in hunter green. The same green was woven with red and white to form the plaid design of the pressed wool kilt. Tucked into a corner, as if freshly polished, was a pair of black leather boots with ornate silver buckles. They'd probably hit Sam at midcalf, where his well-formed muscles would push at the leather, emphasizing his physical power...

*"Ohhhh, God."*

She had no idea she'd also groaned it aloud, until Sam's urgent call came through the door. "Mouse? You sure you're awrite?"

She yanked the door back open.

To surrender her breath to shock once again.

He'd peeled off his T-shirt. To make matters worse—or better—he'd also unhitched the top button of his sinfully fitted denims. The line of tawny hair down the center of his torso, so perfectly framed by the dual ridges of his happy V muscles, joined with a thicker, curlier patch she could just glimpse at the place where his zipper started to part.

*"Damn."*

Out the word tumbled before she could help it, though the syllable was more a breath than an exclamation. She longed to repeat the word, more as a curse this time, as Sam lazed against the doorjamb, clearly and maddeningly aware of what he'd done—and pleased as a cocky knight-errant about the outcome.

"My pardons, lady." As he drawled it, he folded his arms— once more, knowing exactly what he was doing. The new pose magnified the boulders of his biceps, the striations in his forearms, the ripples of his tightening abdomen. "I was just thinkin', no matter what you decide, that I'd get out of these tatters, and—"

"*Stop.*"

Sam froze his fingers on the tongue of his zipper—though not before he got the teeth separated far enough to expose the clear fact that he was commando under the denim. "Right here?"

Jen gulped. Fought like hell to rip her gaze away from the Sam-style goodness that lay beneath his fingers. That beautiful, hard ridge, already pulsing so hard that she was certain his poor penis was gaining some interesting new indentations...

Thank God she had something else to focus on. His outfit was gorgeous, like a costume created for a Highland book boyfriend. If the vest was replaced by a sash and the kilt secured by a sword belt instead of snap closures, she could even turn that setting into something from hundreds of years ago, where he was the laird of his own clan. If they'd lived four hundred years ago, could she have been his lady? Lairds were a lot less picky in the 1600s. Curves, curls, and a talent for rocking high heels were a lot less important than leadership, business sense, and the ability to reload a spring-action stapler in less than thirty seconds. Surely a flintlock pistol wasn't so different.

She pushed the fantasy—make that a few new fantasies—aside in order to answer his query. "Yes," she blurted. "*There.*"

His gaze narrowed with fresh intensity. "Sounds like you've made up your mind."

She copied his pose. Ordered her scrutiny to stay on his face, no matter how valiantly his crotch was trying to sway her determination. "Aye, Captain," she said, though she lifted a stiff finger. "With conditions."

His brow furrowed. "Conditions?"

She stunned him—and, frankly, herself—by managing a little laugh. "Well...one."

He was persistent with the majority of the frown, though the silver flecks reappeared in his eyes, highlighting his flirty tease. "I like conditions."

Her breath snatched again—especially as the man unfolded his arms and took a step toward her. Sultry intent surrounded him like the glow around a candle flame, only with bulging muscles and burnished hair...

Fire that would burn her, if she let it.

But maybe she wanted—*needed*—to let it.

And suddenly, the idea of actually finding that dungeon, on the arm of this beautiful flame of a man, turned her nervous system into a thousand blazing comets of arousal. What would Sam really do with her, *to* her, if they were alone in a play room together? If she were kneeling before him, picking out a safe word for him? If he were no longer Sam at all but purely and wholly her Sir?

One prolonged look in his eyes, and she already saw the possibilities swirling through his mind too. The promise of the new ways they could be together and open each other. The brilliance of what they could share...

Crazily—or maybe all-too-appropriately—her mind was emblazoned with a classic pilot's inspirational quote. *The sky is no longer the limit.*

For too long, she'd been defined by the reaches of what she thought her sky could be. What always *would* be. But then she'd met this man, and he'd showed her how to fly in *his* sky. A sky, she sensed, that he'd forgotten how to soar in as well.

So maybe they both needed this adventure.

And maybe she had to realize that—for both of them.

With a zealous sweep, Jen whipped the clothes off the hook. As she did, Sam pushed away from the doorframe. Good thing, since she shoved them against the two main slabs of his chest. "We're going on a dungeon hunt—but you're going to wear this to do it."

"All right."

The corners of his mouth inched up along with the slow, sultry release of his drawl. Jen stood back, savoring the fact that she'd already pleased him with her decisiveness, watching the ease with which he pulled the shirt off its hanger and then stabbed his arms into the sleeves. The entire time, his stare didn't leave her face. He kept watching, lips quirking, as he buttoned it. Didn't relent as he slipped on the vest, removed his jeans, and then wrapped the kilt around his lean hips. Once the snaps were locked, he smoothed the whole outfit into place— and then swept a gallant bow toward her.

After he rose, he chuckled. Jen didn't laugh. How could she, when her lungs desperately rationed breath? She attempted to school her features but was certain she looked ridiculous, fighting a suddenly dry throat and a womb clenching so hard she trembled.

She needed to jump at him. *On* him. To mold every inch of her naked body against his and beg him to slam her to the floor, hike the kilt up, and then fuck her like the self-respecting Scot he was.

Which didn't exactly keep with the nobler plan here, did it?

"Shit. *Shit.*"

Once more, she let the gray matter exclamations spill

over her lips. Once more, Sam was ready with a smirk that actually made smug humility a thing. "Changin' your mind about wantin' to claim Franz's fortune?"

"Ssshhh." She pushed three fingers against his lips. "With you looking like all my wet dreams, I can't handle you sounding like them too."

He twisted his head enough to capture her middle finger between his lips. Then slid his tongue to the crevice at its bottom. As Jen gasped, he whispered, "Did you just mention wet dreams while standin' here in my bathroom, dressed in that bonnie fine dress, and—"

"Shit!" Her repetition was stripped of its raspy arousal, thanks to the horror that slammed her like the hull of an aircraft carrier.

"Mouse?" Sam murmured.

"My dress." She moaned it while looking down, realizing she was still wearing her basic red shirtdress and matching pumps from the day. While the color of the dress favored her skin tone, it was still about as boring a look as they came. "This doesn't exactly scream 'show me the epic dungeon you're hiding out back, guys.'"

"Speak for yourself, woman." Sam rocked back on one heel, appraising her with a gaze that had gone the shade of a mysterious sea. Not the dangerous, ship-destroying kind. The tempestuous kind that crashed up against the lighthouse where Jen envisioned him taking her and then fucking her in that hotter-than-hell, better-than-the-pages-of-a-book outfit. "On better thought, let me speak for you." He dipped a decisive nod. "The dress is sexy as fuck, woman."

She rolled her eyes. Watched the responding tension at the corners of his own but didn't let it deter her from muttering,

"The dress is meant for a military base accounting office, Sam, not a—"

Her own gasp was her interruption—though it coincided with the one-two swoops of his hands, one at her neckline and one near the hem, each twisting free a couple of buttons. He concluded his "alteration" by grabbing the clip that held her hair off her face and then tousling his long fingers across her scalp, bringing a bunch of her thick waves across her cheeks.

"Errmmm..." She bit her lip but flashed a grin. "Okay, then."

Sam stepped over, pressing himself against her and nuzzling her neck suggestively. "*Not* 'okay, then,'" he rasped into her hair. "You're not just fuckin' *okay*, Jenny Thorne. You're *perfect*. Especially right now."

She sighed. For a moment, just enjoyed the feel of him again, so huge and hard and defined against her...and damn near around her. She inhaled him, forest cedar and ocean spice joined by the starch in his shirt and the musk of his skin.

Holy God, how she wanted him. Yes, this damn swiftly. Yes, this damn badly.

The yearning only got more intense as he cupped the sides of her face and husked, "All better?"

"Hrrrmmm," Jen mumbled. "Yeah. I...I think."

"You *think*?" Sam pressed his fingertips into the indents just below her ears. "Not acceptable, sweet mouse. Come on, now. What is it?"

"Oh, ugh," she rasped. "It's really noth—" But she realized writing herself off like that would only darken the tempests in his eyes at this point. "Cripes, Sam. I mean, look at us! You're... You're a freaking book fantasy come to life, and I'm—"

"Goin' to get your arse pummeled a lovely shade of

carnation pink, if you don't stop with this silly mince right *now*."

But it was too late to prevent the blush that felt exactly that shade. Jen somehow sucked together the rest of her composure and used the fortitude to push away from the hunk in her arms. Well, to attempt to. When Sam didn't relent, she protested, "I'll be fine, okay? Just give me a second to—*oh!* Sam!"

Sam clutched her waist tighter, securing her balance as he bent to finish what he started with his other hand: whipping her panties down, all the way around her ankles. "Mmmmm," he rumbled. "Now look at *that* bonnie sight." With a sultry look up over his shoulder, he speared her with eyes gone the shade of molten silver. "Still think you're not 'hot' enough *now*, missy?"

"Sam." It was a plea, a rebuke, and a gasp in one, the latter happening as he nimbly maneuvered the lace around her heels and then up into his inner coat pocket. "Come on..."

"What? *I* don't get to have one of *my* fantasies come to life?"

"One of your—" Her jaw plummeted. "*You've* had fantasies about *me*?" She lifted it again, battling to work moisture back into her lips and throat. "L-L-Like...this?"

"Without any panties?" He *had* to be a Highland god about filling that in, his posture so focused and his grip still undaunted. "In a dress the color of your nipples when I bite and suck them...and the sweet, tender bits between your thighs when I—"

"All right, all right!" She held up a hand, trying to laugh but sounding like a constipated goose instead. "I get the picture!" And dear crap, how *that* was the truth. She shoved down a deep breath, certain that if she actually wore the underwear now, they'd be soaked. "Can't say I'm actually *comfortable* about it, but I'm also not sure I get a choice about that."

"Of course you get a choice." He stepped back, already seeming to sense how she needed the space for clear thought. "You *always* get a choice. Say the word, and the lace is yours again."

Jen smoothed her skirt. Realigned her posture. Neither move compensated for what she'd felt when he was close. The primal sense of being protected. Safe. Cherished. Thoroughly female, balanced out by the massive presence of his masculinity. To be a damn greeting card about it, she already missed him. But the ache was eased by knowing he still carried a little "gift" from her. A token that been cupped around the most intimate part of her...

"No," she finally rasped. "I...I want you to keep them."

An extended rumble resonated through him as he reclosed the space between them and dipped a kiss along her forehead. "Tell you what?" he said, deep pleasure threading his voice. "Show of solidarity from the smitten dafty in the room. Tonight, I'll wear my kilt in the manner befittin' a proper Scotsman."

She laughed again. It sounded more human but felt a lot more like it'd come from another creature: a woman much more confident and carefree and sexy than Jennifer Josephine Thorne could have ever *considered* in her existence. At once, she inwardly blamed and thanked "the smitten dafty"—while acknowledging that could only be the start of what she owed the man, in *all* his incarnations. The more of him she knew, including tonight's Dom *and* dafty, the more she longed to give so much more to him than her damn panties.

Because, she openly admitted, the more he kept giving in return. Like this latest twist—throwing her into incredulity that must have shown on her face, if his resquared shoulders and resecured feet were any accurate reflector.

Into their little moment of shared amusement, she finally charged, "You're—you're serious, aren't you? About us doing this?"

"You're astute." He twisted his lips until his dimples were deep accents in his cheeks. "But I already knew that."

"I've...I've never done anything like this before."

"You don't say."

Fast glower. "Smartass."

"Hey, first times are fun to share with friends."

She pulled in a breath and frowned. But only for a second. His rejoining smile was enough to shred any resistance Jen had left. In that moment, she wondered how the man had really ended up as a pilot. His ability to push a jet to Mach speeds was nothing compared to his ninja mind trick of disguising utter naughtiness as casual conversation.

So what was their "chitchat" going to be like in a real public setting...like the Scene Lounge?

As Jen watched him tuck her panties deeper into his pocket, a polite smile on his lips but silver fire blazing in his eyes, she finally wrapped her head around the fact that she was truly going to find out.

And that the experience wouldn't be one she soon forgot.

★ ★ ★ ★ ★

"Sam?"

"Hmmm?"

"What happened to the pact we made in the car?"

"The pact?"

"About being good at least for an hour?"

The assertion seemed in need of a visual jab as well, so she set her wine down and stole a glance up at the man. It was a hell of a dirty job, but someone had to do it. Possibly again and again and again.

She could only hope.

Dirt, mud, sludge, muck... She'd take it all if it looked and felt and smelled this stunningly good.

His scent, all rain and sun and man together, consumed her aroused senses. His size, enforced by the plaid draping one of his shoulders and the vest custom-cut for his chiseled shoulders, welcomed her roving gaze. His formidable profile was given more definition by the bar's dim lighting against the ginger stubble along his jaw. Despite all that, his face on the whole was open and congenial, even exchanging an approving smile with a guy who'd ordered the same dark ale as him. "Of course," he murmured. "Good. One hour. I remember."

"So squeezing my knee under the table—"

"Isn't bein' good?"

"There's a difference between *being* good and *feeling* good, Captain."

"But why?" He tilted his gaze in toward her. Gone was the funny guy from his bathroom who used silly Scottish nicknames on himself and smirked while he hid underwear in secret pockets. From the moment they'd walked in here, Sam had become all Dom, all the time—and damn it if that, along with all the kisses of fresh air up her skirt, weren't turning her most sensitive parts into one mass of bare, quivering arousal. "Besides," he went on, his gaze lowering and his lips curling,

"I'm not squeezin' your knee. Not anymore, at least."

He was right. It was no longer her knee. It was her lower thigh and then the middle of her thigh. If he didn't stop, it'd be her upper thigh and then—

"*Sam.*"

He set down his beer and laughed softly, as if she'd just told him a private little joke. The gleam in his eyes was brilliant; the focus on his face was indisputable. "How's that for good, lass?"

She pushed her legs together to keep his hand from sliding higher. He chuckled quietly again, *finally* withdrawing it—

Only to replace it with the other one, meaning he was now fully turned, nearly blocking her view of the glamorous place with his shoulders. The Scene Lounge was a round room, where old Hollywood glam had been masterfully meshed with a Marrakesh brothel. The designers hadn't skimped on the red leather, gold tassels, ornate accents, and nuanced dimness of the ambiance.

Sam smiled down into her face. Jen pressed her legs harder and attempted to glower back. For a moment, he looked adorably nonplussed, as if they were standing in her office and she'd cut him off in the middle of a one-liner, ordering him to sign off on flight assignments. She refused to remember that in most of those moments, she'd yearned to have him in *this* kind of a moment.

Different times, different circumstances.

*Much* different.

"Okay now. Stop." She would've attempted to squirm free, but where did that take her crotch except closer to his fingers? Her utterly naked pussy...his completely determined hand...

To her shock, he acquiesced. "You win, beautiful." Dutifully, he even tugged her skirt back into place. "For now, at least." One swig of his drink later, he added, patting his pocket, "But only because I've got the bargaining chip."

She sipped at her wine, a Cabernet as wonderful as the one they'd started back at his place, before returning coyly, "You going to reveal another fantasy involving my panties, Captain? How many of those *do* you have waiting in the wings?" She cocked her head, battling to copy his slick seduction though she was sure she probably came off more like the socially awkward Muppet who just said "meep" over and over again.

"I've tried not to dwell too much on my fantasies about you, mouse." Though he leaned over close enough to grate it into her hair, his gaze struck out across the room again. "Mistakin' one's cock for the control stick can be a fatal mistake in sixteen tons of speedin' steel."

She clutched her wineglass. Hard. "I was seriously just kidding."

"I wasn't." So gruff. Heavy. A sough of pure lust.

"So...you really *do* have fantasies?" she managed. "I mean, the kind that..."

"Fairly soon after the first moment I met you." He dipped his head, peering closely at her again. "That's fashin' you fiercely. Why?"

"Why?" She arched both brows. "Because I'm a dweeb, Sam. I walk around with my nose in books and my head in the clouds."

"But I like you that way."

"I like me that way too—except when I'm yanked out and have to be reminded that I can't take three steps in dress shoes without falling flat on my face. That sometimes—*most* times—I have the social graces of an orangutan. Like when I can't stop babbling stupid shit like *this*, around someone like *you*, and—"

He borrowed her move from his place, flattening several fingers across her lips. "Haud your wheesht, darlin'. Someone like me? What the bloody hell does that mean?"

She turned her head, freeing her lips. "Sam...please. Don't even try to tell me that you're unaware of it." She arced a finger, encompassing the room. "You turned every woman's head—and half the men's—just by striding in here a half hour ago."

"And your point is what? That I inherited great bone structure and have decent hair?"

"It's a little better than decent." Much better, actually, but she didn't push the subject. He'd started to steam about this. "But no, that's not my point. It's not what you have here." She relished the chance to glide a touch down the side of his face. "It's what you are in *here*." She dipped her caress to the middle of his chest. "You're something special, mister. People see it, *know* it, everywhere you go."

He lifted a hand to cover hers. "And you're not?"

His words still sounded like an accusation. Beneath their weight, Jen squirmed. "I don't light up rooms everywhere I go. I don't fly to the stars and then bring them back down for the earth to revel in." The glow from a wall sconce was a perfect fixation, invoking a vision of Sam's jet against a sunset sky. "That's another fantasy of mine, you know," she said wistfully. "To know what it's like to fly with you."

"Don't change the subject." His retort was instant. Too much so. Her confession had touched him a little, and Jen was glad of it. It was her honest assessment, not some ploy to get him up her skirt—despite how he'd already been there once tonight already. Besides, he was right. She nodded quietly, conceding to that.

"Sorry," she murmured. "You're right."

"Damn right I'm right." Though returning her gaze to his face yielded the fast recognition that they still weren't on the same page. Sure enough, he growled out in challenge, "How the hell can you *not* see what I do in you?"

She pursed her lips. Tried not to get pulled back in by his stare, which was filled with the fiercest predator focus she'd seen in it yet, to the point that her inner radars were already screaming with the man's missile lock on her. "Whoa." She used both hands to T-stab the air. "I thought we were here to find the secret dungeon."

"First things first." He pushed in closer. Issued a low growl so close to her ear, it trailed shivering heat down her neck, between her breasts, and straight into the enlivened nerves at the crux of her thighs... "Answer me."

"First things first?" She twisted her head to find him waiting with obvious expectancy. "I thought the dungeon hunt *was* the first thing..."

"You're evading."

"*You're* evading." But when he didn't let up on his solid silver scrutiny, she dug in her heels on her own stare—though, just thirty seconds later, became the first to relent, diving her gaze back toward her wine. She didn't want to admit to the subtle shift that had just occurred between them, although every hormone in her body wasn't so forgiving. So many instincts screamed at her to turn and duck her head against him and then just pour out every misgiving and insecurity she'd ever had to him. But her will held out, at least long and strong enough to keep her head up and her voice steady as she declared, "You know what? We'll have to agree to disagree on this, buddy. You're a damn good man, Sam, but you can't change what simply is. Even if we didn't live halfway around the world from each other, we'd be living in different circles. Different worlds."

His lips twisted as if he contemplated having to kiss a snake. "What? So you think a woman like Mattie belongs on my arm instead?"

Jen grasped his hand between both of hers, an unspoken plea for calm. "Maybe not her, exactly," she conceded. "But... someone like her."

"*Like* her?" He leaned away. Yep. Avoiding the snake.

"You know what I'm trying to say," she snapped. "Why are you making this so hard?"

His eyes bugged. "*I'm* makin' this—" He interrupted himself, inhaling sharply. Finished with just as harsh a nod. "All right, then. If I belong with someone like Mattie, who do *you* belong with?" He swept an arm out. "Go on. Here's a nice room, full of chaps to choose from. Who among them is *like* the guy you need to be with?"

Jen flinched. What other choice was there, in reaction to the venom in his voice? "Who the hell poured salt into your beer, Mackenna?"

His gaze narrowed. "Excuse the fuck out of me?"

"You heard me," she countered. "Why are you acting like I black-eyed your ego? You're a hell of a lot sturdier than this, Braw Boy." Okay, using his call sign was aiming a tiny bit under the belt, especially in the same sentence she'd mentioned the strength he was more proud of than his looks, but he really was behaving like a bruised boyfriend instead of an out-of-her-league lover. So logically, that led to a pair of conclusions. Either he'd been truly hiding one hell of an ego over the last two weeks, or—

Or the guy really did care for her beyond the realm of just

a couple of friends with epic benefits.

As they said where he came from: *horse shite.*

There had to be some other explanation.

"Okay, Captain Mackenna," she finally mustered the courage to charge. "What the hell's going on?"

Sam finished off his ale. Pounded the glass to the table. "That wasn't an answer to my question."

Fine. Two could play this game.

Jen scooped up her glass and chugged the rest of her wine.

And instantly regretted it.

After crashing into her empty stomach, the wine was instantly shot into her racing nerves and whipped into a cyclone in her head. "All of them." *Liquid courage, don't fail me now.* "There's your answer, Captain. Because every man in this damn room wants to be with a cute little catch like me, right?" Her throat snagged on the sarcasm, making it possible for her pain to seep through. She pushed on, having no choice if she was to save any kind of face. "Damn. I'm so glad *you're* here, because I'd be beating them all off with sticks if that wasn't the case. Story of my life. Men, men, men. Everywhere I turn, it's— *agghh!*"

Her yelp popped out as Sam thrusted to his feet, hauling her right behind. Still reeling from chugging her Cabernet, Jen careened forward. He caught her easily, despite the dark fury still claiming every inch of his mien. While settling her balance, he beckoned a cocktail waitress.

"Captain Mackenna," she murmured politely. "Will you be transferring the evening to private status now?"

Sam's smile was perfunctory. "Fuckin' bet I am."

"Transferring the—" Jen darted her gaze between him to the waitress. "'Private status?' Huh?"

"Very well, then." The server, a leggy beauty with trendy cat-eye makeup, spoke like Jen had commented on the weather. "Right this way."

"Right this way *where*?"

Sam gave her no solid rebuttal but his tighter hold and his harder stare. Jen was able to summon her own glower before he pivoted back around, following Leggy toward a portion of the bar's stylish wall that actually turned out to be a swinging door.

"Hold on a second," Jen blurted. "Sam...is this...did we..." She caught sight of the electronic pad in the hostess's grip, realizing that the screen didn't appear at all like the seating chart of the round room they'd just left. Instead, she spotted an icon of a lock, with the label *VIP* beneath it. But stumbling along behind Sam, Jen didn't feel very "VIP." Skittish colt instincts to the rescue. She backed away until she couldn't— held back by a six-foot-something fighter pilot with launch rockets blazing in his eyes.

"Room three," said Leggy.

"R-R-Room three?" Jen raced her gaze between the hostess and the man still clamping her in an unretractable hold. "Room three of *what*?" But as soon as she really regarded Sam again, she knew. The rigid set of his face, along with the new authority in his stance... "You knew," she gasped, identifying the coalescing logic in her mind. "You *knew* from the second we got here, didn't you? Maybe even before that?"

Nothing about his aura faltered. If anything, his composure smoothed in proportion to the higher flare of *her* hackles, working in tandem with the wine to confuse her even more. "I would never deliberately deceive you, mouse."

"No? Then what the hell *is* this?"

"Someone beating you guys to the spanking bench by ten minutes." The interruption, erupting from behind them, was tied with an all-too-familiar ribbon of humor. Familiar, as in a tone she'd known for over twenty years—ever since it was used to comfort her after Tansie Owens pushed her off the swings on the kindergarten playground.

Sure enough, she spun around to behold the treasured grin and twinkling fairy gaze of her best friend—though Tess's smile and eyes were about the only recognizable aspects of her face. The woman had made up her face so she really did look like a fairy—of sorts. Maybe a naughty fairy. The glam shades of red, orange, and black were angled to make her look wicked yet innocent—at least to her neckline. From there, the sparkled shades spread out to cover the tops of her breasts, which were barely concealed by a tight red corset. Beneath that, layer upon layer of red and black tulle sprung out in a skirt—though again, the description barely fit the look. Tess's naughty bits were barely covered by the frothy flair, from which Jen rapidly averted her gaze. She had a feeling that was exactly the idea. She also had a feeling that her friend's panties were hiding in one of Dan Colton's pockets—though the man slated to become her husband in five days, now strolling out into the hall behind his woman, didn't appear to have a pocket with enough room for the task. The man wore nothing but black leather pants, and they perfectly outlined every damn inch of his—errrmmm—assets.

"Okay," Jen heard herself mutter, tossing her stare all the way to the floor. "*Whoa.*"

Tess giggled. *Giggled.* That was enough to bring Jen's gaze back up for a second. Tess wasn't the giggling type. On the other hand, she'd never known Tess to be the naughty-fairy-in-a-tutu type, either. "Well, hello to you too, missy."

Jen managed to return her friend's fast hug. Kind of. She didn't hug hard, afraid she'd squeeze too much in the wrong places and she'd see more of Tess than she wanted to. Rephrase. She'd *already* seen more of Tess than she wanted to. "Wh-What are you guys doing here?" The woman had half of Atlanta's society page in town for the wedding and a brain-exploding to-do list. Jen had been trying to help out where she could, but Tess's mom turned "control freak" into an art form.

"What does it look like?" Tess replied easily as the guys grunted, fist-bumped, and murmured to each other in ways that made Jen nervous and aroused at the same damn time. When obvious Doms started muttering mysterious things, it was time for submissives to pay attention, wasn't it? But Tess went on as if they were just standing on the corner of Flamingo and Vegas Boulevard, waiting along with the tourists for the light to change. "Franz told Dan and the guys about this place, and we jumped on a reservation as fast as we could. We both need to get away from the wedding insanity—like, *now*."

"Right." That part, she could give with sincerity. A girl didn't put a ring on it with one of the world's most prominent businessmen, in the middle of Las Vegas, without there being some crazy fanfare.

"Got a bonus from the whole thing too. Turns out we won some kind of a contest among the guys from acting so fast, so Master picked up a new paddle and told me to splurge on the new play gear. Like it?"

*Master? Paddle? Play gear?* "Uhhh...sure," Jen all but choked. "Pretty."

"Hopefully it'll match what he does to these."

"Oh my God." So much for pretending they were standing

in a mob of tourists. Or for the way her eyes bulged as Tess turned and flipped up her skirt, exposing the very firm and very bare globes of her backside. It was official now. She *had* seen too damn much of her best friend.

Apparently, and thankfully, Dan seemed to agree. The man reacted to his sub's playful "show" with the speed of a tiger tamer with a wildcat, sweeping over by a powerful step and then hauling her against his side with a powerful pull. Once she was there, he dominated her mouth with a crashing kiss until she visibly melted and audibly moaned.

"Sorry to cut social hour short, gang," he growled once they dragged their mouths apart. "But a certain little ruby needs to be reschooled in showing herself off in the hallway without her Master's permission."

At once, Tess erupted with a cute little yip. While Dan's gaze never wavered from her face, his hand had disappeared beneath her tulle—no doubt giving a subtle preview of what he had planned for his fiery fairy. "Oh yes please, Master. Teach me a *very* good lesson."

Jen watched, fascinated, as Dan only reacted by tightening his gaze and clenching his jaw. But the lack of outward signs aside, the energy—the *power*—flying and flowing between the two was like a blast of sheer electricity on the hushed air of the hallway. Just being a witness to the whole thing, Jen admitted she was fascinated. And enflamed. And so fucking turned on...

Which made it doubly strange when Leggy cleared her throat and arched her sculpted eyebrows Sam's way, a silent request to keep them moving on down the dim corridor. How the woman could still look so bored, after the tease of tantalization Dan and Tess had just given them all, needed to be catalogued as a new mystery of the cosmos. Not that Jen even thought about it once Sam moved back next to her, his eyes filled with silver intensity and his presence radiating more of the potent Dominant flow she'd just experienced from Dan Colton.

She was intoxicated—and it had nothing to do with the wine.

She was soaked—and it had everything to do with him.

She was limp—and it was due entirely to his hold on her. With his hands around her wrists, not his fingers threaded with hers. With his forceful efficiency in pushing right into her personal space, hauling her up against his chest, and dipping his stubbled jaw into the sensitive crook of her neck.

"What do you say now, mouse?" he gritted. "It's still your choice now... Will we have a few more cocktails or a lot more fun?"

Somehow—she really had no damn idea how—she got in a huge swallow. But once her throat oscillated against his prickly jaw, her self-composure was done. Even her irritation with him had vanished. All she could feel was the man's heated focus...his full, thick, lust-driven attention...his desire to give her everything she'd just witnessed between Dan and Tess and maybe more. Oh, so *much* more...

"Holy...shit," she rasped as he swept around to bracket her body from the back, locking her wrists using just one of his hands and yanking her against him with the other hand at the front of her neck. Not in a stranglehold. He didn't need one. This was right where she wanted to be. Right where she'd *dreamed* of being. She just hadn't realized it...until now. "Ohhhhh, holy fuck."

So much for pruning the lust from her gasp. Or feigning that his responding hum, rich and deep and low, didn't affect her in exactly the same way. "Might just happen, sweet one... if you're good."

"G-G-Good?" Jen stammered back. "H-H-How?"

"That's my secret to know and yours to find out," he supplied in a soft snarl. "Now, she said room three. *Walk*."

Once more, Leggy was the picture of baffling boredom. She watched their entire exchange from heavily kohled eyes as if she were just wiping off plastic menus and they were a normal couple having a tiff. Jen wasn't sure if that made it easier or tougher to comply with Sam's order, but she did it, even admitting to all the tingles of erotic expectation through her body as she did.

Down the alluring, thick-carpeted hall they stepped, past numbered rooms that couldn't even be written off as specialty spa suites. No way could Jen ignore what the rooms were there for. After passing room two, the picture was crystal clear. Heavy moans bled through the door. Then a series of distinct smacks, like leather meeting leather. Then more moans and a man's baritone voice crooning distinct words. *Good girl. That's my good girl.*

As they passed, Sam fitted his lips once more to her ear. "You ken what I'm sayin' now, mouse? Good girls get rewarded around here."

She almost snapped around to tell him that good girls usually had more than three seconds' notice to discover they were going into the hidden dungeon with their sexy-as-hell Doms, but it had been an hour and a half since she relinquished her panties to the man, more than implying that she trusted him for whatever crazy turns the night took. But more importantly, she kind of *liked* that part. When was the last time she'd been someone's "good" anything? Even the subject of their little spat was kind of cool. He'd been so bent about her trying to talk him *out* of considering her so special, it had taken him right into full-on fury.

She couldn't remember the last time anyone had ever cared enough to get *pissed* at her.

And once Sam pushed open the door to room three, no way could she deny how he planned to prove it to her even more.

The space was lighted even dimmer than the main room. There was a canopied bed fit for a king, framed in mahogany tapestries and piled with endless pillows. A three-sided mirror stood in the corner with a multilevel stool in front of it, serving a purpose Jen could only imagine—though right now, her imagination ran pretty damn wild.

"In."

His voice was harsh, twisting into her like a newly heated poker, needing no embellishment for her compliance.

But he'd given no stipulation about doing it meekly. "Damn it, Sam. We should talk about this, right? I mean—"

It was impossible to say anything else, with the man's tongue suddenly in her mouth.

Passionate. Powerful. Consuming.

*Ohhhh, damn.*

"Your safe word is *fantasy*. Now in."

After he finally freed her from the next openly carnal kiss, a moan exploded up Jen's throat. She wanted to—needed to—resist but couldn't. Her lungs struggled for air as her stomach battled for the right way up. Her head fought a silvery, lusty fog. Her whole body burst to life, as if this was the first time she and Sam had made out like this.

Dear God. He really was a dream come to life. Every

amazing romance hunk she'd ever fallen for, rolled into one magnificent package. Turning every feeling she had and sensation she felt into something new and brilliant, incredible and illicit...

Especially as she walked all the way into the room and he rammed her back against into the thick bedpost. And kissed her with hard, ruthless possession all over again.

She met his desire with a matching groan of urgent need, hiking a leg around his waist. To her shock, Sam pushed it back down. When he tore his mouth away, she let her face drop into confusion.

"For the *record*, it isn't acceptable that you've compared yourself to the scum on my shoe and then even hinted that—" Whatever he was going to say stunned him into silence. He stabbed a hand through his hair. "Arse and fuckin' parsley, Jenny. We've shared a lot of bloody things with each other in the last two weeks! Do you really think that I would be even *half* attracted to someone like—"

He interrupted himself with another growl. The violence of it curled into Jen's blood, making her instinctively reach back, clutching the bedpost with one hand.

A lot of good that did.

"Fuck it," he muttered, grabbing her free wrist. "I'm tired of tryin' to sweet-talk this into you."

"*That* was sweet talk?"

Bad move. The three seconds she took for the sarcasm were all the time he needed to pivot her around and then lift her other hand to clasp the post. In another flash of motion, he pulled on something hidden in the canopy. A pair of padded wrist cuffs dropped from seemingly nowhere. Holy shit. Did every piece of furniture in this place come with kinky booby traps?

Not that she cared about the answer—especially as Sam wasted no time in latching her into the cuffs.

The second he was done with that, he hiked her skirt up. She was exposed—and completely turned on—from the waist down.

"Ahhhhh!"

And then turned on and screaming—as the man delivered a sharp spank across the center of her bottom.

"Sam! *Oh!*"

Then a second smack.

*Holy crap!*

"What the—"

He cut her short by spinning her back around and kissing her again. Delving deeper. Sucking on her harder. He didn't relent, compelling her head to drop back so he could assault her mouth—doing it as brutally as he squeezed both globes of her ass, rubbing in the heat from the pain he'd just dealt. And God help her, Jen let him—not just because he gave her no choice but because she wanted to. Because somewhere, in her wildest and naughtiest dreams about this man, she'd envisioned him like this. Tearing into her mouth. Razing into her senses. Firing up her pores and skin and nerves...

Exactly...

Like...

This.

By the time he pulled away, her chest heaved, her blood throbbed, and her sex clenched tightly enough to make her moan again.

Especially when he delivered a third blow to her bottom.

A fourth, at twice the impact.

A fifth, intensifying more.

"Shit!" she finally managed past the screams.

"Breathe." His exhortation was practically a Zen chant in her ear. Calm. Soothing. Infuriating.

"Fuck you."

"Fuck *you*, Jenny Thorne." Bizarrely, a smile entered his voice. It twisted with his anger, throwing Jen off. Was she supposed to melt for him or pour molds for new ice daggers?

As he circled in order to look at her directly, though the post was between them, his expression gave her no clues. He was still beautiful, with those dark eyes and ginger waves and jaw like a precipice from his native land.

"Fuck you," he repeated, "for thinking so little of me, that someone like Mattie Lesange could ever meet my needs. And fuck you for thinking so little of *yourself* to presume *you* wouldn't."

Her breath stopped. Well, she knew what to feel now. Giddy astonishment collided with abject remorse, sprinkled with a layer of maybe-this-really-*is*-all-a-dream. "I'm...sorry." And she really was—though that didn't throw a cease-fire onto her confusion. "But men love pretty things on their arms, Sam."

He glowered. "What's that supposed to mean?"

"Not the insult you're taking it as." She shrugged. Remaining covered from the navel up lent her the confidence. "Life is life, friends are friends, and lovers are something completely different. Sometimes, good sex is just good sex, and making more out of—"

He jerked her chin up using two fingers. Stared like she'd just told him the moon was made of bacon. "Is that really all you think of what we're sharing here? 'Just good sex?'"

Confusion tumbled in again. The answer to that seemed

apparent but wasn't. She decided to go for total honesty. "Look...I just don't expect anything else, okay? And it's fine that—"

"*I* should expect anything else."

She ignored the darkness in his tone. "How could you? And why *would* you? Neither of us is a kid. It's great to think of taking home grand meanings from a one-night thing—when you're young. But we're not—"

He stopped her with another kiss. Dug his hand against her scalp, locking her head in place. Stabbed his tongue against hers, as if needing to strip off the words she'd just uttered. When he let her mouth go, he kept his hand in place. Dragged her head back up so he could impale her stare with his. The command in his grip was as compelling as the force in his eyes, once more driving in like that fresh poker, scalding its way onto her psyche and searing its way into her soul.

"I want to spank you again, Jenny."

She swallowed. "I know." Ohhh God, how she did. All the silver spikes in his gaze had told her so.

"I just don't want to be gentle about it."

"I...I know."

He dragged in a rocky breath. "Do you?"

"Of—of course. I pissed you off. And you're a Dominant." *And I want you to punish me. To control me.*

*Yes, please...*

"No." He shook his head fiercely. "No, you *don't* understand. The punishin'...it's done. But I'm not." He pushed in, smashing his lips to hers. "God help me, my burners are just starting to fire." His hand twisted tighter in her hair. "Not a fuckin' thing I feel about you is civilized, woman. It hasn't been for quite a while."

Her senses swam in a thick fog. It felt so good. Everything about him felt so good. "You...really mean that, don't you?"

"I do."

Her lips lifted. Only one glass of wine, but everything was limp and carefree, as if she'd had the whole bottle. "I had no idea."

"Disguised it that well, did I?" He curled a smile of his own. "When all I thought about, walkin' into your little office at Nellis every mornin', was how to get you exactly like this. Wait—no." He swung around to mount the bed, wrapping an arm around her waist to pull her with him. She now knelt on the mattress, wrists tethered to the bedpost and ass high and presented to him. He revised with a growl, "Exactly like *this*."

Jen lowered her head between her arms. The pose, so submissive, also felt completely right. "Thank you for the clarification, Sir."

"*Sir*." Another satisfied snarl rumbled from his chest. "Do you know how much pleasure you give me, every glorious time that word spills across your lips?"

"Don't think I do. But maybe you can just...show me instead?" She finished by subtly wiggling her ass, though it was no small feat. With his hand sweeping back and forth across her cheeks, spreading the heat of his first swats, it was all she could do to be coy. She needed more of him, so damn badly. Needed him to touch her in other places. Illicit places...

"Perhaps I can." But while his voice approved, he pulled his hands away. Bafflement struck but only for a second. A fresh wave of arousal took over—as Sam reached to a control panel embedded in the bed's footboard. After he pushed a button, the mattress began to raise up—but only beneath her legs. She would've laughed aloud, if the action didn't heat her sex in a hundred new ways. A control number bed, the D/s version. Was there any end to what the Nyte's creators had dreamed up in the way of kinky delights?

The next moment, even that cognitive thinking was ripped away. Sam dug his hands into her hips, centering her lower body against the hump. Power radiated off his fingertips as he flowed them in, spreading heat across her buttocks.

A gasp burst off her lips. A growl curled off his.

"Fuck. Me." His hands splayed, kneading her flesh and warming her skin all over again. "So bloody beautiful. So pink and sweet..."

"But...?" Jen went ahead and led where his voice seemed to be trailing and reveled in the approving hum that prefaced his reply.

"But it needs to be red." And just like that, no more approval. Only his touch, back with a rough purpose, echoed by the wolfish edge in his voice. "Your ass needs to bear my mark, girl."

*Take senses, toss into rock tumbler.* But Jen sighed out her gratitude for the ride. How her balance rolled from the magic of his voice and the spreading heat from his possessive strokes along her tingling skin.

"Yes," she heard herself rasp. "Yes. Mark me..."

He snarled low again. "Ask it properly. I want to hear that pretty word from you again. *Say it*, sweet Jenny. 'Spank me, please—'"

"Sir." She filled it in with eager longing. "Yes. Oh yes, Sir, please. Spank me. Mark me. *Oh!*"

The exclamation took over for any more coherent words as Sam lowered a *thwack* across her ass. While her flesh stung, her mind careened. Logic taunted, just beyond her reach.

There was a reason she wanted this so badly, especially from him, but did it matter? All she wanted right now was his touch. All she needed was his dominion, full and consuming and perfect. Sam. Sam. *Sam*. For this moment, for this time, she only existed because of him. Through him.

Another spank. Unleashed power. Reverberations of pain. She screamed. Or maybe just dreamed it.

"Give me 'fantasy' if you need to stop, mouse. I'm only just beginning."

She rolled her hips, letting the sting spread and dissipate. The tingles down her legs and through her sex...were incredible. "Don't stop. Please, Sir."

"So certain." Why did his voice suddenly sound weird? Almost...wicked? "So sure."

The answer came with a resounding crack—though the next impact to her ass wasn't from his hand. It was the harsh stroke of leather in the middle of her left cheek. As Jen struggled to summon a scream, another *whoosh* whipped the air. She took in the musk of the leather—before pain chomped into her right cheek. When he rained another blow to her left, the shriek finally manifested. The right again. Back to speechlessness, fighting to accept the agony that would soon bring ecstasy. Or so she hoped.

*Fantasy.* It already hovered at the outskirts of her mind, tempting her to call out, when a new kind of growl vibrated out of Sam. Jen had never heard a sound like it. Deep. Dark. Dripping with carnality. Coarse with need. "I knew the crop would love your ass, darlin'. Knew that your skin would take my marks so perfectly." Another rumble, twice as entrancing as the first, flowed as he whipped her again: two more blows on each stinging cheek. "Take it in for me, sweet Jenny. All of it.

These memories in your skin...take them into your spirit too. Twist them inside of you. Weave *me* inside of you."

She sighed. "You're already there."

"Not deep enough." He emphasized with another two strokes. "Let the pain open it deeper and then pour me inside the crack. Let me into the places that mean you'll never forget me. That mean you'll never think yourself unworthy ever again."

More smacks. More pain. More spaces, so far inside, that cracked open and flooded with the adoration, strength, and majesty in his voice.

More of herself...surrendered to him.

More of the composure she could no longer hold together.

His passion set her tears free. They burst on messy sobs, and she didn't care. A vision danced across her mind. She was five or six, twirling in the front yard with a "wand" made from a stick and some party streamers. She was magical and perfect... so many years before the world began to tell her she wasn't. Before she became the dork, the brain, the geek, "the weird one."

Now, she danced in the light again. Streamers of pleasure and pain blew across her senses. The beauty of it was...intense. Blazing. Blinding. And everywhere in that heaven, there was Sam. Always Sam. Now leaning over her, brushing back her hair to collect her tears with his kisses. Pressing against her so his heat and strength permeated her body. His satin vest caressed her back, his wool kilt scraped her ass...and teased farther between her legs. As if she needed a reminder of how her body craved him as much as her soul did.

"So beautiful," he murmured. "Damn, Jenny. How beautiful you are to me."

Sensations continued to bombard. The streamers morphed into other images, full of light and lust and power. *His* strength, fused into her through the awareness they funneled into each other...*through* each other. She shivered from the enormity of it. Basked in the perfect, permeating glow of it...

*Of him...*

Sam. Sam. *Sam.*

The teasing swipes of his kilt against her pussy were more instigators of the sensations, filling her with tremulous, joyous shivers and sobs. She was like a jet, guided by him through a canopy of clouds, into the blinding light from above. But then he banked and rolled the aircraft, and she was disoriented. Which way was up? And did she care anymore? She only knew she longed for more. Needed it like her next damn breath. Needed *him.*

"Sam. *Sam.*"

"I know, darlin'. I know."

She whimpered in protest. He *didn't* know. She needed more of him. *All* of him...

A crinkle of foil serrated the air. The kilt didn't abrade her ass anymore. There was furnace heat...and the push of a steely knob at the cushions guarding her intimate tunnel.

"I need to fill you." He prodded in a little more, circling his hips to stroke every sensitive edge of her throbbing entrance. "Will you have me inside you, Jenny? Will you let me fuck your perfect little cunt?"

She didn't remember saying yes. Maybe she hadn't. Maybe he'd just heard the cry that echoed from her heart, resonated through her being, drawing his cock inside her, as inevitable as the sun in her visions.

As undeniable as her love for him.

*Ohhhh, shit.*

She loved him.

Ohhhh yes, she certainly did.

The truth of it punched free as he peeled back her defenses, replacing her barriers with the fullness of his body. Jen let it crash in, racking her in harder sobs, knowing this would be the only time she could. Between the tears she'd already shed and Sam's relentless pace, she'd be able to weep for every woe in the world and get away with it at this point.

"That's it, darlin'." He was none the wiser either—thank God. "Give it to me, Jenny." His words were harsh and hot in her ear. His teeth dug into the flesh beneath. His hand was a clamp of demand on her shoulder, securing her as he shuttled his cock in and out, pounding her with the urgency their connection commanded. "Take me deeper. *Deeper*."

She interrupted her sobs long enough to gasp as he shoved her dress higher. Then shrieked as he reached beneath her bra, tugging hard at one nipple. Harder at the other.

"Sam! *Shit!*"

He twisted her nipple tighter. And again, the other. "*Who am I?*"

"Sir." She panted it out, hissing as he pushed his knees between hers, spreading them farther. "You are...Sir."

He penetrated her deeper. "And who gives you all your pain...and all your freedom?"

"You. Only you, Sir."

He growled low. Changed his punishing pace into a more determined drive. "And if we were still in the bar, who would you pick to take you here and fuck you?"

"You." The confession cracked from emotion. "J-Just y-you."

He released a long breath against her neck. "Christ, Jenny. And I'd pick just you too." His thrusts were so deep, the clap of their bodies reverberated off the walls. The sound barely registered past the blood thrumming through her ears, especially as he snaked a hand between her legs from the front. "Come with me, beauty. Let it all go for me."

She couldn't have denied him if her life depended on it. As his knowing fingers stroked her to orgasm, she wondered if she *was* dying. Surely heaven didn't give this kind of gift and expect nothing in return. Her nerve endings were fire. Her heartbeat was chaos. Every inch of her sex was an inferno, blazing and bright, convulsing and cataclysmic, squeezing over Sam's cock with the needy desperation of a Tolstoy heroine.

*Sam...*

"Jenny. Oh *fuck*...Jenny."

*I love you...*

"Take it all from me, beauty."

*Yes!*

He shoved in hard and then froze. Groaned hard as his cock expanded against her walls and then shot off. Bellowed as he exploded again and again in the dark, tight embrace of her body.

But the very next moment, Sam started pumping again. He threw a leg over, bracing his foot against the headboard, still slicing in and out, as if he hadn't just climaxed with the gusto of a lion.

"God*damn*, woman," he snarled. "It won't stop. I can't—" Another rough groan. Harder, harsher thrusts. "Fuck. *Fuck*."

His lust whipped hers into a new frenzy. Within a minute, Jen felt her sex grab him all over again, clenching his shaft as a new climax tumbled her into darker oblivion. "I can't stop either. I...can't..." Unbelievably, it was better than the first. Waves of white heat demolished like a Biblical storm, ripping screams of ecstasy up her already-parched throat. Her senses dissolved. Her body shook.

Her world was changed.

# CHAPTER EIGHT

His world was changed.

The truth of it wrapped like ropes lashed to moorings in that storm, refusing to be loosened even after Sam released Jen from the cuffs and lowered the bed. It was still relentless as he pulled out, tossed the condom into the bin near the bed, and then collapsed into the mountain of pillows—making sure to take her with him.

Without a word, he tucked her head against his chest, evoking deep intimacy though they lay there mostly clothed. His lungs still heaved, raising her up and down, like he'd just burned through an intense flight. His heartbeat roared like afterburners in his ears.

"Holy God," he muttered.

"He was probably involved somehow," she chuckled back—speaking more of a truth than she likely realized.

Because only a force like the Almighty could facilitate the tempest taking place inside him, even as they lay there in sublime stillness. A storm so forceful, Sam had to feign clearing his throat not to roar out the blaring truth of it.

*I'm falling in love with you.*

Yep. Holy God.

Aside from that, he didn't contemplate or question how he knew it so fully. Didn't want to think about the countless times, missing faces and places now, where he hadn't experienced anything remotely close to this. Hadn't known half the ache of being outside a woman's body instead of staying buried inside the hot, tight home for which *his* body was perfectly, supremely created...

"Well, there's a fantasy crossed off *my* list."

Or endured the celebration in his chest at hearing such soft, satisfied words tumble off her sweet, succulent lips. Or felt free enough to issue a snarky comeback like, "Which fantasy would that be, exactly? Gettin' to play in this starship disguised as a bed?"

"Close, but no." She sidled up next to him, proppin' her chin atop her folded hands, and the recessed lighting turned her eyes into mesmerizin' emeralds. "Getting to submit so fully to you."

Sam growled out his initial approval. He reached for a thick twist of her hair, working the rosewood-colored strands around a couple of his fingers while lifting a shit-eating grin. She returned a look so sultry, his cock twitched again like a badger wakin' up in a cracked log. "It was a fine thing, Jennifer Josephine, gettin' to put my personal signature across your gorgeous backside."

She stirred and then rose a little, treatin' him to a most memorable sight of her creamy cleavage. "Well, okay," she spurted, lips tremoring with half a laugh. "That settles *that* little curiosity for me."

Sam pushed the pillow higher under his head. "And which curiosity would that be?"

"The one in which I wondered if you could possibly turn me on so totally again."

He pushed up, giving himself a better view to really contemplate her pure bonnie features. "You liked it that much?"

She pulled in a breath, closing and then opening her eyes. "Yes, Sir. It was...nice."

He focused tighter on her. He could practically see his gaze darken by a few shades, reflected by her shimmering greens. "A little nice...or a lot?"

"Depends." She met his stare directly, as if able to see that he still didn't fully believe her. "If it was fulfilling one of my daydreams, then just a little. But if this was a fantasy from one of my nights, alone and thinking about you in bed..."

"You've thought about me? In bed?" After she nodded, he pressed, "And...daydreams? You've thought about me at the office too?"

Not that he hadn't thought about *her* in that way at the office. Perhaps a few times.

Okay, so he'd done it damn near every time he'd walked into the place.

Especially when he'd stroll in and catch her unawares, teethin' the bottom of her lip while tappin' out numbers on a calculator, or laughin' from some meme Lola showed her, or just starin' out the window at the tarmac and absently stirrin' her coffee. Perhaps in one of those moments especially— because he'd hoped she was gazin' out at the planes and entertainin' a few ruminations about *him*.

Now that he knew she likely *had* been...

His soul. Sandstone.

Done. Crumbled. In all the very best ways.

"You're a damn hard one not to think about, Sam Mackenna."

No. Not sandstone. Just a slip of sand itself, like the fine silt between the boulders at Sango Bay, ready to be washed out to a sea of emotion from the crashin' wave of her declaration.

What she did to him...what she had the power to *always* do to him...

And what the hell was he supposed to say in return—without bletherin' too much about the tempest truly takin' over his senses right now? At this point, it *all* felt like too much—but at the same time, none of it was *enough*. He yearned to call out of duty tomorrow, climb into the cockpit of a skywritin' plane instead, and plaster the Vegas Valley skies with one message only, over and over again.

*I'm in love with Jennifer Josephine Thorne.*

*Och.* What was the worst that could happen, truly? In two weeks, he'd be buggin' back home. He and Jenny could surely manage an awkwardness tango for that long. Seemed a tinier price to pay than the lifetime that was the alternative: the *what if* of never saying anything at all.

So he took the plunge. Sort of. He tossed out the skywritin' idea in favor of turnin' to the tousled woman next to him and joltin' up one corner of his mouth at her.

And bravin' it out to blurt his heartfelt confession out to her.

"And you're an *impossible* one not to think about, Jenny Thorne."

All right, he managed to keep the *L* word out of it, but the partial exposure was well worth the risk. At once, her features went all gooey and sweet. His senses turned to a matchin' texture of mush. The feelin' wasn't completely uncomfortable, but it sure as hell wasn't easy to keep sustained.

"Is that...a problem?" she finally asked, addin' the most breathtakin' lick along her lips.

"The fact that I can't stop thinkin' about you?" Sam grinned. "No, mouse. That's so *not* a problem."

"But..." With darkening features, she sought out the center of his chest with one of her palms. "But there *is* a problem...?"

He pointed to the foot of the bed, where the cuffs still dangled as proof of the pleasure he'd just given—and taken from—her. "You said that was *a* fantasy crossed off your list."

"Errrmmm...yeah? And?"

He cupped the back of her neck. Massaged upward, dragging his fingers against her scalp. "Well, it was *a* fantasy. And now you're tellin' me you've had others? A lot of others?"

"Errrmmm...yeah." Her gorgeous face crumpled with tighter confusion.

"Well, that leads us to a new challenge."

"A challenge?" Her scowl intensified. "To do what?"

"Grantin' some more fantasies, of course."

She laughed. Loudly. "Is that so?"

He rose to his haunches but kept her gaze engaged with one of his most wicked winks. The hand she'd raised to his chest now rested against his kilt, which fanned across the small space between them. "I should probably tell you I'm pure rocket keen for a good challenge."

She laughed once more. The action brought different lights to her eyes, sparklin' like sugar dust that could have topped the delicious desserts of her gently swaying breasts. He amended the description. They'd be *luxury* desserts, something exotic concocted by one of the celebrity chefs who'd set up shop up and down the famous Strip of this city. It would have to be named after her and taste-approved by him. His mouth bloody near watered from the thought.

"Sayeth the high laird Mackenna?"

Her cute quip distracted him from her chest long enough to explain, "Officially, my name's actually more Irish. But when the famine hit in the eighteen hundreds, someone hopped on a boat somewhere and then stuck his banger where it didn't belong."

She wove a droll quirk over the smirk. "Imagine that."

Sam surprised himself, choosing not to emulate her look. The next second, his logic caught up with his instinct. "You're tryin' to change the subject again." Swift as a ninja, he grabbed up her hand once more. "Why?"

She skittered her gaze away. He was about to push back over and notch a finger beneath her chin, but when she pulled away from his clasp, he hesitated. And instantly wondered why. But then *knew* why. Holy fuck. Two minutes after admitting he was truly smitten with this woman, and he was already a pussy-whipped shargar, backin' down at her every damn whim. And fuckin' happy about it too.

Which meant he was pure delirious when she decided to look back up at him of her own free will, despite the defined resignation across her patrician features. "Sam," she murmured, though she stopped to sit up straighter against the pillows. Then look to her lap. Then fold her hands in it. "Okay, look..."

"I am," he interjected, laying it on thick with his burr, knowing how that turned the woman into a ball of aroused goo. "With pleasure."

He watched the accent do its damage, as he'd hoped it would. But would the gamble work and find its way beneath the noble shell she'd suddenly insisted on? He wasn't certain, even after she started twisting her hands together. She was going for composed and noble but looking more like a real mouse in a huge hurricane, with the stormy green gaze to go right along. And damn it if he didn't feel like a helpless leaf in her storm, swirled and tumbled and helpless to resist its sucking force...

Even after she pouted and huffed, turnin' those gorgeous chebs of hers into even more enticin' desserts, before spewing, "All right, knock it off."

"Knock what off?" he countered, though he fully admitted he was edgin' toward the realm of cheeky wanker. "The lookin' part? Or the 'with pleasure' part?"

A protesting sound ripped its way free from her. "Both," she bit out. "Neither. *I don't know.*" As fast as it had struck, her rage slipped free, leaving a residue of irritation. "Are we really doing this right now?" she snapped. "Because I'm pretty positive you don't believe the let's-just-be-buddies-when-we're-not-bonking thing any more than I can."

"Meaning...what?" he asked, deliberately careful about the enunciation. The alternative wasn't a pleasant consideration. At all. That he gave in to the unease that began scratchin' the edges of his mind, its claws sharpened by the terse underpinnings creepin' into *her* tone. What the hell? They had just connected in a way few lovers ever did. He craved that connection again already—and he knew she did too. So why was she all but shamblin' into a walk of shame out the damn door?

"You know what," she rejoined. "We both do, Sam." She pulled in a long, visibly determined breath. Her release wasn't so steady, mostly because a bunch of fast, hard blinks betrayed her ultimate purpose. She thought if she battled the tears like that, the ball in her chest that had sent them would get the message and go away. He wanted to tell her that would work, but experience had taught him it only made things worse. *Lots* of experience—from the countless times he'd attempted the same damn thing in front of too many therapists to remember.

All the "professionals" and "specialists" the RAF had dug up for him to try. To "fix" him so he was ready enough to fly the most elite missions again. In the meantime, to keep his skills sharp—and perhaps reignite his killer instincts—they'd kept him busy with what he'd perceived as doaty cross-training.

But right now, he didn't feel so damn doaty.

For the first time in a long damn time, he felt...

Guided.

Destined.

In the exact right place, at the exact right time.

Here. With her. *For* her.

And just five minutes ago, he would have counted her right in the same damn clubhouse with him on that. Hell, she would have been shootin' up her hand to be president of the place. And he would have let her. He had no intention of moldin' the beauty to his will except when the lights were down and her panties were off.

But now, Jen looked ready to dive a hand into his pocket, fish out the underthings, and cover her gorgeous bits as fast as possible. More swiftly than she'd manage to wall off the rest of herself from him—though fuck, did she manage to make an impressive show to him otherwise, with her twisting lips and her worried expression. He yearned to yell at her to save it for an audience who'd actually buy the ticket but clamped himself back if only to hear what she had to say now.

"Sam...you're magnificent, okay? The most incredible, intense, funny, sexy man I've *ever* known—because amazingly, you've helped me remember and see and know all that about myself too..."

"But?" He managed to spit it out at a reasonable volume. Pure jings, since he fuckin' hated that word under most circumstances but loathed it with solid ferocity now. It was a polite version of another word he hated. That word was *no*.

"But we're doing this in a bubble," Jenny supplied with too much haste before succumbing to a defensive huff. "I'm not telling you anything you don't know, damn it. It's an *awesome* bubble, okay? The most stunning moments I've ever known..."

"And you think I run around throwin' bubble parties like it all the damn time?"

"I think you know how bubbles work, Captain." Her rebuttal flung his tight, bitter tone right back at him. "But just in case your self-pity is making you a little deaf: bubbles are bubbles because they need to be appreciated in the moments of time that they last. Moments of time like getting four weeks of cross-training in another country—a country that's several thousand *miles* from your own. And because of that, they're temporary. Their beauty only lasts for a few seconds. It has to be appreciated, even intensified a little. But after all that intensity, the bubbles break. Some people are lucky, and they get some pretty goo in the grass even after the bubble breaks. But others—"

She stopped short as he abruptly leaned in at her, using the breadth of his extended torso to fill her vision and the force of his growl to silence her science lesson. "You, Jenny Thorne, are worth every second of the goddamned bubbles. And aye, even the goo in the fuckin' grass."

He had much more ready to say but stilled for a moment, watchin' every tiny nuance of her reaction. Perhaps, tryin' to learn from it. Probin' her face for a clue, *any* fuckin' clue, about the reasoning behind this new attack of her skittishness—but best as he could fathom, her own body was tellin' her exactly what his lips just did. The way she breathed in his scent, watched the depths of his eyes, studied the movements of his lips, even winced at the heavy gulps in his throat...

Christ. She hated having to face the bubble burst even worse than *he* did. So why was she searchin' for the damn pin already?

"What the hell is goin' on, Jenny?" he finally grated. "Why are you sittin' here, the queen of every fantasy *I* can even remember for myself, doin' *this* to us *now*? Don't lie to me, damn it. You want all of what this can be—all of what *we* can be—as much as I do."

A rickety breath soughed down her throat. "Who the hell says I'm lying?"

He tilted his head. Lifted his fingers and dug them against her hairline. "Because if the rest your fantasies really are as fine as mine, you'd want to be thinkin' of *them* instead of startin' the countdown timer to when I—"

"Leave." It cascaded from her atop a terrible sob, which she instantly gulped back. She slammed a hand to the base of her throat, as if ordering it to stay there, but the damage had been done. Several salty globs flowed down her angular cheeks, rushing toward the quavering curves of her mouth. "You're going to *leave*, Sam. And it's going to be fucking hell, and...and..."

As her teary rasp dumped pain into his soul, she ripped that hand from her throat and tangled it into his hair. Sam swallowed hard as she pulled him even closer, clutching his shoulder with her other hand. He turned his head, smashing his nose and lips into her neck, filling his senses with the perfect scent of her skin in this moment. Her own vanilla and cream layered with his distinct spice and the unmistakable musk of the passion they'd shared. *Fuck.* He wanted her to smell like this all the time, every morning and night...and just for him. *Only* for him...

"Hell won't even be the start of it, lass." His voice sounded like sandpaper as breathing got harder and harder. His fingertips shook against her cheek. "But why fight the chance to grasp heaven while we still can?"

She released a soft, shaky sob. "Sam..."

"Please, Jenny." He dragged away enough to ensure she beheld the heat in his heavy gaze. He didn't do a thing to lighten it either. He focused all of himself onto her. Gave her his heaviness and heartache, his darkness and violence, his blazin' need to believe—to *know*—that despite all of it, he still had the ability to see some light. To see *her* light...through all the reaches of his heart and soul. And he did. In the pure magic of her intense gaze. In the silken planes of her rosy cheeks. In the gentle trust of her touch and even the bright offering of her tears.

Holy God help him. He really did love her. So truly and deeply and completely.

"Sam..." She threaded her fingers with his. Compared to his hand, hers was so tiny...and cold. He held her tighter, infusing her with his heat. Still, her voice was redolent with so much remorse. "*Sam...*"

"Jenny." He kissed her again but just with the surfaces of his mouth. "Please. Give me the bubble for a while longer."

"I want to," she finally confessed as they kept brushing lips back and forth with each other. "Believe me...I just want to push the pause button. To have this whole night with you...to beg you to do sweet, dirty things to me..."

"And I would." He growled it before dippin' to take her mouth with more force. The rough groan from her throat and the eager opening of her lips were all he needed to go further. To plunge deeper. To sweep his tongue into every wet, warm crevice she'd surrender to the demandin' quest of his tongue. He only gave her time to breathe as he pulled away for three seconds—long enough for him to promise, "And I will," before his mouth meshed with hers again, and they sought and sucked and bit and devoured each other in a wildfire of lust and need that threatened to best the passion of their first lusty fire. Dear holy fuck, he hoped so...

But just when Sam dug a hand into Jen's upper thigh and pulled, preparing to reposition her so he could spread her and spear his tongue into *other* parts of her, the woman let out a new moan—of protest.

Unfiltered shock caused him to loosen his hold at once. Just as swiftly, Jen scrambled off the opposite side of the bed, not even stopping when some of the curtains caught around her ankle and she nearly fell flat on her face. When she apologized to the velvet drape, Sam almost rolled off and recaptured her.

Almost.

But damn it, he couldn't take away this moment from her—or this choice. Or, goddamnit, the pain that drove it. The agony he saw on her face, even as she blurted a string of *sorry*s to a clump of velvet drapery. The desperation in how she scooped up her heels and then clutched them to her chest. And even worse—no, worst of all—the fear gripping every inch of her form as she jerked her shimmering stare back up to him once more. Clearly, this goodbye was already tearing her apart. Even more clearly, she couldn't face the idea of it being even worse—even if that meant surrendering the joy they'd know now.

Even if that meant how she had to stand there and stammer

out, "You—this—all of it—was beautiful, Sam. *Incredible*. I won't forget it. Ever. I promise. But we let a workplace crush get too far. We both know it. Why should we draw the torture out even further?"

He rested back on his haunches. Regarded her with a newly darkened glare, as the three-paned mirror readily reminded him. The fun little nook where he'd been plannin' on takin' her next so she'd have been able to see how beautiful she was when a real man gave her real pleasure.

Instead, he was on his fuckin' knees in the middle of a gigantic empty bed and gritting through his teeth, "Right. Sure. The protocols and all that. Bet you're happy now, aye? You were really right about your policies, Jennifer Thorne."

"Sam—"

"You'd best get back to all of it, then." He clenched his teeth to give himself enough fortitude for risin' up to a full kneel. If she was going to leave him like a prisoner facin' the guillotine, he was going to damn well look the part and deliver the guilt.

"*Sam—*"

"Good night, Jenny," he muttered. "And goodbye."

With a tight sob, she spun.

On bare feet, she staggered out of the room.

The same way he left the damn place nearly a full hour later.

Ignorin' the joyous screams that bled through the door of Dan and Tess's play room.

Disregardin' the sloe-eyed girl at the reception stand who didn't look so distracted when eyeing his newly solo state.

Oblivious to the glam and gilt of the rest of the hotel, which he afforded just fleetin' glances while making his way to the Lyft queue for his ride back to Nellis.

*One step at a time.*

*One step at a time.*

*One step at a time.*

Even after he got back, heedin' only that mantra to get his ass inside the little house, in the middle of a night thick with cicada song and desert breezes. A night that would have been hours of sheer enchantment world, if Jenny hadn't chosen to run. And his little house, now just a house again...when hours before, just for a little while, her presence had made it into something more.

Something like...

A home.

*One second at a time.*

*One second at a time.*

*One second at a time.*

It was how he slogged through dumpin' the rest of the Cabernet, rinsin' out the glasses, and then wipin' down the countertop that he'd wanted to hurl himself across, even durin' their post-work clownin'. That even then he'd imagined securin' her on, growlin' orders for her to push her hands back and her breasts forward as he sank his link deep inside her and suckled both those sweet nipples until they were the texture of ripe, hard cherries...

With a virulent snarl, he left the fuckin' kitchen. Prowled into the bedroom, intendin' to open his e-reader and get lost in a good, no-women-allowed political thriller, but that was a bigger mistake than wallowin' out in the kitchen. All too clearly, he could envision Jen on all fours in the middle of the mattress, her lovely back arched and a glass plug in her arse, begging him to fill her sopping pussy with his vein-lined erection...

So at midnight, he finally got up, changed into a tank and nylon shorts, taped up his knuckles, and surrendered to a new mantra.

*One punch at a time.*

*One punch at a time.*

*One punch at a time.*

And pummeled the fuck out of the bag in the base gym, not stopping until his vision blurred and his body was soaked.

But obliteratin' even one fuckin' second of memories from bein' balls-deep inside Jenny Thorne three hours ago?

He was radgin' screwed.

There she was, parked right where he'd left her—in the stretch of his heart between desperate love and functional sanity. And as he slumped to a recovery bench, gulpin' on a bottle of water, his imagination damn near stirred her to life before him. She was a sexy hologram of his mind, dressed as *his* version of a sexy fairy. Her face was made up in shades of green to match her eyes, and a collar embedded with emeralds encircled her neck, restin' right beneath the wild pulse of her thunderin' heartbeat. She wore a corset too—though it was one of those keen kinds with the center carved out, puttin' her nude breasts on full display for him.

He almost offered a swig of water to the hologram. Hell, he could even imagine her lips formin' a succulent seal over the top of the bottle. Then the undulations of her throat as the water went down. And the sultry lift of her gaze as he ordered her to get well hydrated because the next liquid in her throat was going to be his come...

And that did it. With a snarl of pure fire, he surged to his feet. Made his way into the gym showers with stomping fury but didn't bother to even take off his shoes before divin' under the spray, where he fisted his furious cock and came with hard, fast vengeance—roarin' her name with every ruthless stroke.

For a long while after, he stood with his hands braced against the tiled wall and his head dunked beneath the pummelin' spray. And somehow found his mind coherent enough to issue two points of thanks, despite the Almighty's refusal to listen to his other pleas of the night.

One: thank God none of the other guys were in here to work off their frustrations in similar ways.

Two: thank *fucking* God for the cold setting on this shower.

# CHAPTER NINE

A shrill *ding* sounded in Jen's ears. Her wireless headphones were synced to her phone, so the text notification came in loud and clear. She whooshed a relieved breath when seeing the message was from Tess, not Sam. He'd gone radio silent since last night, when she'd bolted like a chickenshit from the Scene's heavenly hidey-hole, whether from anger or respect, she didn't know—and shouldn't care.

But she did.

More than she wanted to admit.

With more pain than she thought she'd still be feeling.

Wasn't that what she got here, in return for the humiliation of leaving him like she had? For hurting him in the name of preserving them *both*? That was how this worked, right?

Her heart had no answer. Her intuition, which she'd thought was the mastermind behind that impulsive flight, had also gone silent. She was a ship in uncharted waters. Nothing about being in this abominably deep sea, with a man likely descended from a freaking god of Atlantis, was familiar or predictable or easy.

She just had to hope, by the time she saw him at the wedding, that her head got screwed back on better than this. That she'd know what to say...or not to say. That she'd be able to keep her shit together better than she had last night, when raw fear and an undeniable survival instinct had kicked in.

Because falling further for Sam Mackenna wasn't

anything close to survival.

It was stepping in line for the emotional chopping block. A one-way ticket to complete emotional annihilation.

A death she couldn't imagine being any sweeter...

*Are you here yet?*

Tess's cyber-shriek brought a smile down at her phone screen, though Jen paused her thumb over the keyboard before replying. How to convey the right mix of reassurance and humor that would help her friend—*and* steer clear of any references to the chance meeting with Tess and Dan at Scene last night? Turned out that the couple's "naughty getaway" in the play room had been fortuitously timed, since Tess texted three hours ago to say the salon they'd picked for the wedding—the same one everybody had already rehearsed in—had been destroyed by a herd of rampaging llamas that morning. The gaming company holding its annual stockholder meeting in the main ballroom had rented the twelve animals, who had somehow found their way into the freight elevator and finally been corralled in the salon. Tess had texted, begging for moral support in figuring out a backup plan. It was the perfect diversion from Jen's sappy self-pity fest.

*Just got here, honey. Hang on. I come bearing
a wide shoulder and lots of memes.*

At once, the little trio of hang-on-I'm-typing dots started dancing.

*Good. Meet me on the roof.*

"The *roof?*" But repeating the words didn't change the

instructions. That was really what it said. "Oh my God."

Maybe the play date hadn't helped with enough of Tess's edge—though hell, despite all the heartsickness, Jen had gotten home last night and felt like a soggy noodle. No wonder submissives needed lots of aftercare for more intense scenes. If Tess really had any anxiety left after how Dan clearly intended to work her over, Jen seriously had to get the name of whatever vitamins the woman was popping.

For now, she rushed to the elevators faster than a mob of French Revolutionaries storming the Bastille. She got to the vanilla crystal ones first and wasted no time jumping in. But before that, taking heed of the dead spot she'd likely encounter in the lift, she replied with racing thumbs.

*On my way. Don't do anything crazy!*

At once, another response appeared from her friend.

*04301980*

"Huh?" As she blurted the confusion, it occurred that her own message might have been as baffling to Tess—but it'd be easier to explain herself to a harried bride than lament not saying enough to her stressed-out friend. In a strange way, it also helped to funnel her anxiety from last night into a more useful purpose than simple hand-wringing.

The car couldn't seem to climb fast enough. Finally, the overhead display glowed with a bright *60*.

"What the hell?"

She'd punched the *61* button. The lift itself filled in the answer to that, verbally prompting her to punch a special code into the high-tech keyboard appearing on the lift's embedded touch screen. Suddenly, Tess's gobbledygook of numbers made sense. And though the explanation for the necessity did as well—not every visitor to the Nyte could be allowed to just stroll around on the roof—she also questioned the hotel's wisdom in giving out the access code to people like brides who'd slogged through llama poop in their wedding salon just ninety hours before their big day.

The code was accepted. The car lurched back to life and then came to a rest at the higher floor.

Jen walked out into a glass-enclosed lobby. Like everything about the Nyte, it was decorated sumptuously, but the décor couldn't surpass the view. The entire valley sprawled before her, awesome even beyond the city's parameters. To the left, the cliffs of Red Rock were dramatic against a thousand stars. Her head dropped back, following the twinkling carpet through the glass roof over her head. Up here, the light pollution was diminished to a dull roar, turning the stars into a light show in their own right.

A second of the awe was all she allowed herself, though. She had to get to Tess—

"Miss Thorne?"

She jumped. She hadn't expected anyone up here besides Tess, but the pixie-sized brunette, dressed in a stylish black pantsuit and toting a flashing smart pad similar to the one Leggy had toted last night, smiled like she greeted paranoid strangers every day.

But not complete strangers. The woman knew her name. How? Why?

"Yes?" Next to the beauty, who floated more than walked and smelled like a newly minted angel, Jen felt like a hobo. Didn't matter that she was in her cutest pair of ankle boots along with a pair of trendy, cuffed peg pants and a flowy blouse;

she'd been in the outfit all day and probably looked as wrung-out as she felt.

"Hello. I'm Francesca, the hotel's lead concierge."

"Lovely to meet you, but I'm up here to meet someone, and—"

"Yes." The girl smiled. Seriously, how could so much flawless bone structure be stuffed into one teeny person? "I know."

"You do?" Her heart lightened. Maybe Tess wasn't really out there walking on a windswept ledge, like she'd imagined. If the concierge desk was involved here too, maybe this really was just a minor detail about the wedding. "Awesome. So where is she?"

"Ahhhh..." Francesca peered a little harder at her. "You do mean where is *he*, yeah?"

"He?"

But the question mark in her tone didn't seem to matter now. "Ah," she repeated, this time clipping the word with confidence. "He says it's all ready."

"*He?* He *who*? Where's Tess?"

"Tess?"

"Lesange?"

"Oh." It was better than *Ah*, or so Jen hoped. She wasn't sure, since Francesca the Concierge seemed dually comfortable but nonplussed by her demand. "The *Lesange* of the *Lesange-Colton* wedding for this Saturday?"

"Yes."

Francesca blinked with maddening innocence. "Hmmm. Yes. She's a lovely woman."

"I agree." More blank blinks. "Do you know where she is?"

"Right at the moment?"

"Yes." It took a huge inhalation not to scream the word.

"Sorry, Miss Thorne. I'm afraid I do not."

"But she just—"

"Right this way, Miss Thorne. Everything's ready."

"Everything for *what*?" But the woman was so pristine and polite, which piqued Jen's curiosity even more. Besides that, it would give her a chance to tap—translation, slam—out a message to Tess, asking what the hell was—

As soon as she followed Francesca out the glass doors and around the corner, she paused her fingers somewhere between *Where the hell* and *are you*.

She stood at the edge of a huge rooftop helipad.

Where, indeed, a sleek black helicopter was parked.

With its cockpit door open and waiting.

Where, standing in front of that portal, wind whipping his hair and a black T-shirt and jeans turning him into sin on two feet, was the beautiful bastard who'd been torturing her with radio silence and the MIA treatment all damn day. On freaking purpose. Because he'd been plotting, planning, and then implementing.

*This.*

Because of her. *For* her.

She didn't know how to react—mostly because she didn't know what she felt.

She'd left him last night with his dick in hand—damn near literally—because of a freak-out she still couldn't quite explain, even to herself. She'd told herself it was the right thing to do, especially after breaking so many of her protocols to be with him like that, but once she'd realized the only *right* thing here was him, she'd been out the door, down the hall, and feeling a thousand kinds of utterly stupid. Men like Sam

Mackenna didn't suffer fools, even dorky bookworms they fancied themselves in love with. She'd sobbed half the night away, believing she'd really hammered in the final nail on her coffin with the man.

Now, she was damn sure she'd sob half *this* night away— for a billion different reasons.

And the hugest one of them was standing there, looking pleased as a sexy swami about it. Because damn, had the man already read her mind. Backward and forward. Remembered words even *she'd* forgotten: the claim she'd uttered to him last night in the bar, before they'd gone into the play room.

*That's another fantasy of mine, you know. To know what it's like to fly with you...*

And after they were sated and half-naked, he'd lounged in that big bed and begged her for more of her fantasies—despite how she'd already given him the answer. And now, she realized, even enlisted Tess in his cause. She envisioned her friend now, giggling as Sam explained his plot, totally agreeing to send that text on his behalf. A glance around the deck confirmed it. No Tess in sight.

Okay, so she should've been a little pissed about at least that—but even her best efforts couldn't summon the ire. Simply put, she just didn't *want* to be angry. She wanted to give in to this moment instead. The giddy leap of her stomach at beholding the powerful lines of the helicopter. The girlish flip of her heart at taking in the majestic man next to it. The tender squeeze of her soul when he beckoned to her, palm turned up, long fingers extended.

Still, she shifted on both feet. Twisted her hands around her purse strap. Chewed the inside of her cheek into hamburger.

If she took his hand, she'd be asking for the pain. In her

heart. In every corner and crevice of her *soul*.

But maybe not *all* of it.

Clearly, he planned on piloting the flight, meaning he'd be focused on keeping the helo in the air instead of touching her. They'd be having an adventure in the skies above, not in the sheets below. And a true bonus: she'd be able to watch his beautiful fingers as they flipped switches and mastered controls. She'd marvel at the power in his hands as he handled the stick, guiding them through the stars. No way could he even attempt to spike her lust...

So maybe...this was doable.

What was the harm in letting him give her this? In agreeing to share this exciting adventure with him? They were still friends, after all—and this was one fantasy he could grant to her without fucking her...

She shook her head. Rolled her eyes. Split a huge grin. Then made her way across the pavement, toward the man who outshone every light around and below with the joy of his barely tamped delight.

It was better than she'd ever dreamed.

More sweeping, more spectacular, more shriek-worthy—a fact she emphasized many times over, just to make sure Sam got the point. Perhaps the way he answered her screams, with a smile that turned his dimples deeper than the Grand Canyon and his grin more resplendent than the Luxor's light beam, made it a little easier to cut loose. All the reasons weren't important right now. The feelings were. The freedom of having the sky to themselves. The thrill of the wind whipping at the cockpit's windows. And the awe, turning her into a kid at an amusement park for the first time. From up here, Vegas wasn't a city anymore. It was a wonderland of lights and color and textures, from the bold blues, purples, reds, and greens illuminating the Strip's many icons, to the urban fairyland of gold and white beyond.

But all those belly twists didn't compare to the buzz of watching Sam in his element. He was confident and calm, focused and watchful, though he spared a few glances her way that made even her casual clothes feel tight and hot. Thank God for well-made bras with padded cups, though her nipples were only the start of her body's refreshed need. Observing the man's command of this complicated machine only made her remember how he'd controlled every one of her personal "buttons" and "switches"...and did they absolutely have to position the throttle between the pilot's legs? With a hand gripping the thing like that, his elbow resting on one massive thigh, her thoughts repopulated with a fantasy much different than this one. In it, those stunning fingers were wrapped around his cock. He stroked every lean, glistening inch of his erection, getting ready to feed that mesmerizing length into her eager mouth...

She pushed the thought aside with a pointed cough—though not fast enough to evade Sam's notice. His jaw clenched. His nostrils flared. His stare heated.

Before a hail over the radio came.

"Night wing two, this is McCarran Tower. Do you copy?"

*Thank you, thank you, thank you, McCarran Tower.*

"Copy that, McCarran," Sam responded. "Is course alteration clear and approved?"

"Affirmative," replied the woman on the other end. "Weather is clear. Enjoy your trip."

He gave the appropriate sign-off, but Jen didn't care about the words. The secretive quirk of his lips, along with the steady turn he gave the helo, were another matter.

"Course alteration?" she enunciated through locked teeth.

Sam didn't look at her, let alone answer. The better part of a minute went by. He flipped switches, checked headings, even sang softly. "Sing me a song...say, could that lad be I..."

"Sam?"

"Merry of soul, he sailed on a—yes, mouse?"

Because of the headsets, he could issue the murmur with the slight growl that spoke straight to the tissues between her thighs. Still, she was able to maintain her glare. "*Course alteration?*" she demanded again.

More long seconds. Finally, one side of his mouth ticked up. "Jenny?"

Annnnd more of the damn growl. "What?" She squirmed— and mentally smacked herself for thinking the man couldn't arouse her without touching her.

"Do you trust me?"

She huffed. "That's not fair."

"Neither was you showin' up dressed like that, all glowy and sweaty and delectable, but I invited you for the ride anyway, did I not?"

Well, there went the huff. And a lot of everything behind it too. Now she could only laugh. First because the man was clearly, certifiably insane. Second because she didn't know if she wanted him any other way.

Third because she realized that he was guiding the helicopter toward the vast darkness of the desert beyond the Vegas city limits—and that their next landing very well might not be back on the rooftop of the Nyte at all.

And that despite every damn vow she'd made herself about

resisting him again, she couldn't wait to learn what surprise he had in store now.

# CHAPTER TEN

The first thing Sam had ever noticed about the middle of the desert was the silence. To him, so used to the heartbeat of the sea growing up, meeting the stillness of the desert was like getting acquainted with an entirely new person. The totality of it was like an entity of its own, reclining serenely across the barren section of desert into which he'd just landed the helo.

After he got out and then jogged around the chopper to help Jen down too, she didn't step back from his embrace. Despite everythin' they'd shared back at the Scene just last night, the moment felt as foreign as the wilderness over which they both peered.

At last, Jen coaxed his gaze down to her with the gentle tug of one hand. "What is it?" she whispered into the few inches between their faces.

Sam lifted her fingertips to his lips. "This wasn't exactly a scheduled stop on the tour—nor was this the way you'd been plannin' to spend your evenin'." He intensified his study of her, across the juncture of his mouth upon her skin. "Just makin' sure you're all right with bein' a bit of a hijack victim is all."

She kicked the corners of her mouth up. Just the corners—though that was enough to reassure him that he hadn't completely mucked this all up. That perhaps now, nearly twenty-four hours after she'd fled their room at Scene, she'd had a chance to rethink where she'd gone with the effort at bein' "responsible" about all this. There was responsible, and then there was just overreaction. But sometimes, it took an overture to overcome an overreaction. So he'd decided to overture like fuck. And the look on her face, with the breeze liftin' the hair from her face and the stars illuminating every dazzling green depth in her dancing eyes, made him recognize the decision exactly for what it was.

*I'm a fuckin' genius.*

*And she's the most breathakin' woman on this entire goddamned planet.*

"Hijack away, Captain." She added a laugh that only enhanced her natural beauty, but when he let her hand slip away so he could see her better in the dim light, her features sobered. "What is it now, Sam?"

He ticked his head, indicating his deeper consideration of the question. "You...look different out here. Almost as if you belong in all this wilderness and wind."

Another gentle tug of her lips. "Well, it's not a foreign planet to me, if that's what you mean." She turned her gaze out across the vast plain. "I live in the city now but get out to the more open parts of the valley whenever I can. The vastness of the desert...it's daunting yet comforting. When you feel small, you're able to recognize your place in the bigger picture of things, you know?"

The woman could have dropped to her knees and offered to service him then and there and not gotten him more enervated. He felt like bellowin' out his next words, though they ended up fallin' out with the profound awe he actually felt. "That's the way I feel when hikin' through Glencoe." He chuckled at himself before amending, "And up in the Shetlands. And atop the Cairngorms."

"Yes, yes, and yes. I want to visit them all."

"You do?" He crunched a perplexed scowl. "You...*know* all those places?"

Her tiny smirk was also better than an offer of a blowjob. "In case you don't know already, I'm kind of a fan of Scottish hunks—and their homeland."

"As well as the beauty of your own." He guided the subject back to the here and now because it was too damn easy to think of her in sexy hikin' togs, leadin' him up through the Three Sisters with a follow-me-and-then-fuck-me look on her gorgeous face. And all too easily, he could imagine doin' exactly that...

"Indeed, the beauty of my own," she echoed with a pretty smile. "Thanks to summers at my Aunt Fran and Uncle Chris's ranch out up Kingston and the cute boy who led the hiking club in high school."

"Aha," Sam quipped, scooping up her hand once more. This time, there was distinct purpose to the move. He started leadin' the way toward what looked like a sizable storage shed, about forty yards away. "*Now* I know who I'm up against."

"Well...he *was* a sexy ginger," she returned, easily keepin' up with his long strides. "And, from what I could tell, packing some nice heat under his hiking gear."

He halted long enough to ensure she registered his narrowed gaze—but ignored her sweet giggle while tryin' to wrap his follow-up query in a nonchalant tone. "But you... never found out? About his...um...heat, I mean."

"You mean did I tap that shit with Heath the Hot Hiking Man?" She deliberately nudged him, ruthless in her razzin' about his poorly veiled dig for details. "Well, that would be a huge negative, Captain," she supplied conversationally. "Heath carried a torch for one woman only. Her name was

Mattie Lesange."

He scuffed to a new stop. Jen succumbed to a brighter giggle.

"Well, *now* this is gettin' juicy."

She shrugged. "Well, I wish I had more juice to share than that. I only know that right before senior prom, she broke his heart."

"Hmmmph," Sam returned, starting the trek toward the structure once more. They were close enough now to see the aluminum siding of the big shed, reflecting different textures of gray and silver in the moonlight. "Served that roaster right, then. He should have recognized the jewel right in front of him."

"Well, we were in high school." She squeezed his hand. "Don't tell me *you've* never been that 'roaster' before, Captain Mackenna."

He didn't squeeze her back. Instead, he worked their hands differently so he could lock her fingers between his—linkin' her so solidly in his grasp, she wouldn't doubt a damn syllable of the confession he gave her now. "Never had a jewel like *you* in front of me, mouse."

She said nothing else.

But he felt her take the words in as if he stood still and watched it happen.

And he reveled in the flow of happiness that emanated from every pore of her, until they were standing directly in front of the large steel structure.

Only then did Sam turn and look back down at her.

She wasn't waiting with a responding stare for him. Instead, her scrutiny was directed up at the building. He didn't begrudge a twinge of the uneasiness in her eyes. All on its own, the building gave off an aura of visceral creepiness.

"So..." She drew the vowel out, lilting it up and then down, clearly attempting an infusion of humor to the strangely heavy air. "Should I prepare for the jump scare now or when we get inside? And are we doing Jason Voorhees or Freddie Krueger? Probably Freddie, yeah? Doesn't Jason need a lake?"

Though Sam chuckled his way into it, he cut her short with a hard smack on her lips. He was pure tempted to keep going from there, if only to show her his gratitude for flyin' in and reopenin' such a shuttered part of his soul, but he was eager to get her inside—where the second part of his surprises for the night lay in wait.

Thankfully, she followed him inside the shed with no further hypothesizin' about men with knives in hockey masks. The only thing she did comment on were the pair of pretty benches out in front, freshly painted in a Mykonos blue and sportin' little holes in their bases as insertion points for optional sunshades. Though he'd only been in Vegas for a couple of weeks, Sam already knew the coverings were essentials if anyone was goin' to be out here between June and September.

The door was secured by a padlock, which Sam released with a key from a ring in his pocket. Once inside, he reached for light switches and found them right where Frank had told him they'd be.

As the illumination kicked in, Jen took her first step across the threshold.

Then halted.

Then gasped.

"Whoa."

Sam cocked his head. "Okay." And emulated her drawl

on the vowel, though definitely not with the same flair she possessed for off-the-cuff mirth. "Does that mean...you like it?"

"Does the Starkiller dwarf the Death Star?"

And had she really just said that? And was this him, still holdin' back from plungin' a hand into his own chest and givin' her the whole of his hopelessly smitten heart?

Instead, he took delight in watchin' her peer around the whole place. It was damn near a designer showroom, with no sign of the aluminum walls from outside. The interior space was walled in polished wood, reflecting warm hues beneath the bright track lighting. A stacked-stone fireplace was surrounded by big leather couches draped in thick throw blankets, all but begging for someone to curl up in them with a good novel and a glass of wine. The open-plan kitchen—separated from the main room by a wide bar framed by wrought-iron stools—was small but outfitted with up-to-the-minute appliances. The same industrial motif defined a spiral staircase to their left, leading to a loft bedroom.

"*Whoa*," she repeated after well over a minute of gawking.

Sam nodded. "Same thing I said when Frank showed me snaps of the place." His counterpart from the USAF squad was a decent but enigmatic guy. Despite his Thor-hot looks, he'd never kept a girlfriend longer than three months.

"Is this place his?" She threw a sardonic look over her shoulder. "And if he's coming all the way out here to do the deed, how is he holding on to any woman?"

"It's not entirely his." Sam sidestepped any more discussion about Frank and his shag count. "It began as a way station for miners but sat empty until the nineteen forties, when Nellis came into its own as a base. An officer bought the property and refurbished it as a place for him and his mates to unwind, away from the constant noise of the base."

Jen slid a teasing smile as he tugged her across the room. "Noisy? Why, we're just a bunch of sweet little...mice."

Though he tossed back a wink, he kept the rest of his face placid. He liked the tiny skitter of arousal that caused across *her* features, though. "When the man passed on, he willed all of it to his squadron. It's remained that way through the years, with everyone pitchin' in for upkeep and renovations."

"The booty-call commune, eh?"

Though she emphasized with a tinklin' laugh, Sam again didn't match her mien. Instead, with focused somberness, he stopped and turned back toward her. "I've never been here, mouse."

Jenny brushed a gentle hand down his arm. "Not even to get away with your secret thoughts?"

"My secret thoughts and I haven't been on speakin' terms for a while." He didn't give her a chance to reply. While flashin' her a refreshed smile, he relaced their fingers. "Want to see the upstairs?"

Jen resisted. "Sam—"

"Drop it." He locked his visual deflectors firmly back into place. Even if the woman dug in and insisted on a "talk," it would get her nowhere. But luckily, she clearly wanted to see the rest of this place. So did he. Everythin' was stunning. Several generations of men had put their unique touches into the place. Sam was humbled to be here.

Humbled...and aroused.

As. Fuck.

The loft contained another plush sofa and a huge, gorgeous bed. A chocolate-colored comforter was spread over the bed, with equally luxurious pillows outfitted in soft white shams. On the other side of the room, a spacious bathroom possessed a huge Roman tub.

Sam deliberately lingered.

But Jen didn't.

"Wow," she blurted, already turning back toward the stairs with a forced smile plastered on her lips. "It's very...errrmmm... nice."

"Nice." Sam echoed it on a chuckle he kept cryptic. "Well, Frank tells me that's only the start."

"What do you—"

Sam stopped her short by flipping the switch in the wall next to him, also exactly where Frank said it would be. As soon as he hit the lever, the wall trembled. And then the wall next to it, along with the floor. A high-pitched whir consumed the air, making the whole chamber feel transformed into a freight elevator. He was happy to know the impression wasn't solely his, as soon as Jenny let out a yelp and practically leapt into his arms. She clung to him even harder as the roof started moving.

No. Sliding.

*Holy hell*. He expressed as much in an amazed gasp before murmuring in soft amazement, "This is pure barry."

The "light switch" he'd flipped was actually an activation button that ordered the roof to retract, revealing a skylight the size of the entire bed, exposing the billion stars in the sky overhead. A smaller door retracted directly over the bathtub.

Lights? Who the hell needed lights?

The answer to that was as easy as rememberin' the rest of Frank's instructions and punching the second button in the wall—which doused all the track lighting over the main room.

At once, Jenny let her purse plummet to the floor. Her jaw

dropped the same direction. "Oh my...*wow*."

In the sudden darkness, the stars seemed to zoom closer. And though Sam had flown so close to those miniature suns, through night skies a lot like this one, it had to be one of the most dazzlin' sights of his life.

Entirely because of the beauty by his side.

With her head jerked back, her gaze full of wide wonderment, and her mouth parted in a delighted smile, Sam swore he could have goggled at her for as long as she wanted to gawk at the sky. But though his soul swore the oath, his cock was already fashin' hard about it. *Hard*. Bloody tadger felt like every damn star in that firmament had fallen through the glass roof, embedded itself beneath his flesh, and was now twinkle-twinklin' the shit out of his achin' flesh.

That was before Jen made it all worse—and better—in one perfect swoop.

With a sigh of mesmerizin' delight, the woman slowly turned away from him. Not on purpose. She was just so dazzled by the spectral light show, she forgot where she was even standin'—

Until she wasn't standin' anymore.

The bed was right there, her perfect excuse to simply flop back and better enjoy the spectral panorama through the window. The second she was down, she released another huge gasp and reached a hand up toward the sky. "Holy crap. It looks like it could all just ripple at my touch."

Sam allowed himself a low, satisfied rumble. He walked to the edge of the bed but didn't join her on it. Right now, with the meteor shower in his pants, just the idea of it was epic daft. He forced his mind toward the opposite end of the mental spectrum. *Dirty gear grease. Post office lines. Frank's belching version of "Uptown Funk."*

No use. The star shower still raced up and down his cock. Did she know? Did she see how hard he battled to stay chivalrous, when thoughts of attackin' her here and now were like a thousand exploding suns in his senses? That all he could think about was fitting every inch of himself against her delectable softness before makin' love to her for hours beneath that canopy of endless stars? That he wanted to watch the soft glow of them reflect in the emerald glory of her eyes until the mists of arousal clouded them over?

Before she started screamin' for him.

And beggin' to him.

Pleadin' for him to finish her off...

And he would. So gladly. Kissin' her everywhere outside as he fucked her everywhere inside...

It was *really* time to step away from the bloody bed.

Except the woman herself had him doubling back on his intention *again*. This time, with hardly any movement at all. She merely pushed up to her elbows, hardly aware of what she'd done to push her gorgeous breasts so tight inside her silky top. A blouse with delicate pearl buttons that would probably slip free of their nooses with one easy twist of his fingers...

*Think about Frank's belchin'. Or mission debriefs that last forever. Or reality TV.*

"This. Is. Outrageous." Her declaration, along with her impish grin, detailed exactly how she intended the word—and effectively banished every belchin' fortification from his mind. As warmth suffused his chest and heat kept torturin' his toorie, his legs had suddenly turned to blocks of lead. He couldn't leave the side of the mattress if the fuckin' place caught afire.

So he did what any self-respectin' Highlander would do.

Butted a hip against the thing and then folded his arms like a cocky genie. "I had a bit of a ken you'd like it."

"Bullshit," Jen volleyed. "You had a little 'ken' I'd *love* it."

As she tacked on a spurtin' little laugh, he opened his mouth to whip back somethin' just as lippy, but the universe had other plans. The universe—or heaven itself. Or maybe hell. He had no fuckin' clue, nor the inclination to dissect the whole matter, since he was still dealin' with the bollocks blast of sheer, insane emotion that hit him before the woman could even finish with her adorable giggle. As if fate itself had retracted the roof of his goddamned heart, Sam couldn't escape the resplendence and fullness of what he felt for this woman...

What he'd always feel for her.

*Dear, bloody fuck.*

He wasn't just in love with her.

He was utterly, permanently smitten.

Bound to her.

Blinded by her.

As metaphors went, nothing could have been more perfect, since the backs of his eyes cooperated with a pure fine burn. It worsened as he gazed down at her, takin' in the dark-green sheen in her irises that betrayed her own soppy battle.

They were both helpless and motionless, gaping and gulping and fighting this lunatic *pull* of their minds and hearts and souls, silent yet potent as a star about to go supernova. Their silent but catastrophic gift to the cosmos. Nothing would ever be the same again. *They'd* never be the same again.

"Shit." Like the amazin' warrior she was, Jen shattered their silence first. All she could do was rasp, but every intonation tore into his heart like a scalpel soaked in tears.

"Shit. *Sam.*"

The hitch in her voice caused the snag in his breath.

"Jenny," he finally growled.

Oh aye, he *did* growl. And along with it brought one knee up to the mattress so he could loom over and then in, threading all five fingers of one hand into her wind-tossed waves. Tellin' her, in no uncertain terms, that he wasn't afraid to really do this...to fly into the explosion with her. But she had to be willing to face it too. She had to *make him* throw that lever for lightspeed. She had to *show* him...somehow...

"Somehow" got its answer fast. *Thank fuck.* He had no idea what spurred her to push up a little more, turnin' her face against his palm, but the simple beauty of it felt like the fulfillment of his destiny—even if all destiny was going to give them was right now. He'd take it. Every ragin', ravishin', punishin', *perfect* second of it.

Like the one in which she abandoned the frame of his hand...and turned her face toward the bulge in his crotch. And then rested her mouth on it. And then sweetly, silently, deliberately leaned in—until she was biting at the stiff fabric.

"*Jenny.*"

He wasn't sure if he groaned it or sobbed it. He was damn sure *that* definition didn't matter. Were definitions even a pertinent concern once the world seized on its fuckin' axis? Because nothin'—not a damn bloody *thing*—was more vibrant or relevant or important than what she blatantly offered with that dulcet nip of her gorgeous lips. For the first time in *years*, every fuckin' thing in his senses—the memories, the anger, the frustration, the loss—was gone, phased into nonexistence by his utter need to feel all of this, to connect to all of this.

To build a bridge over all the leaves in his crazy waters.

So he could get back to her.

Only, always now, to her.

"Jenny." His voice wasn't any stronger, but at least his touch was. Somehow, he found her scalp again and dug his grip in harder against the back of her head. In response, she smiled against his throbbing center. Cheeky minx. *His precious mouse...*

"Oh dear *fuck*." And now, apparently, the shrewd lover who'd already gotten the drift about how he liked her teeth against his denim too. "Woman...when you take my banger like that...*shit*! Jenny!"

"Ssshhh." She grabbed his empty belt loops, yanking him closer.

"Wait. *Wait*." He moaned it but had to shove even that into his throat for the volume. But the interruption wasn't negotiable. Because he needed to be clear with her before she bloody near made him jizz in his jeans with the magic of her talented teeth. Talented *teeth*? How was that even a thing? And how did he not know by now that any fuckin' thing was possible with this glorious goddess? Fighting back what his brain did with *that* imagery, he managed to spurt, "*Mouse.* I...I really didn't bring you out here to—"

"I know that, Sam."

"I—I have the highest respect for you, Jennifer Josephine." Which he might have indulged a good skoosh of laughter about, if his intention wasn't purely serious. Even so, he had to be the world's biggest wanker, tryin' the fuckin' line on the woman he adored while her mouth was makin' best friends with his cock through his zip.

"All right." She threw away a bit of her coy pout, instead makin' room for an irritated moue. "So...you don't want to, Sir

Galahad?"

Well, *that* made his scowl hellishly easy. "Galahad is fictional. And English."

"Okay. So, you don't want to, *Sir Robert the Bruce*?"

He caressed her cheek, unfurling an approving smile. "I didn't say *that*."

"Hmmm. No." And the minx was back again—now taking the initiative to twist the button beneath her mouth free. "You certainly didn't."

At once, he felt his smile drop. Bloody hard for a man to keep grinnin' when a woman had her face an inch from his crotch and was workin' down the zip that would free his throbbin' tadger.

And was lickin' her way through his short and curlies along the way.

"Jenny. By everythin' that's fuckin' *holy*..."

"*Psssshhh*." She pushed the zipper all the way down to its base. That aligned her fingertips with his baws—a fact she took full, naughty advantage of. "There's nothing holy about you, Sam Mackenna. And I want to explore it *all*."

He couldn't manage anythin' more than a taut groan as she stroked his tender sack, taking sweet little nips at the flesh just beneath. She slipped her other hand up beneath his shirt, roller-coastering her fingertips over the ridges of his abs before descending her mesmerizin' touch again. Her nails scraped into his skin, following the seam of muscle down into his thrummin' crotch, where she played with the nest from which his cock sprang like a proud pine in a dense forest. But not for long. She trailed her hand upward again, and this time Sam helped her by shucking the shirt all the way. He rolled onto the bed, sighing roughly while letting her caress and claim him in any manner her pleasure took her.

*Holy God.*

*Her mind-blowin' pleasure...*

His whole body quaked as her hands came back to center. This time, she flowed her touch up and over his cock, rubbing him from balls to crown with steady, sure exploration. Along the way, she'd let a finger or two wander off from the straight line of her hand to follow the jagged curves of his veins, which pulsed at his skin with increasin' demand.

"You're so beautiful," she breathed.

"You're so incredible," Sam whispered back.

"You make me feel powerful."

"And you make me feel helpless." His voice cracked on the declaration, but he didn't care. He hiked his hips, seeking her touch with the brazen need of a mongrel craving an ear scratch. Only this was more than an itch. This was raw, relentless, ragin' need. "Don't stop. For the love of *fuck*, don't stop."

She didn't, thank all that was holy—but after she teased and tormented him longer than he should have allowed, Sam finally twisted his hand against her scalp again. With another yank, he snapped her head back until it was possible to sweep the brunt of his gaze over her. She took his breath away. Her stare was glazed with lust, and her chest was pumping with full breaths. But he wasn't prepared for the moment she parted her lips and then stuck her tongue between them, as if starving for every drop of the white drops that burst from the throbbin' slit at his erect tip.

"So what will I say now, darlin'?" His voice was just as hot and molten as the liquid pearls on his dick. "You know, don't you?"

"I can hope." She whispered it as soon as he jerked his hips again, dealin' as best he could with the white rockets burstin' out his cockhead. He never knew he had this much to give in precome. Already, he wondered what this orgasm was going to be like. Jesus *Christ*, he already needed to come...so fuckin' bad...

And damn it if the gorgeous woman, with her uncanny erotic ESP, didn't know that—and fully capitalize on it.

By keepin' her gaze firmly locked to his...

While dippin' her mouth back in and formin' her pretty lips over the top of him.

Just the top.

That was enough.

*More* than enough.

Sam growled. Long and low and hard. Used his other hand to shove his jeans down to his thighs. Thank God he'd gotten hopeful after his shower and chosen to go commando. With all of his sex officially free, his cock bobbed up stronger and stiffer than ever, the tip weeping all over again with the evidence of his need. And aye, he had even more precome to spare as soon as Jenny glided her nose down to his base, inhalin' with open greed and appreciation. Her own scent curled around his senses too, all sugar and wind and woman, fillin' him until he felt damn near like a god.

She breathed him in once more before adding the sorcery of her mouth back to her slow, sweet worship. With wet, adoring nips, she made her way back up his steel-hard stalk. With a breathtakin' sigh, she closed herself all the way back over his tip again. Then out came her tongue—just the tip—working all the way into his slit, cleaning out his juices until a whole galaxy of stars invaded Sam's brain as well.

"Jenny. Oh, my sweet and fuckin' *sexy* little mouse. Your

mouth. Your incredible, hot *mouth*..."

"Not as incredible as how you taste."

Though she pulled up to give him the words, she didn't stray her lips from his flesh for a second. The vibrations of her words against her tip...and then the way she finished them, adding the one and only word that could completely undo him...

"Sir."

*Fuck.*

He *was* a god.

And now needed to prove it—by spreading his grip along the back of her head and guiding her mouth into the most perfect position possible...

*Aye...*

"Open your mouth, Jenny."

*Ohhhh, aye...*

"Wider. Let me see your tongue."

*What you do to me, lass. How you fulfill so many of my fantasies.*

"Perfect." He worked his cock along the center of her tongue. "So warm. *Fuck.* So soft. Jenny. *Jenny.* Your *mouth*!"

He bellowed it as she closed completely over him, lettin' out a long and lush moan with her eager swoop of control. At once, any remainin' drops in his slit were hers. His whole head was hers. His balls were hers. His fuckin' *soul* was hers...

His veins beat against her tongue. His flesh swelled against her lips. His hips clenched as he struggled to ease into her slowly, but her impatient mewls urged him otherwise. "Don't be careful," Sam dictated from locked teeth. "For fuck's sake, don't be tender."

*Because I'm not goin' to be.*

He thrust into her a little harder. A little more. Tightened his grip on her head as the demand in his cock beat louder, seeking the perfect heat at the very back of her throat.

"Breathe," he urged. "Through your nose. That's it, sweet girl. Take me deeper. *Deeper.*"

And then he was there. Stabbin' all the way into her heat, fuckin' her mouth as completely as he could. Consumin' her with all the lust in his body, the desire in his spirit, the need in his senses. But incredibly, the woman groaned as if she craved more. She dived her hands beneath him, grabbing the spheres of his ass with lusty vengeance. With every lunge he gave her with his dick, she dug harder into his glutes. And aye, it began to hurt. A lot. But God help him, he didn't want her to stop. The jabs helped him hold back, drawing out the exquisite ecstasy of this union even longer.

"Aye," he encouraged her between some of his harsh, heaving gasps. "Make it hurt, my beauty. Harder. *Harder.*"

As she groaned and mewled and slurped around his cock, he forced his eyes to crack open just a little. Just enough to behold his cock invadin' her mouth and the shimmering puddle of her saliva at his base.

"Damn," he grunted. "Damn, damn, *damn*, Jenny." When she responded with another lusty little sigh, he continued, "My darlin' *a leanbh*. You love this, don't you? You *want* me takin' your mouth like this, with every inch of my cock?"

"Mmmmm hmmmm."

Luscious little minx. He'd never been happier the angels had handed him a girl who devoured sexy romances like candy—and had the passion and talent to service his cock like it was a stick of the same molded sugar. Jesus, she was even well-read enough to know that repeatin' the exclamation would stimulate him even more if she hollowed her cheeks at the same time. But not even that little trick affected him as profoundly as the stare she lifted up to him as she did. A look that conveyed so much more than how deeply this was turnin' *her* on.

It was a look of spot-on, well-rooted, take-this-and-deal-with it confidence.

Clarity in how sexy she was. How beautiful she was. How worthy she was.

All the sexiness and gorgeousness and worth that *he'd* seen in her from the very start.

Perfection.

She was sheer, incredible *perfection*.

Exactly the incentive he needed to combine a growl and hiss into the same blissful eruption from his lips—just before increasing his pace into hers.

"Yes," he praised. "That's it, Jenny. Take me deep. Take me down your throat." But as she closed her eyes, focusing on doing just that, Sam tilted her head back, compelling her stare back open. "Stay with me, *mo muirnín*. Watch me, my darling. Look at every shred of desire I have for you. Every dirty, wicked thought I have about you. You'll be seein' it all, Jenny. You'll be lookin' at every way I adore you...every way I need you."

*I need you.*

The words drilled through his body, pulsin' up into his sex...and all of his soul. Because that wasn't an idiotic idea, right? Hotwirin' one's cock to their heart? What could possibly go awry with that...

Except everythin'?

But there was the not-so-small matter of keeping her gaze locked to his. Of watching every raw, wild emotion across *her* face as he swelled and thickened and hardened inside her. As the stabs of his cock tore new moans past her lips. As her eyes darkened to the shade of green smoke, so full of her own desire and dominion that he had no choice but to let her into all the places in him where the thickest shadows of his own soul still thrived...

Confirming one unalterable truth.

Jenny Thorne really was his soul mate.

And selkies really lived. And the monster of Loch Ness was really lurkin' around in the muck of that place.

Soul mates only existed in fuckin' fairy tales. And now that he'd reminded himself thoroughly of it and she didn't have to worry about the helicopter morphin' back into a pumpkin, he refocused on enjoyin' every moment of this. *Only this.* Every drop of its erotic magic. Every thrill of its growing arousal. And aye, he made sure Jenny beheld it too. The profound pleasure she brought him. The welcomin' heat she gifted to him. All the ways she opened him back up to how breathtakin' life could be.

How happy *his* life could be.

That was when the truth of all this struck.

She made him feel like a god...

Because she was a goddess.

And for right here, right now...*his* goddess.

He just couldn't get too attached to the feeling.

An affirmation that couldn't have been better timed—for as it struck, he summoned the fortitude to pull away from her, draggin' in shaky breaths as he reached his hands back through his hair. Already anticipatin' how she'd fire off a puzzled pout, he was also ready with a laugh-choke combo that did little for his air supply but a great deal for her vampy little grin.

As he rolled off the bed, shoving back his hair once more,

he shook his head and cleared his throat. "Do *not* move," he was finally able to order with convincin' dominion, pointing a mocking finger at her. "I'll be right back. A muckle manwhore like Frank has got to have *one* box of condoms in this place."

So much for dominion. The second he muttered it, Jen burst out with a definite giggle, utterly tramplin' on the gist of his order even if she complied in theory. But he couldn't help his charmed chuckle as she waggled a jokin' finger of her own and then ordered, "*You*. Gorgeous male-type specimen. Get your finer-than-fine ass back here."

As he slid back onto the bed, she busied herself with reachin' for her purse. The next second, she pulled out her little makeup bag—and from *there*, she drew out a foil packet emblazoned with the Nyte's logo. "Courtesy of the wedding salon ladies' room." She offered it up in triumph. "The one hotel in Vegas that *really* sticks to the marketing slogan."

Sam flashed a wide smirk. "'What happens in Vegas...'"

"Something along those lines."

He jumped one of his brows. "And I had you marked as the *lotion* pilferin' type."

She pouted. "They *were* free. And they're super pretty."

"I don't care if you held up the attendant and shot out the security cams." His voice was as rough as his jaw, which clenched in all the best ways as he tore the foil open with his teeth. Before he pulled out the latex, he nodded toward the center of the bed. "Get naked for me, beauty. I want to see all of you—right there."

She rewetted her lips. And then rasped, silkier and sexier than he'd ever heard from her, "Yes, Sir!"

No point in tellin' her how that sweet acquiescence affected him. The evidence jutted straight out as she returned to an air of cute and coy, unbuttoning her blouse with sensual little tugs. The little temptress kept up the flirtation after removing her bra, trailing both hands over her erect nipples, pulling until they became firm berries of arousal. Only after Sam let out a low rumble did she finally say, in a teasing murmur, "But I've been at work all day. I'm probably covered in old sweat."

She was rewarded with the gulp that corded Sam's neck... and the darker danger in his eyes. "And soon you'll be drenched in new sweat. Now get those pants off. I need to see every fuckin' inch of you."

His tone brooked no more dawdling. Wisely, she didn't. But just as Jen finished removing her pants and boots and then scrambled to the center of the bed, he made her freeze—with his astonished growl.

"What the bloody—"

Jen pushed up from the pillows, alarm painted across her face—until she spied the reason for Sam's outburst. At once, her face changed—as she pressed her lips together, clearly tryin' to hold herself in from wild giggles. "Well, that's certainly...keeping it different."

"*Different?*" Sam gestured at his erection with a sharp sweep. The condom was stretched tightly over his wang, from the juncture of his heavy balls to the proud crown at the top. Although now that peak was...

Decorated.

Unfortunately, there was no better way to phrase it. The rim between his head and frenulum was accented with a ring of bright-blue latex, serving as the base for a row of small rubber spikes. The resulting look was certainly some bampot's idea of a little exotic mixed with a lot of erotic.

He wasn't that bampot.

"Well, at least it's a great color." Jen attempted a helpful smile. "Bolt blue!"

Sam was ready to maintain his answerin' scowl—until the woman brought up one of his favorite American heroes. He didn't have many, mostly because there were plenty to idolize in Scotland and they tended to kick ass the world over, but Reece Richards' alter ego was an American legend who surpassed boundaries of geography, topography, and nationalities.

Because of that, his mouth started twitchin' too. How could he resist his adorable little woman, with her eyes twinklin' at him, her dimples flashin' for him, and her naked curves callin' to him? And fuck him, she was Team Bolt on top of bein' a *Star Wars* geek and a sassy little kinkster.

He'd hit the cosmic jackpot.

And was so thankful for it, he almost stopped right there and mouthed a long *thank you* to the Almighty.

Instead, he saved up the gratitude for the heat in his eyes while prowlin' closer to her, scootin' up the mattress one steady knee at a time. "You really like it, sassy mouse?"

She returned his heated stare with wide, watchful eyes, as if he were a tiger that had suddenly slipped its chain. He could really live with that analogy—and showed her so with a stealthy slide of his right hand around her left ankle.

She barely held back a gasp as he tightened his fingers, sending visible goosebumps up the length of her leg. "It's...it's... errrmmm..."

"What?" He swung in, clasping her other ankle.

She let out a long, velvety mewl as he glided his fingertips up the back of her calves. "Kind of...exciting." She rolled beneath him like a feline in her own right, her nude curves so feral and graceful, responding to all his caresses with matching flows of movement that captivated and awakened him. Ignited and inspired him...

"Excitin' sounds very, very fine." He skated his fingers behind her knees. Dipped his head to nip at the insides of her thighs. "Oh aye. So fine."

"Mmmmm." Her intention seemed to be a seductive hum but came out more as a strangled choke. And *that* was very fine as well. "Yes. I think 'exciting' could serve us very...*very*...oh!"

Two more kisses, higher on her thighs, made her squeal and shudder. And rendered him officially in heaven. Bollocks on the fact that he was capable of rainin' fire on an enemy from ten thousand feet. This was the only incineration he was interested in ever dolin' again—from two inches of altitude, where the damage could be gauged in this goddess's heated twists, tantalized shivers, and passionate sighs. And what about hittin' the ultimate target? That was the best part of all: the buck of her spread thighs, fully exposin' all the pink, wet glory of her plumped, ready sex, just waitin' for the full impact of his hard and achin' missile...

"Sam! Enough teasing, you bastard! I need you!"

Oh, now he had a *new* favorite part.

The "provoking incident" of her "return fire."

Which he was thrilled to cut short after just her first volley—by diggin' a pair of brutal grips into the curves of her thighs. Then tuggin' hard, without any more of his sweet and sultry shit about it, to align her body perfectly beneath his.

"Bastard?" He flashed a smirk, pouring on a mixture of allure and antagonism at once and rejoicin' in how that dilated her irises. Despite the evidence of her arousal, he went ahead and taunted lowly, "Good bastard...or bad bastard?"

"I—I don't know," Jenny stammered. "Ohhhh, shit." Her limbs quaked as Sam rolled his hips—scraping her pretty, sensitive nether lips with the nasty blue spikes that poked from all around his girth. Those perfect, incredible little teasers... "Y-You're driving me crazy, damn it. I—I can't think—"

"Then don't." He stamped a fresh underscore of command to the words. "Just stop thinking and feel it, my beautiful Jenny. Feel me. *All* of me."

But suddenly, despite her passionate dictates, the woman had started to hold back. Sam could ken it as sure as the air in his lungs; there was fresh tension in her muscles along with the strict line that now comprised her lips. She clung to it even as he seduced her more with the latex she'd called full-on *excitin'* a few minutes ago—but that wasn't nearly enough. For some reason, her surrender had been yanked off the table—ever since the moment he'd pierced her gaze with his own and ordered her not to just take him but feel him.

*Damn it.*

She was at it again.

Wantin' all of the sex but none of what it now represented between them. Oh aye. She craved all the teasing strokes of the wild spiked condom and even the rockin' climax they'd bring, but none of what he was askin' her—*ordering her*—to give him in exchange. Her truth. Her vulnerability. The honest, real, gory, scary passion that *he'd* been willin' to expose to *her* already...

That was, as she would say, bullshit.

But now he just had to find a way of showin' her so.

And set himself to the task with a purpose that might turn *him* into a bloody superhero.

Intense or not, he already had the ideal starting block.

Or, more accurately, the commencing condom. Thanks to the Nyte Resort and their dedication to makin' every mate's sexual swim a safe one, he already had the ideal tool to taunt her sweet pussy in ways he hadn't anticipated. With deliberate gyrations of his hips and tantalizing taps with his cock, he soon had Jen lurching and shivering under him again. The second her higher sighs punched the air, he moved to phase two. With deepened snarls, he nuzzled her neck. With calculated pressure, he tugged at her nipples, stroked her outer thighs...and went for the ultimate clincher in circling her clenching asshole.

But as soon as she moaned and bore down, hoping to get more of him inside her sensitive entrance, he purposely pulled back. Then, coiling his muscles to assist, all the way up.

He descended his gaze over her body, restrainin' himself even more. The effort was *not* fuckin' easy, especially with her hair already lookin' freshly fucked and her lips so plump and berry-red from bein' fucked by him. There were new temptations here as well. The engorged erections of her nipples. The sight of that bright-blue condom, ready to protect his length as he plunged home inside her...

But not yet.

Almost. There.

*Almost. There.*

Which was why he locked his teeth and held back just a little more. And stared down over all of his gorgeous Jenny again, takin' note of every tremor, quiver, shiver, and shake that led to his overridin' instinct about how this was goin' to go down next.

Which was why he lifted back up, until their faces were in line again—

And let her have it with his surest, sexiest half grin of

ultimate triumph.

Instantly earnin' himself what had to be her most incredible scowl.

Incredible—as in needin' to be capitalized and practically spelled out in twenty-foot neon over the bloody Vegas Strip itself.

Incredible—as in the woman looked ready to crumble from the force of lashin' it at him.

Incredible—as in that was right the fuck where he wanted her. *Needed* her.

"Goddamnit, Sam." Her wince was just as harsh, but she didn't look away. Not this time. Not when she clearly, fully intended that he see every square inch of it, proved as soon as she drove a hand up into his hair and twisted as if her life depended on it.

Sam wasn't sure *his* didn't.

"Jenny." He poured all of himself into the syllables, makin' damn sure she knew she wasn't in this emotional whirlpool by herself. And that if the spinnin' waters pulled her down, he was damned well going to follow her into them. "*Jenny.*"

*I'm here. I adore you.*

*I love you.*

"Stop." She almost hissed it, as if she'd somehow heard everythin' he'd said. His heart was thunderin' so hard with the force of his vow, he wouldn't have argued it. Because, of course, selkies were real and he really *was* sure he'd seen Nessie of Loch Ness once, right? "*Stop*, okay?" She gritted her teeth on the words now. "You're tearing me apart."

He dropped his forehead atop hers. "Good." *Welcome to the fuckin' club.*

"Damn it." She dropped her hand. Squeezed her eyes

shut. "You really are a bastard."

He was actually grateful for her sarcasm. Told her so with a rueful wince. "Yeah? Well, the bastard says to spread your legs for him, beauty."

She spat back a watery laugh. "I should tell you to go fuck off."

"But you won't." He took his voice into a register barely above a whisper. Into the tone of a command that would resonate into every pore of her body and awareness of her soul. Because that was exactly where *he* felt *her* inside his own bein'...in the fibers of what made him a creature reborn. By her. For her. "You won't—because denyin' me is like cuttin' out your own heart."

"Shit." She said it slowly, shakily...as she parted her thighs for him.

Then again as Sam moved into her with his first hot slide. And his second. And his third. And all the slow, tantalizing thrusts after that—delivering the sensual swipes of those blue latex spikes against every inch of her juicy little clit, fadin' just a little bit more of her control.

She reached for him again. Hung on with a grip that would surely leave deep red marks along his shoulders—or so he hoped—sighin' and gaspin' with every new, deeper plunge of his throbbin' length, helpin' him climb for the pinnacle they both sought with growlin', surgin' exigency.

"Oh, Sam. *Sam!*"

He was shakin' sorely himself but sucked in enough air to whisper back. "Aye, *a ghrá geal?*" *Yes, my beloved?*

"Tear. Me. Open."

Her snarl worked through him like quicksilver. Settled at the base of his spine for excruciating moments before spreading across his ass and injecting itself into his swollen, screamin' balls. He tucked his head against her neck, prayin' like fuck for the strength to hold on as he braced her waist with hands that felt stiff as goddamned Lego bricks. He was likely markin' her soft skin the same way she'd bruised him—*not* a thought he needed right now—but it helped him secure his grip so he could ram her body harder around him.

Her screams started.

But not the telltale tremors through her channel that he sought.

Not the tremors he longed to give her.

He growled out his greedy approval at her shrieks nonetheless, thankful there were only bunches of cactus and a few coyotes around for miles. Dear *God*, the sounds this passionate creature could make. She was magnificent, now becoming *his* uncaged tigress, so fierce and savage, scratchin' him harder and yellin' at him louder, as if challenging him to find a way to fuck her harder and bruise her deeper, before she gave up the screams of her ultimate, searin' surrender.

*Soon. Oh God oh God, please let it be soon.*

"Sam. *Sam!*" she finally cried. "I can't—I don't know if I can hold it—"

"Don't you *fuckin'* hold it." His face locked into a thousand angles of his own tension. As he kept rammin' her, still working to brand himself on every inch of welcoming tissue inside her, he raised a hand to her forehead. For a moment, he left his grip right there, before twisting his fingers into her hairline with brutal force. "Now, Jenny." The words seethed from between his teeth. "Let me watch it. *Now.*"

And finally, he tore her apart.

Just as she ripped him into a thousand shards of rushing,

relieving ecstasy.

The orgasm bloody killed him.

His heart stopped as the heat blazed in, crashin' his blood and evisceratin' his senses. "God," he groaned. *"Fuck."* He plunged into her with merciless force, his shaft retreating and then reentering with long, hard strokes. He was nothin' but ripped, raw glory, splayed beneath the desert stars, never wantin' to be whole again. But that was exactly what Jenny Thorne did the very next moment. She melted him back into one piece as he kept shuntin' inside her, giving her every last drop of come his balls could squeeze and punch into his strained, and soon utterly drained, cock.

At once, he wanted to let out a hysterical laugh. Had he really thought *he* could make his mark on *her*? As he curled his face back into the curve of her neck, the truth blared at him with agonizing clarity.

*She'd* marked *him* for life.

Forever.

Holy God, he hoped so.

Especially as she kept clinging to him. Desperately, unbelievably, milking even more out of him. With one hand latched against his scalp, her fingers tanglin' in his sweaty hair, one sweet little mewl from her had him pumpin' yet again, wrappin' her hair all the way around his fist this time. Ferociously, they clung to each other. Passionately, he fucked into her. Then suddenly, once more together, they came again—twice as hard. But he slowed as Jen's scream pierced the air, also doubled in force.

"Shit," he muttered. "Am I hurting you, *mo luaidh*?"

"Y-Yes." She swiveled her face, punctuating with a ruthless bite in his neck. "But don't you dare stop."

Inspired by her move, he sank his teeth into the flesh beneath her ear. Filled her sex with more of his passionate possession. "I want you to feel me inside you for weeks," he growled. "I want to walk into your office, bid you a good mornin', and know that the sound of my voice makes your cunt wet from rememberin' me. I don't even want you to sit without feelin' the pain I've given you...the marks I've put on you...inside and out."

# CHAPTER ELEVEN

Nasty words...breathed into her with the solemnity of a vow.

The former fired into every inch of Jen's body. The latter sang to every hollow of her heart.

The collision destroyed so much of her will, making it impossible to hold back her whispered confession in return.

"I'll never forget you, Sam Mackenna. Ever."

He pulled his head up a little—just enough for her to see the effect of her words across his face. She wasn't sure whether to feel good or bad about it. He looked like he'd just been drawn and quartered but hadn't been able to process the torture yet.

"I'll never forget *you*, Jenny Thorne."

As the promise left his lips, the come exploded from his body. He didn't look away for a second, baring the apex of his passion to her. His brow crumpled. His cheekbones jutted, stark against his skin. His teeth gritted until a guttural groan spilled out.

He was the most beautiful thing she'd ever seen.

He was the ultimate dynamite to her defenses.

At first, she thought she could contain the damage to a couple of sobs—but after those tumbled out, the truth was clear. The torrent was just starting. The tears rushed out, violent and consuming, destroying everything in their path, including any self-dignity she had left.

She shouldn't have gotten into the helicopter with him. For that matter, she shouldn't have even let him get into the elevator with her, that handful of hours ago...now feeling like years.

God. All the stupid love songs were right. Maybe, with the right person, it was possible to live a lifetime in one night. And yeah, just *maybe*...Sam *was* her right person. Maybe fate really had dealt them the wild card—that this one time in a million, the hunk and the geek were perfect for each other.

But they'd only ever own it for this one night.

How could she afford to think otherwise? In ten days, he'd be five thousand miles away. *But Elgin, Scotland isn't exactly the surface of Mars, Jen.*

Right. So she'd just...what? Decide to pop in casually in a few months, telling him she was "in the neighborhood" on holiday? The idea alone made her squirm, wondering if Sam already smelled the desperation on her. Behavior like that only worked for women in rom-coms and nighttime soaps. The last time she checked, her name wasn't Bridget Jones *or* Cookie Lyon. Sam would give her his politest smile while taking her out for a Dundee pie and a pint—and then put her on the next transport back home. The whole time, he'd hide glances that questioned if she really *was* from Mars.

No matter what kind of obstacles they'd both hurtled to truly find each other, they'd still done it in the wrong damn place. At the wrong damn time.

The truth of it torpedoed harder. Sobs erupted from deeper in her chest. She fought them hard—so damn hard. There were bigger things to grieve about. *Much* bigger things. But right now, nothing felt that way. Nothing felt better than giving in to her selfish pain. Of caving to the knowledge that once the sun rose, her romance with Sam Mackenna would be over—and there really wasn't a damn thing to be done about it.

"Sam." She wrapped herself around him, hanging on as if her life depended on it. At the moment, it just might have. *"Sam."*

He rolled to his side, keeping their bodies entwined in every sense. His cock still filled her, warm and strong. His arms encircled her, protective and sure. His voice flowed over her as he brushed his mouth across her face, capturing her tears. "It's all right. It's all right, my sweet mouse."

"I—I—"

*I love you.*

The words hovered, thick and demanding, in the very essence of her breath.

*Just say it!*

But she couldn't. The words bore all of her heart, and she needed some of it inside to keep living after he'd gone. *Somehow...*

He understood. The new shadows in Sam's eyes, velvet as winter twilight, told her so. But he didn't stop there. He leaned in, gently sucking that air from her, as if drawing her truth into his being. As he exhaled, his face warmed with a look of wonder and joy. He'd heard the words anyway—in the place they mattered most. She knew it with a certainty as solid as her heartbeat, as irrevocable as her breath.

"I know," he finally whispered. "And Jenny? I—"

"I know."

And she did.

Only then did the tears stop. No. She chose to make them stop. Acceptance bred stability, if not complete peace. What good would it do to hurl more sadness at it all? Nothing could be changed. The truth...simply was. She had to accept it like a moor accepted the rain.

And eventually, rain brought the spring.

She closed the thoughts off. Spring was *not* on the mental menu tonight. She refused to ponder fluffy bunnies and daffodils when she could savor her last hours encased in steely strength, wrapped in complete warmth.

Surrounded by Sam.

She nestled against his chest, pressing a hand next to her cheek to listen to his heartbeat.

*Remember this sound. Save it, savor it, commit it into the deepest parts of yourself.*

But her senses betrayed her, succumbing to the perfect heat and protection of his embrace. With the thrum of his life in her ears, she gazed up into the stars and followed their hypnotic peace into sleep.

★ ★ ★ ★ ★

"Eternal sunrise, eternal sunset, eternal dawn and gloaming, on seas and continents and islands, each in its turn, as the round earth rolls."

At first, her poetic whisper only earned her the continued thumps of Sam's heart, steady and strong beneath her ear. But after a few seconds, he scraped a hand through her hair in time with the wind against the window, accented by the lusty coos of the roadrunners and the sharp barks of the coyotes.

At last, he even gave up a sleepy hum. "John Muir before six, lass? You really are the geekiest sex fiend I've ever met."

She flashed him a scowl. "And how many sex fiends *have* you met?"

A smile tugged his lips. Just as swiftly, it faded. He lifted his hand to her hair again, letting the strands trail from his fingers, over her shoulder. "Only one who's taken much more from me than that."

Less than ten seconds. Less than twelve words. He had her blood tingling, her chest flipping, and her heart breaking all over again—especially as he drew her down for a long, wet, lingering kiss. But as soon as he parted her lips and swept his tongue out for more, Jen forced herself away. Two more seconds of feeling his tongue like that, and she'd be getting hot and stupid with him again.

"We—we need to think about getting back." Her hair and makeup appointment was at eight. That had to be less than two hours away by now. "Time for real life, my laird-lord on high." Despite the fact that he'd never appeared more like a perfect dream, the peach-and-gold dawn making his chiseled nudity glow.

"I should roll you over and spank you black and blue for that nonsense," he cracked. "But you're right."

"If you want the last word here, that feels like a damn good place for it."

He sat up, leaned over, and reached a hand to L-frame her face. With the other, he guided one of her hands to the center of his chest. "My 'last word' to you comes only when this stops beatin'."

Jen struggled to laugh. It *was* ironic, right? That by staking his devotion on the beats of his heart, he'd stopped hers from working?

From possibly ever beating the same way again.

In just a month, he'd changed her. Moved her. Made her breathe, hurt, soar, seethe, laugh, cry, and live as she never had before.

In just a month, she'd learned what it was to be in love.

Why had she deluded herself that the truth of it would just...fade? That real life would be the magical blowtorch, razing everything back to the way it was?

★ ★ ★ ★ ★

Even a week after Tess and Dan's wedding—which was beautiful and llama-free, thanks to a frantic last-minute venue change to the Scene Lounge, and Sam bowing out at the last minute due to a "buddy in the squad" needing a roster switch— she couldn't find the right target lock on her life. She'd made all the right motions. Had done all the right things. Had kept herself insanely busy—converting the wedding into a retro-themed "Casablanca" vibe instead of the Michelangelo-meets-Liberace thing was a great excuse for that—and had also worked out like a maniac every day, along with a hell of a lot of shopping therapy.

But even with Lola kicking her toosh on the latter two, Sam found a way to sneak into every other thing she did, thought she had, breath she took. At the gym, she was certain she saw him in every golden-haired hunk with pecs of steel and the biceps of a god. In the mall, she saw a pair of track pants that instantly created a new fantasy for her: him in *and* out of them. While Lola was ogling handbags in the Coach store, she sneaked into Scottish Heritage and found a pin that would look perfect with the colors of his plaid. Lola had cockblocked her in the nick of time, threatening to drag her to mid-Strip for watered-down margaritas and an evening of getting hit on by every drunk frat boy in the city.

But she still hadn't learned her damn lesson.

She blew Lola off by blaming it on the man's pheromones

still invading the desert air. Once he was gone, she'd get good and pissed about exactly how *he'd* been dealing with all this.

He got a slight bye for the frenetic days between their field trip to the desert and the wedding. She'd been so consumed with getting work done and holding Tess's hand, nobody saw anything but the top of her head for days. Then after the wedding, she secretly thanked Captain Mackenna for his consideration of her exhaustion level by that point.

Two days after, she was sick of "consideration."

Three days after, the frustration became fury.

Now, just two days before the Scottish squadron was set to board their transport back home, she sat with her elbows on her desk and her head in her hands, forming a teepee over her phone's text screen. Sam's face taunted her from it—along with a text asking whether he could bring her back something gooey from Zapatas.

She hadn't answered.

Because it felt better to ignore him.

Because if she was really back in the hey-we're-buddies-want-some-Zapatas box for him again, she probably didn't want to know it.

Correction. She *definitely* didn't want to know it.

So she resorted to what any woman who'd been threatened with drunk frat boys would.

She was ignoring him. But now realized, in hindsight, that it was actually her bait. Would he come in to rib her about the silly radio silence? That was what the old Sam would do. The pre-desert-confessions Sam. Did she really want that Sam back, sauntering in to give her some cheeky jokes, some smooth charm, and a few dorky fangirl thrills, after everything they'd confessed to each other and exposed to each other this last month?

Maybe she did.

Which was so damn pathetic. Transparent.

But no different than what she was about to do.

Okay, a little different.

Different to the tune of five thousand miles.

She gazed at his tiny avatar picture again. She had a few bigger ones in the photos folder, but this was her favorite, snapped as he'd come in after a kick-ass training hop one day. His hair was sweaty and tousled, his grin wide and bright.

How she loved him.

How she wanted to capture that smile on his face every day. To share yummy wine with him every night and her blow jobs every morning. To massage the aches from his shoulders and kiss away the demons from his deployments. To let him call her his sexy, sassy little mouse...and to feel his hand on her ass when she stopped believing it for herself.

She wanted their one night every night.

Because of that, she was going to ride the elevator to the roof again. Then jump off the building.

Figuratively, of course.

But just as terrifyingly.

If she wound up on the sidewalk as a symbolically smashed pancake, so be it. Better a pancake who'd tried than a ball of batter who'd stayed in the bowl, playing life safe.

The decision blazed through her, firing down her right arm. *No second thoughts. Do it.*

She lifted the pen waiting on the desk and then signed the document she'd completed this morning in perfect detail.

The second she finished, Lola appeared. Her friend walked over, scooped up the paper, and then let out a slow whistle when taking in her frantic autograph on all the right lines.

"Well, blow out my bonnie bagpipes," the woman uttered. "You're really gonna do this, then? A transfer to Lakenheath?"

"Aye." Jen blushed furiously when the joke fell flat. It was better than *her* doing the same thing, she supposed. She recovered by snatching the sheet back at once, feeling strangely protective about it. Maybe if she played the rest of the charade cool, Lola would go along with her charade in front of the office. "Having the squad over here has made me think...about things. A lot."

"Yeah." Lola smirked. "*A lot.*" She tapped at the phone resting on the desk—still open to Sam's text page.

Fine. So much for the subterfuge. But despite the heat flooding her cheeks, Jen kept her chin high. The rest of her justification wasn't so feigned. "The base is five miles from Cambridge University," she asserted. "They've got amazing public education courses."

"Right. Sure." This time, Yoli hopped onto Lola's snarky bandwagon. "Cambridge. *There's* a reason to upend your life."

Jen maintained her stance. Cambridge was going to be a pretty good part of the pancake consolation package, if everything came to that. *If.* She wasn't committed yet. As long as the transfer request was in her hands, she still had the chance to shred it and forget it. Once she walked the sheet across the office and dropped it onto the right stack, wheels would officially be in motion. She'd already talked to the hiring officer at Lakenheath. They badly needed someone like her in the personnel office, so her request would be fast-tracked for processing.

Every step she took across the tiled floor was like a rifle

shot in her ears.

*Think of other things. Focus on the logistics first. They're safe. Stop at the PX for moving boxes. Call the utilities companies to set dates for shut-offs.*

*Practice what you're going to tell Sam...*

Okay, so logistics wouldn't work.

She had no choice but to grit it out, step by agonizing step. The hugest change of her life.

For a man who'd never even said the damn words to her.

*You never said them either, girl. When it was time for the big three, you wussed out on him too. Maybe that's why he's stayed away.*

She was halfway across the office, the transfer request still clutched in her shaking fingers, when the thunder of footsteps in the hallway had all the girls turning around.

Not just any footsteps. These paces carried the cadence of leadership. The boldness of fearlessness. The unmistakable overture of testosterone. A great deal of it.

And they were all, after all, only human...

Though the anticipation quickly mellowed into resignation when everyone realized the ruckus was only Skip Tremaine's normal pre-arrival fanfare.

"Ladies!" Tremaine opened both arms like a circus conductor—an image making everyone giggle, since he was still in flight gear. "Eyes up. Attention, please. I have an announcement."

Again, everyone laughed, though shuffled over out of respect for the guy. Cat Five got excited about a lot of things. Murmurs rippled through the group. Some speculated he'd announce the commissary had agreed to reinstate Taco Tuesdays. Many more banked on the guy revealing his newest

ANGEL PAYNE

tattoo.

When everyone was gathered, Tremaine rocked back on his heels. "I'm pretty fucking excited to tell you all that I've talked one of the world's finest jet jockeys into hanging up his combat wings and joining us here at the training center. He's an outstanding pilot and an exemplary human being, with the patience to put up with my special brand of bullshit. I'd ask you all to make sure he feels right at home, but you've already handled that task with your usual class and style. Well, you big braw boy, stop skulking in the hall!"

Tremaine's last few words were drowned by the hoots, shouts, and applause that broke out before he was done.

*Braw Boy.*

Sam's call sign.

What. The. Hell?

Jen barely treaded water in the storm surge of the celebration. She stood, frozen as ice, jostled as everyone rushed and crowded the grinning guy who'd entered behind Tremaine. Well...she assumed he was grinning. From here, all she could see were the gold halo of his hair and the crinkles at the corners of his eyes, as well as the gusto with which he hugged every last person in that throng who greeted him.

Which, damn it, made her love him even more.

He always had something for everyone: a warm smile, a listening ear, a compassionate hug. There was a reason Tremaine had pursued him. People were inspired to be their best for him and with him.

But what if he didn't have anything left for her?

She didn't—couldn't—dare to have hope about the reason for his bold decision. No matter how much of the "new" Jenny he'd brought to life during their fantasy night, enough of the old girl existed to make her hang back, still rooted to her spot, clutching the paper she'd been a few steps from filing.

A few steps.

Ten feet away from landing herself across the world from him again.

"Jenny?"

She blinked and looked up, just in time to watch him part the crowd, approaching the counter at which he'd camped so many times just to shoot the shit with her. This time, he didn't stop at the shelf. Parked one hand on the ledge and vaulted right over.

He landed directly in front of her.

As the room fell to silence, Sam cupped the sides of her neck. "Jenny?"

She lifted her head. He was dressed in flight gear too—and damn, it looked even better from up close. "Yeah?" she finally whispered.

His lips twitched, unveiling an expression she'd never seen on his face before. Was he...nervous? "Say somethin'. You look like a bomb just dropped."

"Hasn't it?"

More of the nervousness. It entered his eyes now, turning them into shadows. His hold slackened. "Then you're not pure jings about this?"

She blinked again. Lifted a hand to his broad chest, directly over his heart. "Oh, God. *Sam.*" She wasn't handling this right at all. If her dreams really were coming true—if he'd given up the green beauty of his land and the familiarity of his home to come live in the desert, with *her*—then a simple, albeit epic, word like "jings" wasn't enough to contain the joy she felt...or even a fraction of her heart's exultation.

"Well, that's fine, then." He stepped away. Yanked his hands back, fingers stiff, as if he were suddenly sure he'd break her. "I guess I...jumped to conclusions I shouldn't have after our time together. Now I'm in a world of sorry about it too." In a guttural growl, he added, "To both you and me."

"Sam!" But her plea didn't stop him from whirling from her—forcing her to race around, plant herself before him, and shove the sheet in her hand right into his. "Tell me *who* was the one assuming things, Captain Mackenna?"

His stare was still dark with fury. As he read the first line of the request, it changed to confusion. Then as his lips moved over the text, exploded with astonishment. "Lakenheath?" His head snapped up. "You were going to—"

"Ten more seconds, and it would've been submitted." She closed the gap between them. Uncaring of who watched or even took a damn video—and she wouldn't put it past Lola, because this was *much* better YouTube fodder than her cats singing old Rod Stewart tunes—she lifted a hand to his perfect, rugged face. "And you would've been worth it, Sam Mackenna. All five thousand miles."

His gray eyes smoldered once again—but this time, in all the right ways. He didn't veer that beautiful stare as he tore her transfer request in half, tossed both pieces over his shoulders, and then reached out for her...

And crashed their mouths together.

Jen was conscious of more woots and claps, but she barely heard the din past the rockets blazing across her senses, the happiness exploding in her heart. Sam wrapped his arms around her with the same jubilance, his grip as dominant as his kiss, his groan matching the need in her sigh. His tongue rammed between her lips before dancing with hers, leaving her with no mistake about who got to lead. No way was she about to argue. No way did she want to.

A part of her almost didn't believe this was happening. Their love story was the long shot, not the sure thing. The hot, graceful Scot and the mouthy, gawky American. The warrior who'd lost himself in the violence and the book nerd who insisted he'd been there all along.

Two people who never should have met.

Two paths that never should have crossed.

A bridge that never should have happened.

A love that wouldn't accept that bullshit.

Especially when souls were meant to be together. When spirits were meant to love. When hearts were meant to be transformed.

As soon as Sam let her breathe again, Jen used the opportunity to speak the truth from such a heart: the one threatening to thud its way right out of her chest. "I love you, Sam Mackenna."

His dimples became craters from his answering smile. "As I love you, my beautiful hen."

A delighted laugh bubbled up. The endearment was a Scottish thing, used pretty casually in his country, though he'd never said it over here. With his utterance now, he conveyed a message that made her eyes sting all over again.

He was home.

She was going to make sure he felt that way, each and every day. He was her gift, and she'd never stop being grateful for it—which meant no more looking in the mirror and seeing everything she wasn't.

She was more because of him.

She'd *be* more because of him.

As she framed his face with her hands and looked deeply into his eyes, she also saw the more she'd given back to him. The new peace in his eyes. The new trust in his smile. All the leaves in his stream, flowing so beautifully and boldly in every full, happy breath he took. He dazzled her now more than ever—and knowing *she* was the reason just made this moment even more of a miracle.

Even the sarcastic snort on the air, courtesy of Lola, didn't fade her shine. "Hen?" the woman guffawed. "What the hell happened to 'mouse'?"

Jen precluded her reply with a laugh drenched in pure, permeating, exalting, exhilarating joy. "She got conquered. And loved every damn second of it."

Continue the Honor Bound Series with Book Ten

# *Ruled*

**Coming December 11, 2018**
*Keep reading for an excerpt!*

# EXCERPT FROM *RULED*

## BOOK TEN IN THE HONOR BOUND SERIES

"Hot. Really hot. And hard."

"No way. Slow and sexy."

"Girl, please. Look at his posture."

"*Looking.*"

"And that says 'slow' to you...how? That man likes being large and in charge."

"Can't we just wish he prefers both? *A lot* of both?"

"Maybe he'll let one of us explore the issue further."

"After we're done with the dog-and-pony show tonight."

"You mean after *Tracy's* done with it?"

That was it. The banter between her two closest friends finally made Tracy Rhodes choke on her "soothing" cup of tea. She set the cup down on the dressing table, swiveled in the high makeup chair, and unloaded two rounds of exasperation at Gemini Vann, aka her Chief Counsel, and Veronica Gallo, her Media Secretary. At the moment, however, they were distracting thorns, numbers one and two. "Not helping with the 'relax' segment of the schedule, girls."

*Relax.* If that were possible. Down the hall, an army of Las Vegas Convention Center staffers readied a hall that would soon seat thousands. In a little over an hour, all those seats would be filled—with people waiting to hear what *she* had to say. About a subject she knew all of three damn things about. Okay, two and a half. She needed all the help she could get.

That officially nixed relaxation.

Calm. Maybe calm was achievable—though that depended on getting five minutes of deep breathing. Time sure as hell laughed at that one. Sound check was in ten minutes, followed by half a dozen this-can't-wait phone calls and then a meeting with local schoolchildren. And space? Fifteen people in a twelve-by-twelve dressing room might be *someone's* idea of space, but she wasn't that someone.

There were a lot of "someones" she never thought life would turn her into by now.

Widow.

Single mom.

Entrepreneur.

Vice president of the United States.

Annnnd there went the possibility of calm.

Before her nerves could start their usual run with that, Gemini came to the rescue, holding out a bottled water. With eyes half a shade lighter than hers and the same somewhere-between-blond-and-brunette hair, many mistook Gem as her sister. Neither of them refuted the claims. Why bother when it might as well have been truth?

"Better to ask forgiveness, right?" The woman's blue-silver gaze sparkled. "So...errrmm...sorry, boss?"

Tracy took a second to think of a good zinger as comeback. It was all the opening needed for the strawberry blonde poised at the other end of the mirror. Veronica, actually *looking* like a Veronica instead of the shortened version of Ronnie she preferred, pointedly cleared her throat. "You mean *sorry, Madam Vice President*, right?"

Gem snorted. "She was my pinky-swear bestie long before she was DC's darling. She'll be the same long after they've moved on to the news cycle's next favorite flavor. Still"—she nodded Tracy's way—"sorry, *Madam Vice President*."

Tracy stifled a chuckle. "You're forgiven, Madam Counsel to the vice president."

Gem glanced across the room again. "Just for that, I'm ogling the new guy again."

"Not if I beat you to it." Ronnie sneaked in a long stare at the cluster of men near the door—"men" seeming the worst ration of a word for the sight. At least ten better definitions came to Tracy's mind for the dark-suited group.

Giants.

Fighters.

Leaders.

Alphas.

Rulers.

Annnnd that did it. She was now a member of the gawk-a-thon too. And that was a surprise...why? With the turn her life had taken in the last year, there'd barely been time for a little self-induced fun in the sheets, let alone activities like—gasp—a date. And if she could even find the time for that? What then? One couldn't trade small talk about the job over dessert and coffee when most of that information was classified. One couldn't invite a guy up for a nightcap when Secret Service was opening the car door and the street address was One Observatory Circle.

Even if that wasn't the case, she had to consider Luke.

Like she did in every decision she made. In every breath she took.

*Well. Speak of the handsome devil now.*

No. Not a devil. Despite the glints in his eyes and the cant of his grin, her son would always be her perfect gift from heaven. A little extreme? Of course. A thought process she'd have to revise one day? Definitely. But not today and not now, even if staring at Luke meant she had to keep looking at the suited hunks, now engaging him in caveman-worthy fist locks and shoulder bumps. The lump in her throat swelled bigger as she watched his attempts at reciprocation, all gangly limbs and fifteen-year-old bravado, clearly worshiping the warriors who joked around with him—

Until he locked gazes with the new arrival to the gang.

The one who made the others, even with their linebacker shoulders and towering thighs, look like his wimpy kid brothers.

The one who still had Gem's and Ronnie's tongues dragging on the floor.

The one who turned her kid into a speechless slab.

Especially the next moment, when he turned and gripped Luke in a thoroughly masculine handshake. With their hands locked, the man's fingers stretched halfway to Luke's elbow.

"Holy shit," Gem rasped at the sight.

"Holy *something*," Ronnie seconded.

"Sssshh," Tracy admonished. "He's talking."

And she didn't want to miss a second of it.

Because his voice was the most alluring thing about him. *Dear. God. That. Voice.*

Deep as his dark, watchful eyes. Formidable as the shoulders straining at every stitch of his jacket. Warm as his caramel-colored skin but cool as his control. It was the kind of voice she could imagine in the front lines of battle—but also at the pulse points in her neck. And other places on her body...

Holy. Cow.

Well...holy *something*. Cows weren't exactly at the mental forefront at the moment. Stallions, maybe. Or mambas. Maybe even werewolves.

No, no, and no.

Pumas.

Dark ones.

Ding, ding, ding. *When the metaphor fits...*

**This story continues in**
**Ruled:** *Honor Bound Book Ten!*

# ALSO BY ANGEL PAYNE

**Honor Bound:**
*Saved*
*Cuffed*
*Seduced*
*Wild*
*Wet*
*Hot*
*Masked*
*Mastered*
*Conquered*
*Ruled (December 11, 2018)*

**The Bolt Saga:**
*Bolt*
*Ignite*
*Pulse*
*Fuse*
*Surge*
*Light*

**Secrets of Stone Series:**
*No Prince Charming*
*No More Masquerade*
*No Perfect Princess*
*No Magic Moment*
*No Lucky Number*
*No Simple Sacrifice*
*No Broken Bond*
*No White Knight*

**Temptation Court:**
*Naughty Little Gift*
*Pretty Perfect Toy*
*Bold Beautiful Love*

**Cimarron Series:**
*Into His Dark*
*Into His Command*
*Into Her Fantasies*
*Into His Sin*

**For a full list of Angel's other titles,
visit her at AngelPayne.com**

# ACKNOWLEDGMENTS

To my sisterhood of friends and support, thank you for selflessly putting up with the neurotic, crazy writer: Victoria Blue, Eden Bradley, Jenna Jacob, Shannon Hunt, Lorraine Gibson, and Martha Frantz.

To Jennifer Mitchell, for all the ways you show me what a huge heart really looks like. This Sam is for *you*, babe!

To Connie Deuning, for showing me all the forms kindness can take. You're incredible!

Special thanks to all my sisters in the Obsessenach fandom. Hope you all enjoy my fun tribute to our favorite guy!

A special thank-you to the readers who have believed in and loved the Honor Bound men throughout the years: You've been through the haters and the lovers, the bad times and the good... I cannot begin to express how much you all mean to me.

To the editors who have helped my "little love story that could" become one of the most emotional projects I've ever finished—I am so grateful! Thank you, Melisande Scott, Jeanne De Vita, and Scott Saunders!

# ABOUT ANGEL PAYNE

*USA Today* bestselling romance author Angel Payne loves to focus on high-heat romance starring memorable alpha men and the women who love them. She has numerous book series to her credit, including the action-packed Bolt Saga and Honor Bound series, Secrets of Stone series (with Victoria Blue), the intertwined Cimarron and Temptation Court series, the Suited for Sin series, and the Lords of Sin historicals, as well as several standalone titles.

Angel is a native Southern Californian, leading to her love of being in the outdoors, where she often reads and writes. She still lives in Southern California with her soul-mate husband and beautiful daughter, to whom she is a proud cosplay/culture con mom. Her passions also include whisky tasting, shoe shopping, and travel.

Visit her at AngelPayne.com

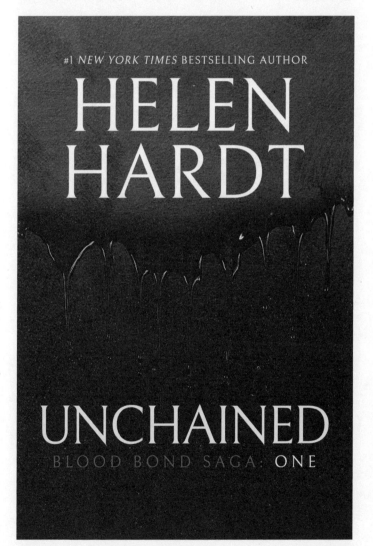

# EXCERPT FROM *UNCHAINED*

## VOLUME ONE FROM THE BLOOD BOND SAGA

# PROLOGUE

### Dante

I used to dream of severed human heads.

They hung above me, their skin gray and pasty as the elixir of life flowed out of them. I inhaled, and the metallic scent of iron infused itself into my cells. It was the iron and other nutrients in blood that our bodies needed, but that wasn't the scent that drew us, the scent we craved.

Humans don't realize they each possess their own scent beyond perspiration and pheromones, a fragrance that comes from their very life force—their blood.

From one neck, a drop of citrusy blond female fell onto my tongue. From another, the leathery and musky flavor of a brown-haired male, this one muscular and full of testosterone. A third fed me with the floral flavor of a female redhead. Redheads were rare, and their blood tasted better than the finest Bordeaux. Redheads with green eyes tasted the best—a lusty concoction laced with essence of lavender yet acidic enough to make a vamp's mouth water for more and more.

Then there were the dark-haired ones with light skin—those who, somewhere hundreds of generations ago in their family tree, were descended from a vampire. Their blood was the ultimate concoction, the Champagne of plasma. Bold and tannic yet fruity and divine. Peach, plum, blackberry. Leather, coffee, the darkest of chocolate. Tin, zinc, laced with violet and apple and estrogen. Even the men smelled of traces of milky estrogen.

All this plus the one-of-a-kind flavor unique to every human.

I lapped it up, gaining strength, finally able to pull hard enough to release my leather bindings.

I roared, flexing my muscles, ready to bolt—

But before I could escape my prison, my eyes would open. I always awoke.

Those fragrances had been denied me for years, perhaps decades. But I remembered, my memory exaggerating each aroma. The only scents in my enclosed space were the remnants of the two human servants who fed me. Who tortured me.

*She* would be hovering above me, gazing at me with her cold, evil eyes before she bent down and sank her fangs into my neck.

*She* never drained me, only took enough so *she* could maintain her control over me and keep up her own strength. The worst days were when *I* had to feed.

*She* forced me to drink from her. I had no other choice. I needed blood to survive, and hers was my only option.

Feeding from her kept my muscles from atrophying, even though I couldn't move much while in captivity. A good thing. The only good thing.

The dream of sustenance pouring into me and giving me

the strength to break free recurred again and again, but escape was always only that—a dream.

Until the day it wasn't.

**This story continues in**
**Unchained: *Blood Bond Saga: Volume One!***